PERFECT MATCH: MY MERMAN PRINCE

PERFECT MATCH

I. T. LUCAS

NICK

*M*y building was quiet this time of night, deserted save for the architect burning the midnight oil on the twelfth floor and the lawyer on the twentieth, who had been sleeping in his office for the past month and a half. The guy was so damn lonely that he was making up things for me to fix so he could talk to someone.

Perhaps I should hook him up with the psychologist on the ninth floor.

The problem was that David couldn't afford her. He'd been kicked to the curb by his wife, and his legal practice wasn't doing that great either.

I doubted he liked me.

David just needed to vent to someone about his troubles, and I was so far removed from his social circles that he felt comfortable confiding in me.

Unlike him, though, I was a man of few words and preferred working without anyone watching me—a habit from my Special Ops days that I found difficult to change.

Still, David was a good man who was going through tough

times, and I could spend a few minutes with him and call it my good deed for the day.

Besides, I needed to practice talking to people in non-military jargon. I sucked at small talk, but I wasn't the type to let a disability of any kind rule over me. I would conquer it the same way I conquered every other obstacle in my life.

David smiled when he saw me. "Hey, Nick. Thank you for coming."

"No problem. So the blinds are giving you trouble again?"

They weren't. I'd fixed them last week.

"Uh, yeah. I can't get them to shut. Can't sleep with all that light coming in."

"I've got you covered." I grabbed my toolbox. Pretending to do things to the lever, I asked, "So, how's it going?"

David's shoulders slumped with relief. He always waited for me to ask, probably because he felt awkward about dumping his troubles on me, but I didn't mind. "You wouldn't believe what she's asking for now. My dog."

"Oof. That's a tough one."

His soon-to-be ex was not a good person. She was vicious and vindictive, and I often wondered what David had done to her that was so bad.

He hadn't cheated on her, that I was sure of. The man was still in love with his wife.

"I know, right? Who takes a man's dog in a divorce?" He would know better than anyone. He was a divorce attorney. "Do you think she's doing it to punish me? Because in my experience, when someone does something so personal in a divorce, they are trying to punish their spouse. And if they want to punish you, they still care."

Given what David did for a living, how the hell could he be so naive?

There was no way in hell she cared. Not after what he'd told

2

me about her. "I'm not sure that's always the case. I've seen people do horrible things to others just because they could."

He looked at me as if he was seeing me for the first time. "Should I ask?"

"No." I never talked about my former so-called career. Couldn't even if I wanted to.

The only reason I was still breathing was that I knew to keep my mouth shut and lay low. With what was stored in my head I was a national security risk, which had been made abundantly clear to me upon discharge. If I reneged in any way or even accidentally let things slip, I would be taken out.

Opening his mouth, David gave me another assessing look and then decided to close it.

Smart guy.

Well, except when it came to his wife, but that was typical. Men were rendered stupid by beautiful women, and David considered his soon-to-be former wife a looker.

Thanks to many surgical enhancements, she might have been considered beautiful by some, but fake boobs and puffed-up lips weren't my thing. I liked my women soft and natural.

Then again, I wasn't looking for a trophy wife or any other kind of wife.

There was no house with a white picket fence in my future, and definitely no wife and two and a half kids. I was damaged goods, and I had enough brains to realize that I should limit myself to hookups.

Hell, I didn't even have a pet.

David let out a sigh. "How did things deteriorate so terribly?"

"It might be just a tactic to force you to make concessions on other things," I suggested. "You said she plays chess, right? Maybe you should make a countermove?"

He brightened. "Yeah, I should." He ran a hand through his

thinning hair. "I'm a divorce attorney, for heaven's sake. I know how these things work."

I gave him a smile. "There is a reason doctors don't perform surgery on family members. The same is true with nearly everything else. You need to have some distance to think clearly."

He nodded. "I should hire a colleague to represent me."

While he continued telling me about his wife's crazy demands and how he'd been hoping for a reconciliation, I pretended to fix the blinds.

"Well, you should be all set," I said when he was finally done. I showed him that the blinds worked properly and put my tools away. "Just remember not to pull the string too hard."

"Thanks, Nick." He rubbed the back of his neck. "Don't tell anyone I'm sleeping in my office. I didn't read all the lease bylaws, but I'm sure that's against the rules, and you could get in trouble if anyone found out."

"Your secret is safe with me, David."

NICK

*A*fter packing up, I went down to the twelfth floor for the next ticket on my list. A flickering light bothered the pretty architect who had been working late every night for the past few weeks.

Hoping she would be gone by the time I got to her office, I had deliberately seen to David's ticket first. It wasn't because I didn't like her, but because I liked her too much.

Jessica Dare was too sexy to ignore, but she wasn't hookup material, and I didn't need complications.

Still, when she stayed alone in that office, I felt compelled to check on her. The building had good security, but I knew better than most that there were ways around the surveillance cameras and other safety features. Besides, the threat might come from a co-worker who knew that Jessica was working late and decided to pay her a visit when no one was around to stop him.

An attractive young woman wasn't safe alone at night and shouldn't be staying in an empty office by herself.

Maybe she didn't want to go home because she was avoiding something? Or someone?

As images of Jessica being mistreated flitted through my mind, the old aggression that I had worked so hard to suppress surfaced. If she was still there tonight, I would ask her a few questions, and if she was having trouble at home, I would do something about it.

Don't be an idiot. What didn't you understand about lying low and keeping your head down?

Counting back from ten, I doused the anger with a torrent of pure will and let out a breath.

The old Nick had died along with his identity, and a new Nick had been born. The old one had been a dangerous operative and a keeper of national secrets. The new one was a custodian of broken blinds and flickering lights.

Ladder hoisted over my shoulder, I made my way past the half-tucked chairs and around the standing backlit desks that artists favored. As I passed by her, I caught a whiff of her sweet perfume.

The woman smelled like dessert.

She hardly looked up from what she was doing until I came close enough to see her sleepy smile. "Oh hey, Nick."

"Hello, Jessica. Working late again, I see."

"You're working late too." She leaned back in her chair and twiddled her pencil. "Sorry to make you come up for this." She pointed at the light above her desk. "It doesn't flicker all the time, but when it does, it's distracting, and I lose my concentration."

She spoke a little too fast, and a pretty pink blush spread over her porcelain-cream cheeks.

Interesting.

She hadn't done that before. Was she showing interest?

I hoped I was reading her wrong. She was already hard to resist as it was, and it would be even harder if she started to flirt with me.

Don't flatter yourself.

Perhaps she was shy and people made her nervous. Was that why she preferred to work at night? The open-style layout of the architecture firm didn't allow privacy, and introverts didn't like to be surrounded by people.

"No worries." I gave her a bland smile. "I'll fix it for you in no time." Climbing my ladder next to her desk, I noticed her drawing. "Is that a library?"

"One day it will be."

I wasn't sure I should ask more questions. She was always tight-lipped and seemed extra tense.

When I slid the cover from the light fixture, dust snowed onto her drawing. "I'm so sorry!"

Jessica loosed a huff, either irritated or trying to blow it off. "It's fine. My idea was a little dusty to begin with." Chuckling at her own pun, she crumpled the drawing and chucked it into the trash. "I need to start from scratch." She pushed her fingers through her long cherry-chocolate hair.

It was one of her best features—rich, thick, and glossy—and the things I imagined doing with it would have shocked her.

Thankfully, I had a well-practiced poker face, so she didn't have a clue.

Or maybe she did.

A sexy woman like her probably had men ogling her left and right.

I felt lousy about her drawing, though. I had barely gotten a glimpse, but I was sure it didn't deserve to be trashed.

"Why did you throw it away? From what I managed to see, it was not half bad."

She snorted. "Not half bad is not going to cut it."

"It was okay until the sprinkling of dust that fell on it. I'm responsible for your design's untimely demise."

She sat up and cast me a shy smile. "It's not your fault. I just have too much on my mind and not enough caffeine in my body, and that design lacked inspiration. Sometimes it's better to start anew than try to fix something that's not working."

"Let me make it up to you." I climbed down. "I'll get you coffee to fuel up, and you can tell me what's bothering you and get it off your mind. I'm an excellent listener."

For a moment, I thought she might take me up on it. But she hesitated. "Thanks for the offer, but I should get back to work. This library isn't going to design itself."

The pretty, shy blush bloomed on her cheeks again, and for once, I couldn't control the response it evoked. Thankfully, my coveralls were loose and hid the evidence.

Damn, if she weren't working in my building, I would have kept at it until she overcame her shyness and agreed to talk to me. Instead, I nodded and climbed back up.

Ignoring the ache in my left calf, I removed the old fluorescent bulb and replaced it with a new one. From up there I could see down Jessica's blouse, and the view was spectacular.

I couldn't force myself to look away.

"Are you okay up there?" She asked.

I chuckled as I climbed down. "Must have zoned out. All these late nights are getting to me."

"Understandable." She looked at me with assessing eyes. "But that's when you usually work, right? You don't fix things during the day."

"Not unless it's an emergency."

Jessica frowned. "When do you go home?"

This was home, but she didn't need to know that.

"If there is an emergency, I get the call at home and come over."

"Oh, yeah. That makes sense." She lowered her eyes to the blank page in front of her.

Even though it was a bad idea, I couldn't help but continue our conversation. I wasn't ready to be done with her yet. "Phelps sent me a long list of nonsensical items to fix in his office, so I assume he is back in town. Is that why you're stressed?"

Her boss was a conceited jerk who thought he was a god because he was a famous architect, and his work appeared in magazines. Luckily for his large staff of junior architects and other support personnel, he frequently attended shows and conferences or met with out-of-town clients.

Her pencil darting over the page, Jessica shrugged. "He is a contributor, but he's far from the only thing troubling me."

I wanted to ask about those other things, but it seemed as if she was tired of the conversation and wanted me to leave.

"Is there anything else I can do for you?" I asked, not expecting her to come up with anything.

Lifting her head, Jessica smiled. "It's so nice of you to ask, but I have nothing else." She chewed her bottom lip like she wanted to say something.

"I think there is," I encouraged. "Come on. It's only nine o'clock, and the list Phelps sent me won't take three hours. I need something to do to fill the time until my shift ends."

It was a lie because I didn't have to answer to anyone and could leave whenever I pleased, but she would find it believable.

"It's embarrassing." She lifted her empty coffee mug. "The coffee maker is acting up. It tastes off, even after I ran the cleaning cycle. Well, I hit the button for the cleaning cycle, and it didn't seem to work." Her expression was both embarrassed and apologetic.

"I'm happy to look at it, but that might be a call to the company that put it in."

She flushed redder than before. "I'm sorry I troubled you. The coffeemaker is not part of your job."

"It's no trouble at all. If I can't figure it out, we can call the company. No big deal."

She smiled again. "Thanks, Nick. You're my hero."

Been a while since I'd been one of those. "Be right back."

I left for the break room and fiddled with the water line. Sure enough, there was a hard water clog. Once I got it taken care of, I returned. "All done."

"That was quick."

"Yeah, I threw some vinegar in and—"

She lifted her hands in the air. "No, no, don't tell me. It'll ruin the magic."

It was nice to know Jessica could be silly sometimes—she was always so intense.

"Okay, I'll spare you the gory details." I winked.

"Thank you so much. You are saving my career, for without coffee, my muse is nowhere to be found."

I cocked an eyebrow. "Really?"

"I'm serious. I can't do my job un-caffeinated. How can I repay you?"

Don't say blow job.

"I'm happy to help. I have stuff to do in Phelps's office, but I'll keep it quiet." I hesitated. "Tell me when you're ready to leave, and I'll escort you to your car. It worries me that you are all alone up here and then down there. It's not safe."

"Oh, Nick." She put a hand over her heart. "It's so sweet of you, but you have nothing to worry about. The only way to get into the building or the underground parking is with a swipe card or to go through the guards in the lobby, and there are surveillance cameras everywhere. I feel perfectly safe working here late and then going to my car."

The naïveté of civilians was astounding. They truly believed they were safe until shit happened to them, and then they realized that they'd been living in a fake bubble.

I forced myself to smile. "I don't want to scare you with horror stories, but just promise me you'll be careful."

"I will. Thanks again, Nick. You are a lifesaver." She smiled.

"If I'm done before you are out of Phelps's office, I'll let you know when I'm leaving."

"Thank you."

Nodding, she looked down at what she'd drawn so far and started absentmindedly sucking on her pencil eraser.

Damn.

I struggled not to let my imagination run away with me at the sight and left for Phelps's office.

His printer was not in my job description, but he would whine if I didn't check it, and his office was a suitable location to watch her from. One inner wall was frosted glass, so there was no—

Wait, where'd she go?

I'd looked down for three seconds at the wires, and Jessica was gone, most likely taking a coffee break now that the water line was clear.

She isn't your responsibility.

When Jessica returned, there was no coffee mug in her hands, so she must have been to the bathroom.

The wiring to Phelps's printer was fine. I wasn't sure what he was complaining about and left a note on his ticket that he should call his IT department, then left his office.

As I worked on the rest of his list, I kept glancing at Jessica through the glass partition. She seemed absorbed in her work, but from time to time I caught her looking at me through the glass.

When our eyes met, she smiled, I smiled back, and then we both went back to our respective work.

Damn, Jessica Dare was really weakening my resolve and making me reconsider my rule about not getting involved with anyone working in my building.

I was done with everything else on the list in under two hours, and as I collected my tools, I decided that I wasn't done with Jessica. I wanted an excuse to talk to her again.

JESSICA

"*H*ow is it going?" Nick asked as he thrust a paper coffee cup at me.

When had he left Phelps's office? I hadn't heard him open the door or noticed him passing by my desk.

"How did you do that?"

He smiled. "I got pretty familiar with your coffeemaker earlier tonight." He was still holding up the paper cup. "I thought it would help you focus and be done faster."

Nick hadn't answered my question, and I wasn't comfortable asking again.

Since Phelps didn't have a secret passage from his office straight to the break room, I must have been so absorbed in my work that I'd been oblivious to what was going on around me.

After Nick had disappeared into my boss's office, a new idea had popped into my head, a clear picture of how the library should look, and I'd wanted to sketch it quickly before I forgot the details.

Smiling, I took the coffee. "Thanks."

He grinned as if I had just accepted his marriage proposal. "You are most welcome."

If I didn't know any better, I would have thought he was flirting. But the sexy custodian had had plenty of chances to hit on me before and never had. For the past two weeks, I'd spent every night late in the office, and he had popped by on each of them pretending to check on this or that, but I knew he was checking up on me.

It was sweet of him to worry about my safety, but regrettably, he hadn't shown any genuine interest until today. Not that it was any reason to get excited. Exchanging a little more than a few friendly words than usual didn't mean he had a sudden change of heart.

It shouldn't hurt that he could so easily ignore me, but it did. I wasn't a great beauty and could lose a few pounds, but I wasn't a hag either.

The only indication I'd gotten that he wasn't entirely indifferent to me was when I caught him staring at my cleavage from his vantage point on the ladder.

There were no rings on his fingers, no discoloration that a wedding ring would have left behind, but he could have a girlfriend, and that was why he was keeping his distance.

"I'm afraid to get near your new drawing." Nick leaned slightly forward to get a better look. "But I'm curious. Can you lift it to show me?"

"It's just a preliminary sketch." I grimaced. "If I want to make it by the deadline, it should have been half done by now."

"Phelps?"

"Obviously."

"He seems to ride everyone pretty hard."

If you're game, I'll ride you pretty hard.

Oh my gosh, where did that come from?

I knew very well where. Handyman Nick was rugged and sexy, kind of rough-looking in all the right ways. Dark hair, dark eyes, thick muscles. His corded forearms alone were fantasy material, and combined with the panty-melting smile, the man could have starred in every naughty novel I had ever read.

Feeling my cheeks getting warmer, I looked down at my drawing. "Mr. Phelps is pretty strict about deadlines."

"The library is the assignment? Or is it part of a larger project?"

I was a little offended. Getting assigned the library was a big deal, even if several of my colleagues were working on the same thing and only one of us would be selected to complete it. Then again, how would Nick know that?

Perhaps he thought that all our firm's projects were designing skyscrapers.

"It's the assignment, and I'd better get back to work." I twiddled my pencil but kept my eyes on him for the simple reason that I couldn't look away.

"I'm distracting you again," he said with a hint of disappointment in his voice.

"It's not you, Nick." He was, but I didn't want to offend the guy. "It's just late, and I'm not fit for conversation at eleven o'clock at night. I have a lot on my mind."

Like why was I pushing the sexy handyman away instead of flirting with him?

Because you don't know how.

I didn't even remember how to talk to a guy about anything that wasn't work-related, let alone hint that I was interested. The last time I flirted with anyone was in college.

Nick smiled easily. "The best conversations happen at night. That's when people are too tired to lie or be polite."

I chuckled. "That's true."

He took a chair from the workstation next to me and straddled it. "So, tell me, Jessica, why are you the only one here working on a library project that seems like it should be handled by a team?"

That was a departure from what he'd said before. How

come he suddenly realized that the library was a big project? Had he been looking through Phelps's files while in his office?

Nah, it was a stupid thought.

Nick was the custodian of the office building, not an industrial spy. Although truth be told, he didn't look like any handyman I'd met before.

"You're right. It is a project for a team, but it is also my ticket into an office of my own, and I'm not willing to let a bunch of inexperienced interns screw that up for me, and that's who Mr. Phelps will hire for a team because they're free."

"So he's picky and cheap? That tracks. Not a good combination."

"No," I said with a sigh. "But he's not all bad. If I knock it out of the park with this design, he will promote me. I just need to prove myself."

It was the story of my life. I always felt as if I had to prove myself to someone. First my parents, then my ex, and now my boss.

Nick crossed his arms on the back of the chair and leaned his chin on them. "Maybe you know the answer to a question I've always had."

With conscious effort, I pried my eyes from his sexy forearms, "You brought me coffee, so you are entitled to three questions."

He grinned. "I'll start with just the one—why do libraries always have so many damn windows?"

That was disappointing. I hoped he would ask whether I was single or whether I was busy Saturday night.

Besides, the answer to that was so obvious that I was starting to doubt the guy's intelligence. "So the patrons can see what they read, of course."

He laughed. "Desk lamps could accomplish that. It's just that I've always preferred a quiet little den with a big leather armchair and a fireplace for my reading. Why don't any libraries ever offer that?"

It sounded nice, but the answer to that was as obvious as the first one. "For the same reason libraries don't have coffee shops. Most are severely underfunded, and the room you're talking about would be expensive. Also, you can't have an open fire in a library, so the fireplaces would have to be the simulated kind, and those are costly as well."

"Everything really comes down to money, doesn't it?"

According to my lawyer ex-husband, it did.

Wouldn't Charles get a kick out of my night?

The truth was that having a friendly conversation with a blue-collar handyman instead of another dull dinner with my ex at the Senator's house was a considerable upgrade. "Yes, but money isn't everything."

"True." He craned his neck to look at my drawing and pointed. "This detail here—that looks like a built-in bench under the window."

Was the abrupt change in subjects because Nick sensed that my mood had taken a nosedive?

I thought I had better control over my facial expressions, but apparently Nick had seen right through me.

The guy was surprisingly perceptive.

I chuckled nervously. "You have a good eye. My half-drawn sketch is crude and incomplete, but you were still able to make out what it is supposed to be." I pointed at the large window I'd drawn and the sun rays bathing the enclave in light. "Since the bench provides seating under a large window, it should be perfect for you."

He smiled. "I didn't ask about windows because I liked them for my own reading pleasure. I do my best work in the dark."

As his deep voice sent a shiver through me, I had to fight images of handyman Nick using his nighttime skills on me.

I should stop it right there and send Nick on his way. My

casual crush on him was deepening, and I couldn't afford the distraction.

During the day, the office was too noisy for me to concentrate on my project, and if Nick kept showing up at night, I wouldn't get any work done then either.

Maybe I should just work from home. It wasn't as if I had any distractions there, but the thought was depressing.

I've been all work and no play for far too long, and chatting with Nick was a rare treat. I wasn't willing to give it up.

My divorce had been hell last year, and knowing that my ex-husband would disapprove of a tryst with an uneducated handyman made the time with Nick feel delightfully forbidden.

Charles no longer had a say in my life, but I relished the thought of his disapproval. If I ever got to go out on a date with Nick, I would post a picture of us in a passionate embrace on social media. Heck, I would even add a caption about Nick's incredible handy skills, hoping that Charles and all his snooty buddies saw it.

I could just imagine the sour face he would make.

Regrettably, that was all happening only in the fantasy I created in my mind. My brief chats with Nick were not a tryst, and I couldn't bring myself to be more forward and move things along. On his side, he seemed content letting things be what they were—surface-level conversations of the "Hi, how are you?" "Fine, thanks." variety. Tonight's conversation was a fluke.

A nice fluke.

I didn't know what to say next, so I lifted the cup and took a sip. "Cinnamon?"

"I've seen you sprinkling your coffee with it. Did I do it right?"

Talk about perceptive. Charles had never noticed and

wouldn't have even if we were married for fifty years. He had never even made me a cup of coffee, either.

I was fighting tears and a tight throat as I tried to answer with a steady voice. "It's precisely how I like it. You are a very insightful and caring man, Nick."

A practical stranger, who had no romantic interest in me, had noticed what my husband had failed to notice over the years we'd been married.

How had I made such a colossal mistake?

Nick laughed. "You might be the only woman who has ever said that about me."

"Then you're hanging out with the wrong women," I blurted before I could swallow the words.

Perhaps he would get the hint.

"That seems to be my MO," he joked. "The bench—I've never seen that kind of built-in in a library before. Seems more custom than most. You said they're underfunded, but you're putting in an effort that would call for money. Who is the client?"

Evidently, my hint had fallen on deaf ears, and Nick had changed topics again to avoid the grenade I'd just dropped at his feet.

Swallowing the disappointment, I forced a smile. "Good eye. The governor commissioned the library, and he wants it to be elegant and practical. I thought that the built-in bench should have a nice swoop in the back as part of the esthetics instead of pillows." I forced another smile. "That way, rowdy patrons won't have anything detachable to throw at each other."

It was a miserable attempt at a joke, but Nick laughed none-theless.

"Is that a common problem in libraries? Wouldn't you get shushed by a librarian for throwing pillows?"

I laughed, too. "Uh, yes, but I've been to some of those

reading hours with my niece and nephew, and the kids get very excitable, so it seemed prudent to have some non-throwable options."

"Your niece and nephew, but not your own kids?"

Excited butterflies took flight in my belly. Finally, a personal question.

"I don't have kids. You?"

"No." As he looked longingly at the drawing, a muscle feathered in his square jaw like he was holding back. "I always wanted some but never saw them in the cards for myself." He cleared his throat. "So, this library means a promotion for you?"

Once again, Nick had changed the subject, and my heart fell. "Only if my design is chosen. I'm not the only one vying for the opportunity."

"That's why you're working so hard, right?"

I nodded. "Senior partners don't get where they are without putting in the hours." Something Charles never understood about my work.

He'd wanted me to be available for all of his social functions and to always look perfect, which required visits to the hair salon and the manicurist, and shopping for clothes. Some women might enjoy that, but I wasn't one of them. I preferred spending my time creating rather than consuming.

"Of course. Someone like Phelps isn't going to promote anyone without being forced to. He's too cheap."

"Exactly. I was up for a promotion last year, but...." *Don't trauma-dump on the hot guy* "...life got in the way. You know how it goes."

Nick didn't need to hear about my messy divorce.

He nodded, and his handsome face fell into seriousness. "More than most, I'd reckon. Well, I'll let you get back to work."

I reached out for his hand before he stood up and gave it a squeeze. I wasn't sure what made me do it other than the need to touch him. His hand was rough and warm and so much bigger than mine. "Thank you for the coffee and the chat. I feel like I haven't spoken to another person in weeks."

"I thought you might need it. The coffee, I mean. I very much enjoyed chatting with you." His smile tightened when his gaze dipped to my mouth. "See you around, Jessica."

"Wait, um," I thought fast for anything to keep him from leaving, "I don't know if you have the time, or if it's something you do, or if I need to put in a ticket, but my chair squeaks. Sometimes."

And on this day, the phrase flimsy excuse found new meaning.

"Why didn't you say so? Stand for me."

I did, trying to do so elegantly and without sticking my boobs in his face.

He sat on it. No squeak.

But I didn't expect one. "It only happens when I adjust it up and down."

"That's usually the cover shaft around the pneumatic cylinder. I'll get some oil and see if we can't lube it up."

Shaft? Lube? Is he choosing these words on purpose?

"I'll be right back." Nick turned around and jogged to his cart.

I was glad for the short reprieve. I needed to catch my breath and plan my next move with Nick, but his backside looked so delectable that I wasted that moment ogling it instead.

4

NICK

*A*s soon as I turned my back to Jessica, I allowed myself a satisfied smirk. Her blush indicated that she'd picked up on my word choices, and it had evoked precisely the images I had in mind.

Why did I do that while having no intention of pursuing anything with her?

Well, a guy could dream. Besides, it was only harmless banter, and she looked like she needed it.

Yeah, you're such a nice guy.

I knew what I would be doing as soon as I got back to my place tonight, and I would be thinking about Jessica Dare and her cute blushes while I was at it. The image of her ample cleavage would play a big part in my fantasy as well.

Cracking my neck to distract myself, I dug through the cart for the oil and black nitrile gloves.

I could feel her eyes on me the entire time, and when I turned around, I got proof that it hadn't been my imagination.

Her eyes were all over me.

I smiled as I snapped the gloves on and flipped the chair over. "Let's see about this shaft."

"Yes, please," she said breathily, leaning against her desk to watch me work.

Observing her from the corner of my eye, I saw her absent-mindedly fiddling with her neckline, her finger running up and down the seam, and if I needed any more proof that Jessica wanted me, the slight parting of her lush lips and the lowered lashes supplied it.

Did she imagine me rubbing oil on a different shaft?

Did it turn her on?

I was crossing the line, or maybe I had already crossed it, but I was too caught up in the game to stop. Hopefully, Jessica was still capable of rational thinking and would stop this train wreck from getting out of hand.

"That should do it." I flipped the chair over. "Good as new."

"Thanks, Nick. It's been driving me crazy."

"Anything else I can lube up for you?"

Her pouty lips parted in surprise as she arched a brow, and her cheeks went from pink to red.

"Since I have the oil out and the gloves on, I mean."

"Oh, right, uh," she stammered as she glanced around, then pointed at her neighbor's seat. "John's chair sometimes squeaks, too." An obvious lie.

"You got it."

Again, her eyes were fixated on my hands while I slicked the shaft.

"Sit on it for me."

She let out a nervous giggle, then sat on the chair.

"Move it up and down."

She did, and her breasts bounced beneath the silk blouse when she landed. "Might be too loose now."

"It works better when tight enough to provide a little friction." I crouched next to her and adjusted the tensioner. "Try again."

She did, and this time, I was up close for the bounce.

Damn. "I think it's good."

I remained next to her. "Then I guess my work here is done."

Neither of us moved for a breath. My inner animal told me to pounce, but I kept him in check.

Jessica smiled politely and sighed. "I guess so." Then she left for her own seat.

The ass on her—

"Thank you so much, Nick. Have a good night."

I searched for something to ask about. It came in the form of a large blue envelope sticking out between some folders. I gestured to it. "You get mail here?"

I thought I'd seen her blush before. I was wrong. She was crimson from the question. "Uh, nothing."

"That doesn't really answer my question, Jessica."

Another nervous laugh. "Sorry, I'm just tired. No, I don't get mail here."

I snatched the envelope before she could stop me. Thick paper with embossed lettering. Whatever it was, it was expensive.

"Perfect Match Studios," I read the small embossed print.

Their commercials were all over the place, but I'd paid them little attention. I had no interest in a matchmaking service, traditional or one that used virtual reality headsets to create beautiful illusions.

Jessica's lips tightened into a thin line.

Was she using the service?

I shouldn't have continued teasing her, but I couldn't help it. "Perfect Match doesn't have an office in this building. Strange that they would get their mail here."

"It's mine," she said, snatching the envelope from my hand. "I brought it with me."

"Is it a present?"

She could easily lie and say yes, and given the way she worried her lower lip, she was contemplating it.

"I've been debating shredding it," Jessica admitted. "And I don't have a shredder at home."

Oh, hell. I hoped I hadn't ruined her plans for approaching the matchmaking service. The way she was responding to my minimal flirting, Jessica was obviously lonely and starved for male attention. I was a good-looking guy, but even though she knew nothing about me, what she did see was not suitable for a well-educated, career woman like her. Girls like that dated lawyers, doctors, and computer engineers, not lowly handymen.

"Forgive me for asking," I said in a gentle tone, or as gentle as I could summon. "Why are you having second thoughts?"

She groaned. "Because it's embarrassing."

I sat back down. "How so? Everyone is using dating sites these days. And this one looks classy."

My words must have reassured her because she leaned toward me and said, "If I tell you, you can't hold it against me or make fun of me."

"I never would. I promise."

She nervously licked her bottom lip for a breath and I stifled a groan. Those perfect lips were not for licking nervously. They were for gliding up and down my shaft.

Then she finally admitted, "It's a virtual reality fantasy thing."

I frowned. "I thought that Perfect Match was a match-making service."

She laughed. "I'm not looking for a husband, and that's not what Perfect Match Studios are about. Well, not directly. Some people end up hooking up with their fantasy partners in real life. I just want to have fun, and having it inside a virtual world seemed like a good idea, but I'm having second thoughts."

So that was what the service was offering—virtual hookups.

My interest was piqued.

"It sounds exciting. Why are you getting cold feet?"

"It's the whole becoming a different person thing that scares me. They say the simulation is so immersive that you even forget who you are. You choose a fantasy—they have pre-made and custom—and you live that fantasy for three hours, but the simulation makes it feel like it has been days or even weeks. It's like having a fantasy vacation, and God knows I could use one."

I had to know what Jessica Dare fantasized about. "Which fantasy did you choose?"

"I didn't choose anything. I don't know if I'm going to do it."

I smiled. "Come on. I'm sure you have a particular fantasy you wanted to live out in the virtual world."

"I do." She crossed her arms under her ample breasts, making them appear even bigger. "But I'm not telling you."

I laughed. "Why not?"

"It's too embarrassing."

"Okay, no problem." Pretending to stretch, I reached around her for the envelope and snatched it again.

She batted at my hand coquettishly, but I opened it up and pulled out the brochure as she huffed in defeat. "I just want to know what Perfect Match Studios is about. I won't read your selection, I swear."

"You can't because I haven't selected anything."

"Then why fight me for the envelope?"

"Because I left out a detail, and I know you're going to judge me for it."

"We shall see," I flicked the brochure open and read aloud, "Welcome to Perfect Match Studios…blah blah, immersive… full body experience…. Wait, this isn't a fantasy like *Dungeons and Dragons*…." I'd guessed that already, but I pretended to have just found out. "This is about living out your sexual fantasies. That's amazing."

I meant it.

Hell, I was intrigued.

Jessica's cheeks were the color of beets. "That's why I didn't want to tell you."

"Huh." I scanned the brochure more thoroughly.

Perfect Match Studios provided a fully immersive virtual reality experience. Customers filled out a questionnaire describing the fantasy they would like to enact and the type of partner they desired to share it with, and once the software found them their best match out of all the applicants, a session was scheduled. The two could be in different locations, but they got hooked up to a virtual reality machine at the same time. In the span of three hours, the participants got to experience days or weeks of living out their fantasies. Some even reported that their virtual adventure had lasted months.

It reminded me of *Total Recall*, which was one of my favorite sci-fi movies.

While inside the experience, they were represented by an avatar and had no memory of their real lives. The software provided a fake history of who they were before entering the virtual world. But after it was over, they remembered everything about their adventure.

It seemed too good to be true, but even if it was half as good as the brochure claimed, it was worth a try. "I like your idea of a vacation."

She laughed. "Right? Who wouldn't want a romantic vacation that takes only three hours but feels like weeks?"

"Absolutely." I flipped through the pages describing the different environments and types of adventures available. "This is fascinating. I did not know the technology had come this far along. And you can customize one of their pre-made fantasies too. That's smart."

"You're not making fun of me."

"Not at all. Why would I?"

"Well, you know. The matchmaking aspect."

She was probably embarrassed about the sexual component, not the matchmaking.

I flipped through the pages, pretending I hadn't read that part yet. I'd been trained to speed-read and absorb everything, but letting her know that would just lead to questions that I couldn't answer.

"Oh, I see," I said as I got to the relevant page. "You get paired with a real person who is interested in a similar fantasy as you are, and it could be anyone. That's incredible."

She giggled. "Yeah. You choose your avatar, so you can look like anyone or anything, and you get to live out your fantasy with a random stranger."

"That's not random. Not really. You must have a lot in common for the software to pair you, and you choose the same fantasy. That's probably more than what most couples who meet conventionally have in common."

"Yeah, I guess that's true."

I looked up from the brochure. "I am dying to know which adventure appeals to you the most."

"No way. I'm not telling you."

"Oh, come on. Is it the *Beauty and the Beast* thing? *Sleeping Beauty*? *Red Riding Hood*? *Cinderella*?"

"What makes you think I would do anything so mundane as a fairytale?"

"Those stories are universal for a reason. Isn't it every girl's fantasy to be rescued?"

She rolled her eyes. "Is it every guy's fantasy to be a rescuer?"

"Yes."

She laughed. "Well, it is not my fantasy to be rescued. Not technically, anyway."

I went out on a limb. "Do you want to do the rescuing? Play the role of the dashing prince?"

More giggles. God, she was sexy. "No! I'm not telling you!"

"Good, I don't want you to."

"Since when?"

"Since I started having fun guessing. What was your favorite movie as a kid?"

She took a breath. "Don't you need to fix some more things?"

"Nope. I'm done for tonight, and so are you." I motioned to her drawing. "You need to let the idea marinate before you continue."

I was talking out of my ass, but I didn't want this to end.

"Yeah, you are right. I made good progress tonight, and I'm too tired to continue." She smiled bashfully. "*The Princess Bride* is my favorite fairytale."

"Good pick."

"What's yours?"

"*Jaws.*"

"Really?"

I nodded emphatically. "It's a perfect film."

"Not really a kids' movie, though."

"Sure it is. It's great for kids. You've got a cop, a couple of bullies, a scientist, and a big fish. Educational on every level."

She giggled again. "Kinda bloody, though. Not really age appropriate."

I shrugged. "Kids should know that violence comes at a price, so they don't choose violence as adults."

"Fair point."

"What was it about *The Princess Bride* that made it your favorite?"

"The sword fights," she said without a moment's hesitation.

"See? Kids like violence."

She laughed, and it made me smile. "They were cool, but not just the sword fights. I liked the idea of a romance that didn't come easily. Wesley had to work for Buttercup and vice versa. In all the other fairytales, if there is a romance, it's simplistic.

Real love is hard won and requires sacrifices and compromises along the way."

"So you were a romance expert as a kid?"

"No." She rolled her eyes. "My parents got divorced when I was a teenager, and I learned how difficult it could be."

"I don't think love should be hard," I said as if I had a clue. "With the right person, it should feel natural."

Jessica nodded. "Yeah, it shouldn't be forced, and it shouldn't require pretense. I would like to find someone I can just be myself with and have quiet times and maybe the occasional sword fight."

I laughed. "So, you want a guy to sword fight you?"

"Maybe. In my fantasy."

I lifted my hand to stop her. "No, no, you swore you wouldn't tell me. I'm still guessing, remember?"

"I don't think you'll guess, but please, keep trying. It's cute when you try."

"You think I'm cute?"

Her breath caught in her throat, and she blushed. "I think it's cute when you try guessing. I didn't say anything about you being cute."

"Well," I leaned a little closer, "it's cute when you're coy."

5

JESSICA

*D*id he just call me cute?

I'd gotten so caught up in our wordplay that I wasn't sure anymore. But I was positive that we were flirting, and I didn't want it to end. "So, any other guesses?"

Nick's dark eyes felt heavy on my skin as he looked me over. "If you want a sword fight with a guy, then maybe you don't want to be the princess. You want to be the villainess. Maleficent?"

"Hardly."

"Ursula?"

Warmer. "I do not want to be Ursula."

"Damn. You're a tricky one, Jessica Dare."

"I like to keep people on their toes."

"Okay, tell me."

I shook my head. "I haven't even told my best friend about this. I can't tell you."

"But—"

"Honestly, I'm not sure I can go through with it. You have to fill out a questionnaire, and according to everything I've read, it is thorough. It breaks down your psychology, childhood memories, kinks, and everything that makes you who you are. I don't know if I want that kind of information available to anyone."

"The brochure says it's completely confidential."

I shrugged. "Lots of companies say that kind of thing, but who's checking to ensure that they are actually as tightly confidential as they claim? Besides, if hackers can get into bank accounts, I'm sure they can get into Perfect Match's database."

"Fair enough, but I don't think that's what's holding you back. What are you really afraid of?"

"What if the experience doesn't live up to my fantasy?" I admitted my real fear.

It was bad enough that my real-life relationship hadn't lived up to my fantasies. It would suck if the virtual world disappointed me as well.

"So, you don't want to tell them what you want because someone else might read it, and you are afraid of disappointment. But succumbing to those fears means you'll never get to live out your fantasy."

I nodded. "Right."

"Are you always so careful to the point of denying yourself what you want out of life, or just when it comes to having some fun?"

His insightful question cut to the bone. I hadn't seen it coming out of our playful banter, and it blindsided me. But he had a point. I'd lived my life too carefully, and what had it gotten me? A divorce from an asshole who had seemed perfect on paper.

"That is an uncomfortably accurate assessment, Nick."

"Forgive me for being blunt, but it sounds like you're more interested in being safe than happy. That can't be any fun."

I shrugged. "You're not wrong. I've always been the responsible one. I'm the mom of my friend group. When I go out with my girlfriends, I'm the one who corrals everyone. I make sure no one disappears." I pulled open my bag and showed him the contents. "I even keep granola bars and hand wipes in my purse, just in case."

"You definitely need a vacation. Maybe one where you get to do whatever you want. In a perfectly safe fantasy land," he hinted.

I snickered. "Yeah, probably." I stowed my bag and took the brochure. "But it's also costly, and I have other things to spend that money on. It was a nice thought, though." I tossed it in the garbage.

"That is not the shredder."

Shit, he'd noticed. "Yeah, I thought I'd be slick and grab it after you left."

He laughed hard. "You're into this."

"I don't know." I squirmed in my seat, still waffling. "I deserve a vacation, don't I?"

"When was your last one?"

I huffed. "Three years—no, four years ago. When my husband and I were working on our marriage."

"You're married?" He sounded put out.

"Divorced."

He breathed an exaggerated sigh of relief. "Glad to know I wasn't flirting with a married woman."

"So you were flirting? Past tense?"

He teased, "Well, I mean since I know now that you're a weirdo with deviant fantasies and all that, I should be careful."

"Hey!" I slugged his shoulder, which set him laughing.

"Nice hook." He rubbed his shoulder and smirked. "And yeah, I was flirting. Still am."

Nick had given me honesty, and he deserved some in return. I licked my lips and admitted, "*Little Mermaid*. That's the adventure I would choose if I decided to go for it."

"Really?"

"But not like the movie or, God forbid, the book."

"What's wrong with the book?"

"Old fairytales were awful. I don't even want to tell you all the details, but they do not end up together in the end. She gets turned into sea foam and pines away for him forever."

He cringed. "That's terrible."

"Read it only if you want nightmares." I shifted gears. "My fantasy is the same idea, but gender-swapped. A merman prince who is fascinated by the human world."

"So you can be the object of desire?"

I giggled. "Something like that. Anyway, he makes a deal with the sea witch."

"For his voice? Ursula's voice was kinda husky in the movie."

"No. For a position in his court when he becomes king. If you remember, they kicked Ursula out of court and exiled her, so what she really wants is a position of importance. He agrees to give that to her in exchange for having legs when he touches dry land and a fishtail when his feet touch the sea again."

"Huh. That's an interesting spin on the fairytale. I love it."

"Thanks, but," I held up the brochure again, "I can't do it. Can't justify the expense on such a silly thing." I began to rip the paper, but he grabbed my hand to stop me.

As his fingers brushed against mine, a spark jolted through me.

"If you don't mind, I would like to take the brochure."

You can take whatever you want. "Um, really?"

"I might try it."

There was no way he could afford Perfect Match Studios on his salary, but there was no way I would tell him that.

"Sure, go ahead." I let it go, and he pocketed the brochure.

"Thanks." He looked into my eyes for a long moment before pushing to his feet. "It's late. We should both call it a night."

No! Don't leave!

But he was right. I took a deep breath and let it out slowly.

33

"Yeah. I'll just tidy my desk, collect my things, and be on my way."

He lifted his tools off the floor and then turned toward me again. "You've never told me who you are in the fantasy. Just who the guy in the fantasy is."

"Can't I remain a woman of mystery?"

"If you want," he paused, "but who does the merman fall in love with?"

"That's just another way to ask the same question."

"I'm persistent. It's one of my worst qualities."

"A princess, of course."

"Is she as bland as the prince in the fairytale?"

I laughed. "No. She is super rebellious, and her father can't wait to marry her off. He accepts a marriage proposal on her behalf from a pompous baron in a neighboring kingdom. The guy who seems perfect but is really just an asshole. She hates him, obviously."

"Understandably. I've known too many guys like that myself. I hate the baron already."

I laughed. "Solidarity, huh?"

"Of course," he grinned cheekily. "So, how does she meet the merman?"

"She runs away from the kingdom and is set upon by bandits. The merman just made his deal with the sea witch, so he walks out naked from the ocean, sees what's happening, and helps her beat the crap out of the bandits."

"Your merman is very confident."

I smiled. "Confidence is sexy."

"It is. Especially in a woman." Nick looked down at the brochure in his hands and held it up to me. "I think you should do it."

"What about you?"

"I'll look up their website. But it sounds like you need this as a visual reminder to take yourself on vacation or do something else to have fun. Stick it on your fridge at home or put it on your nightstand."

"That's a good idea. I should plan something fun for after I get my promotion."

"Convinced you're going to get it, huh?"

I crossed my fingers. "It's about time the universe did something nice for me."

He nodded. "Who knows? Maybe we would get paired on a virtual adventure together."

"It's anonymous, remember?"

"We shall see." He winked and walked over to his cart. "I'll walk you to your car."

"It's fine. You don't have to."

He gave me a stern look. "I insist."

6

NICK

$\mathcal{I}$ could not recall the last time I'd had more than a ten-minute conversation with a woman that didn't lead directly to sex. And the last time I'd had one with this kind of lighthearted yet flirty banter...maybe never.

Most women I spoke to were on apps or at clubs, where everyone was trying to get laid, and no one played coy about it for long. It was strange to admit it, but I liked that my conversation with Jessica didn't end with us hooking up in the supply closet.

Despite her vehement protests, I'd walked her to her car, expecting it to be some beaten-up old clunker, but she drove a brand-new Audi. Junior architects didn't make much, so she either came from money or had gotten a generous divorce settlement.

I didn't know what I'd expected, but I'd been a little disappointed when she thanked me with a shy smile, hurried to get behind the wheel, and drove off as if someone was chasing her.

Had I pushed too hard? Or maybe she'd been embarrassed about her car because she thought I would think less of her for driving a luxury sedan.

That was cute.

It had been a long time since I'd had any challenge. But when it came to Jessica Dare, the real challenge was being the man of her dreams. Not in the real world, though. There were too many variables.

She worked in my building, which would complicate things, and since my discharge, I had been all about living a simple life. More importantly, though, Jessica was a genuinely good person, and she'd been hurt before. She deserved better than the likes of me.

But in a virtual reality fantasy, I could choose to be an entirely different person, and since I would be represented by an avatar, Jessica would never find out who had shared her adventure. It was the perfect hookup with the ideal woman.

I had to make it happen.

When I got to my place, I tossed my key in the wooden bowl by the door and walked past my walnut brown leather living room set and into my office.

The espresso machine in the corner called to me, and I gratefully answered her call, making myself a double.

My usual nighttime routine was an espresso while reading a classic piece of literature in my leather armchair by the fire, but tonight I was on a mission to check out the Perfect Match website.

Looking at the price, I whistled low, piercing the silence.

Damn.

No wonder Jessica was so hesitant—each session cost thirty-five hundred dollars. I could afford it, but it was a hefty price tag for something that could be downright hokey.

When I clicked over to the environments and adventures section, I expected to see video-game-style graphics—good, but not perfect.

I was wrong. After watching several simulations, I had to concede that the Perfect Match virtual world looked incredibly real. It was like watching a live-action film, not playing a video game.

If that was the experience they provided, it was well worth the cost.

I registered, paid the initial fee, and a minute later, got a link to the questionnaire I had to fill out.

It started with pretty mundane questions, which were easy to answer, but by the time I got to the third section, that was no longer the case.

Hell, I hadn't been asked such intrusive questions when I'd been recruited to the Special Operations Unit, and given that the secret service had done an extensive background check on me and every member of my extended family, including a third cousin who had moved to Thailand, that was saying something.

I wasn't shy about what I liked, but some of those questions surprised me. Things like, "Have you ever spanked someone? If so, rate your experience. If not, would you like to? Please provide details below."

By the fifth page of similarly invasive questions, I realized that I had no idea what Jessica's preferences were. If they didn't match mine, we might not get paired even if I chose the underwater adventure and requested a merman avatar.

Time for some subterfuge.

Though it was after one o'clock in the morning, I knew I could call Ed.

He and all his hacker buddies were fond of the adage, "Time is a construct," and his insomnia had helped make him a legend in their community.

After our almost simultaneous discharge, we'd kept in touch for a while, but it had been months since we'd spoken. Still, I knew Ed wouldn't turn me down. He might initially resist, but we had too much history together for him to refuse.

He answered on the fourth ring. "Nick? Is that you?"

"Not hello? Not hi? Just my name?"

"I've been running penetrations for three days straight. Be glad I answered the phone at all."

I smiled. "Any sleep in that time?"

"Sleep is for the weak. What's going on?"

"Can't a guy just call to chat with an old friend?"

"Not at one in the morning. Spill it."

"There's this girl—"

He laughed hard. "I should have known."

I wasn't sure if I should be insulted, so I changed the topic. "How have you been, man?"

"Busy, as usual. I took a couple of babies under my wing, and I'm teaching them to fly, but they're fish out of water, and now I'm having to clean up after them."

"I think your metaphor fell apart there, Ed."

"Yeah, well. Be glad I can make complete sentences. I'm too old to stay up for three nights in a row. You still see some of our old buddies?"

"Not really." I was ashamed to admit it, but civilian life got in the way. "You?"

"Nah. I hear from Toby and Vin sometimes, but that's about it. They had a job for me last month."

I nodded silently. I did not want the details of whatever the job was. It could have been legit, but knowing those guys, it was not. Being former Black Ops meant asking for details of any post-service job could get you killed. "Nothing too serious, I hope."

"No worries. The Feds aren't gonna come knocking on my door anytime soon. It's just some light smuggling, moving some FAA docs around to prevent them from catching on. You know. Kid stuff."

If Ed was talking so freely, the call must be encrypted. I wasn't a tech guy, and I had no idea how to shield a call, but my phone had been modified by Ed himself, and I had no doubt that he had layers upon layers of security in place. A good hacker knew how to shield himself from other hackers.

I chuckled. "If that's kid stuff, I'd hate to see the elementary school you went to."

He laughed. "Most of the time, I'm working white hat, but when the old gang needs a favor, I'm the guy. How about you? What's keeping you busy these days? Still making things go boom?"

"Uh, no, not since everything with my leg."

"Right, right, sorry. I forgot."

"No big deal." My calf ached to tell me otherwise. "Actually, I bought an office building."

"Oh, right, you were into saving your money, playing the stock market, all that adult crap back then. Must have panned out for you."

"Yeah. I bought Amazon when it was still pretty low and sold it high before the crash."

"I can hack the market if you need a wallet boost."

"No, no. Nothing like that. I mean, thanks, but I'm set. Wait, is that how you've been making money?"

He chuckled nefariously. "You don't want to know."

"I'm sure you're right."

"So, the office building—I bet you don't let anyone else touch it, do you?"

"What makes you say that?"

"I remember you back in the day. You refused anyone helping you to set up your charges. You had to be the one to set them up and the one to set them off."

I shrugged. "I admit that I have trust issues, especially when it comes to explosives."

"You are a control freak, Nick. Are you still operating in the shadows and playing Mister Invisible? Once your charges blew up, no one saw you again. What was it Toby called you again? The Phantom?"

"The Phantom Menace. Damn *Star Wars* nerd."

He laughed hard. "Right. You were one too. How many missions did you save everyone's ass with your kabooms?"

"Too many."

"So, what about this girl?"

"She works in my building, and since none of my renters know I own it—"

"Wait, what?"

I tensed up at the thought of admitting it. "I use a shell corporation for the ownership, so I can do the maintenance myself. Like you said, I'm a control freak. And I have rules about the people in my building. I don't get too cozied up to them. I let them think I'm the handyman."

"You own the building, and you're doing the maintenance yourself?" Ed sounded incredulous, but knowing me as well as he did, he shouldn't have.

"My life savings are in that building. I'm not letting it fall into disrepair."

"You know you can hire out for that kind of work, right?"

"Pfft," I huffed, "and let someone screw it up? No, thank you. Anyway, the girl—"

"How are you going to nail the girl in your office if you can't get cozied up with your renters?"

"Being awake for days at a time has worn on your sense of conversational decorum."

"I had it extracted so my other senses are heightened."

I snorted a laugh. "Anyway, about the woman. Her name is Jessica Dare, and she's into this virtual reality fantasy thing called Perfect Match…." I explained the details to him. "…and I want to be her perfect match. That's where you come in."

"It'll cost you."

"Fine."

"And I'll have to know all your deepest, darkest secrets, so I can match you up to her profile answers." He chuckled. "I still have enough decorum left not to ask you what I suspect, and you can be sure that no one other than me will have access to that info, but you need to be okay with me reading through it."

"I don't know what you suspect, but I'm not a deviant."

Given what some of the questions implied, I was almost vanilla.

"Uh-hah..." The jerk sounded doubtful.

What did he think? That because I liked to be in control, I was into whips and chains?

"There is nothing there that will shock you. As long as you keep it confidential, I don't mind you reading it."

"Good to know. Once you're done with the questionnaire, send it to me so I can get to work."

"Hell, no. You are only getting the relevant sections."

"Come on, man, I caught you on base with those two girls from Kansas." I could hear the grin in his voice. "What did they call it again? The Missouri Compromise?"

"They were from Kansas City, not Kansas, and they called it the Tallahassee Tango, but I'm not sure why it was called that."

"Yeah, so I know already how much of a pervert you are, Nick."

"Right back at you, Ed. I will never get the image of you and that circus clown—"

"She was a mime, and you know it."

I grinned. "Like that makes it any better."

"Sure, it does. Mimes are French and classy."

"Whatever you say, man."

7

JESSICA

I got home after midnight but was still wired as if it was the middle of the day.

It was all the coffee I'd consumed.

Yeah, it definitely wasn't the heavy flirting with Handyman Nick.

Walking into my beautiful penthouse had the usual calming effect, and as I set my things down and kicked off my shoes, my shoulder muscles immediately began to unkink.

The apartment and the car were the only good things I'd gotten in the divorce. Well, that and a determination to never fall for the wrong guy again.

With floor-to-ceiling windows in every direction, an enormous terrace, a gorgeous view of the water, a sauna, and a jacuzzi tub, my home was like the love child between an exhibitionist's fantasy and a high-end spa. But being on the top floor of a twenty-seven-story building that was the tallest for many blocks meant I didn't have to worry about prying eyes.

Well, if someone in the taller building three streets over had a telescope and wanted to spy on me, they could, but I wasn't going to worry about it.

I poured myself a glass of wine and headed to the jacuzzi.

The primary bathroom was done in soothing earth tones, and the large square tub was the centerpiece, with pyramid-style steps all around. The decor included bamboo and pale greens, just like in a real spa.

That was the whole point, as I had told my ex when he complained about it being too relaxing. Charles had a thing about never unwinding. He'd claimed that he needed to keep his adrenaline level high to do his job well.

Wait. Why was I getting bogged down thinking about him?

Ugh. My therapist was right. I should focus on forward, not backward. I turned the water and jets on and poured in the lavender bubble bath while waiting for the tub to fill.

Focusing forward was hard.

The one drawback of keeping the apartment was that sometimes I could still hear Charles's voice, whining about the Viking kitchen equipment, or complaining about the view from the terrace not being good enough, or the housekeeper not doing her job right, and a thousand other little things that did not meet his high standards.

Nothing was ever good enough for him.

Including me.

I shrugged off the thought along with my bra and carefully stepped into the water.

Extra hot. Perfect.

I sank into the bubbles and got comfortable on the seat, aiming my low back against my favorite jet. Closing my eyes, I released a long breath and all thoughts of Charles.

I should stay single for a while.

What man could compete with this tub?

Nick.

I giggled at myself for the thought. As much as he was handsome, flirty, and probably very good with his hands, there was no future with the handyman.

God, I sounded like the perfect snob.

It wasn't that I had something against dating a blue-collar man, though. It was that our backgrounds were so different. Aside from a little flirtatious banter, we had nothing in common. We were not compatible.

On the other hand, I had tons in common with Charles, and look where that had gotten me.

Maybe commonality was overrated, but the point still stood. Nick was a blue-collar man with no opportunities for advancement in his career. We'd probably disagree over politics, music, film, and books...there was no chance we would see eye to eye on things, and constant disagreement had ruined things for Charles and me.

I'm not going through that again.

But those arms and that ass...

I wanted to give it a squeeze while we made out. To grab on to it as he thrust—

Oh my.

My hand stirred, tracing a line between my breasts as I imagined Nick's rough, warm hand there. Touching me. His hand glided on my wet skin and cupped my breasts, his thumb toying with my nipple.

Hearing my moan turned me on.

Imagining his face over me while he touched me...my other hand—his other hand—drifted lower.

In my mind, we had been on a date, and he took me home. We'd had a good time, and I knew where this was leading. He hadn't seemed surprised or intimidated by my apartment. I was the only thing on his mind.

It was the one thing I had wanted from Charles for all those years. To be the focus of his attention for longer than two minutes of nothing-special sex. I wanted to be seen for what I was. A woman made of flesh and ideas and longing. A woman who deserved to be cherished in every way imaginable.

45

Nick would do it right. I was sure of that. The details he noticed...hell, he even knew how I take my coffee, and we'd never been on a date. I had years with Charles, and he had never once even offered to make me coffee or noticed that I always ordered cappuccinos when we'd been out.

My ex hadn't noticed many things.

Nick had a keen eye for details and the way he looked at me...like I was the only woman in the world.

He would be such a good kisser. I was sure of it.

As my other hand drifted between my legs, I thought about those full lips—half smiling, half smirking, his hair—almost black but not quite, his devilish dark eyes, the way his jaw feathered when he thought hard or focused.

I imagined the press of those lips on my throat as he made his way down my body, his two-day stubble brushing between my breasts.

I shivered in the water the way I would shiver under him.

Because of him.

Rocking my hips made the water gently slosh against the sides.

I imagined Nick's tongue circling against me there as he slipped a rough finger inside and made me cry out his name. Heat warmed through me, and the pressure built in my core.

He drives me to the edge, making me beg for more, and just when I can't take it anymore, he pulls me to him and thrusts inside.

I came, shaking and gasping.

Panting in my tub, all alone, my head swirling, I sat up and started giggling.

It was such a naughty, brief fantasy, something I rarely indulged in. I usually left my sex life up to my romance novels and rechargeable devices. I never made them about people I knew. It seemed safer that way.

Men on paper couldn't let me down.

After cleaning up, I toweled off and went to bed. But even

after all that, I couldn't stop my racing mind. I needed something more.

Pulling on my pajamas, I went to my office. I had to stop toying around with the idea of doing something and just do it. My laptop had seen little use lately since I was too absorbed in my work. I'd been consumed with the desire to get promoted to senior partner in the firm so I could shove it in Charles's face.

The Perfect Match webpage was still open from the last time I'd browsed through it, so I refreshed it and clicked on the registration tab. I paid the fee, and less than a minute later got a welcome email with a link to download their extensive questionnaire.

There was an option to fill it up online, but I preferred doing it the old-fashioned way with a pencil on paper, so I could go back and change some answers if needed. I also wanted to sit on it for a few days before submitting it to ensure I was comfortable with my choices.

At first, the questions were general in nature, but when I got to the part about sexual preferences, I decided that I needed a break.

After making myself chamomile tea to calm my nerves, I returned to it.

Ideal partner description:

I sucked on the eraser end of my pencil and thought about tall and muscular, with thick, corded forearms, dark hair, dark eyes, and lips that I wanted to bite—

Nick. Dammit, I'm thinking about Nick again.

But is that so bad? He's a living, breathing fantasy.

He's a handyman, for goodness' sake. But isn't that in the top ten of straight women's fantasies? After all, that means he'll be good with his hands.

I couldn't stop thinking about him while I went through all the questions.

Spanking? Huh. I'm not opposed as long as it's playful. Nick looks like the guy who could be into that. Blindfold? I'd have to trust the guy—wait. I trust Nick. This is in a fantasy. It's not like I'll be doing any of this for real. But why do I trust Nick?

I wasn't sure why I trusted him, but I did. Being around him was like being with someone I'd known for a long time, which was absurd given that I had first met him a couple of weeks ago, and we hadn't exchanged more than a few words until tonight.

We were essentially strangers to each other, but we clicked.

Besides, he hadn't initiated the flirting, and it had been all me. In fact, he'd been reticent and hadn't pushed for anything other than convincing me that I should go for the virtual adventure.

Nick would make one hell of a merman.

I giggled to myself, just thinking about it.

Then my body flushed warmly, thinking about him swimming toward me. All wet and determined to get to me. Splashing up and down in the waves, dark eyes focused on me until he held me in his arms and...

Ugh. If I don't finish this questionnaire now, I will never be done.

I went back to checking off boxes, but my mind kept churning in the background.

Something about Nick made me trust my impulses again.

After making such a colossal mistake with Charles, I had been wary of dating, not trusting myself to pick someone who was right for me.

Perhaps after nearly a year of living like a nun, my senses had gotten confused by Nick's masculine pheromones, and I was making another mistake. But that was my logical mind thinking. My gut was very comfortable with Nick.

Besides, I wasn't even going out on a date with him. I was just basing my fantasy on the handsome handyman. There was no harm in that, right?

But what was it about him that made my gut disagree with my mind?

Perhaps I felt safe with him because he'd been so accepting of my strange fantasy? I could have told him that my fantasy was to have sex in space, and I knew he would have been cool about it. But that only meant that he had an open mind. It didn't mean he was a rock of stability and devotion.

I stalled on a handcuff question when the answer suddenly came to me.

Nothing I had done was a joke to Nick. He'd liked my designs and had listened to my explanations. He took me seriously, and that was the hottest thing about him.

Almost.

I returned to the physical description of my perfect lover and added a note in honor of Nick—*a well-muscled ass.*

8

NICK

*I*t was strange to dodge Jessica after our sexy banter, but having more than one sincere conversation with a woman could lead to trouble.

I didn't want to become attached or make Jessica think I wanted more with her.

This was going to be a virtual hookup, nothing more, provided that Ed came through and we got paired. I hadn't heard from him yet, but I trusted him to get the job done.

By Thursday, I'd managed to avoid working late every night for almost a week just so I wouldn't have to worry about running into her for some unsupervised sexy talk. Still, I missed her laugh to the point where my resolve wavered on two separate occasions, and I had to stop myself from getting out of the elevator on the twelfth floor.

That was until today.

I had another ticket from damn Phelps.

The pompous know-it-all couldn't figure out how to close his air-conditioning vent, and according to him, it was too cold in his office. Even though the thermostat had been replaced. Even though he could have adjusted the blinds to let in more light. Even though he could have done a half dozen things aside from bothering me and making me stay later than I wanted to.

"There you go," I said, standing back from the vent. "It's closed. It should get more comfortable for you soon. Anything else you need done around here?"

Mealy-mouthed annoyance wrinkled his nose. "There's a smell."

I sniffed the air. "What smell? Describe it."

"Chemicals or something."

"Could be the oil on my cart."

"No, something like paint thinner."

Had he not realized I had that, too? "Might be the paint thinner on my cart."

"Get it out of my office. I don't like it."

"Whatever you say." I forced a smile and shoved the cart out of his office.

I was eager to escape his attention and his floor before Jessica arrived. Phelps reminded me of every guy who was drunk on a modicum of power and wielded it to make themselves feel better about their insecurities.

"Oh, Nick?" he hollered behind me.

I kept my facial muscles frozen in place.

Just smile. Don't kill him.

I turned around to face him. "Yes?"

"The smell is gone."

"Good. So it was the cart. Have a nice day."

"You don't play poker, do you?"

Yes. "No, why?"

"A few of us like to play on the weekends, and we just had an opening. Interested?"

He was inviting me? A handyman? To join him and his snobby buddies?

Hell no. "Thanks anyway, but I have plans."

51

He looked me up and down. "I bet someone like you has girls lined up around the block."

I chuckled, not at all interested in continuing the conversation. "I stay busy enough. Have a nice day, Mr. Phelps."

"Yeah, you too." He sat behind his desk, his eyes flicking between me and his laptop.

It was bizarre. He had never tried to be friendly before, or what would pass for friendly in his world. I tried to shake it off.

It was just a weird moment. Nothing more.

Jessica breezed through the other side of the open floor plan, her eyes on her phone. I ducked out and around into the break room, pretending to be checking a light. From my vantage point, I watched as she set her things down at her desk and prepared for her day. She wore a sharp blue suit, something more professional than her usual attire.

What was the occasion?

Phelps's eyes were on her from afar, oozing unwanted lust her way.

It was gross. I grunted, "Men."

"You said it," an old woman in the break room said with a nod. Her three-packs-a-day voice and blue eyeshadow made me wonder if she'd been a truck stop waitress in the eighties. "They're the worst."

I smirked at her. "We really are."

"One of the bastards out there break your heart or something?"

"Haven't been heartbroken in a long time." The only time was in middle school when Veronica Shushom refused to be my Valentine. "I'm just over my gender, you know what I mean? Guess that makes me a cynic."

"I'm not overly fond of any gender, to tell you the truth." She sipped her coffee. "But cynicism has never let me down."

Glancing at Jessica, I was glad to see her absorbed in whatever was on her desk. I could sneak by her, and she wouldn't notice me.

"I should get back to work," I told the break room woman.

"Good luck out there, son. We cynics need luck."

"Then good luck to you, too."

I rolled the cart quietly and as fast as possible to the elevator without looking back. Pressing the button for my office floor, I glimpsed Jessica as she stood.

Damn. Was she coming this way?

I pressed the button again, hoping to make the doors close faster. When they finally slid shut, I let out a relieved breath.

I couldn't see Jessica anymore.

Mental note—call the elevator company to get them to make the doors close faster.

Avoidance was the only way to prevent developing feelings for Jessica and vice versa. She was too pretty, too charming, too sweet. I couldn't deny my attraction to her, and being around her made it worse.

When she had stood, my heart had raced. What the hell was that about?

The doors opened to my office floor, and as I walked in, my phone flashed to tell me I had a call. Checking the caller ID, I saw it was an unknown number.

That was never good.

I was expecting a call from Ed, but his number was programmed into my phone, and he would have been a known number.

On impulse, I answered instead of declining the call.

"Hello?"

"Nick, it's the weirdest thing—"

"Ed?"

"Who else?"

I chuckled to myself and sat behind my desk. "Did you switch phones?"

"Yeah. I dropped mine in the toilet by mistake."

"Still clumsy, eh?"

"My fingers are dexterous. That's all that counts."

"True. So, what do you have for me?"

"Your Perfect Match thing is weird."

I remember being amazed by some of the implied kinks in the questionnaire, and given my past, I thought I'd seen and heard of everything under the sun.

"It's a glorified online dating service. Do you mean the kinky stuff, or just generally weird?"

He laughed. "No, man. Not the good weird. It's their encryption. I've never seen anything like it."

"I didn't think there was a type of encryption you were unfamiliar with."

"Neither did I. I can't crack it."

I was stunned to hear him admit that. "But you hacked the White House."

"I know, right? Anyway, I researched the owners to get to the bottom of it, but guess what?"

"What?"

"It's owned by a corporation that has two parent companies, which are owned by other corporations etc. It's a maze that requires a forensic accountant. What's really strange is that until recently, Perfect Match was owned by two guys. They sold it, and apparently the new owners want to keep their identity a secret, and they are doing a damn good job of it."

"Who were the previous owners?" I asked.

"Gabriel Barnes and Hunter Anderson."

"So go through them. I bet they left a back door to their company's database. That's what I would have done."

"Yeah, me too. But I have to find out what's happening and who the new owners are."

"Why go to all the trouble? What does it matter who owns it now?"

"Dude, my pride is on the line here. How dare they be untouchable?"

"Sounds like you're sinking a lot of time into this."

Ed laughed. "And I'm getting to the bottom of it because it doesn't make sense. Why would a glorified online dating service, as you have so aptly called it, have this level of encryption? I can break into banks, hospitals, schools, and government facilities with relative ease, but not a dating site? It's humiliating. I can't just let it go."

He had a point. I wondered about something but was too cautious about saying it on the phone. "You might be in over your head, Ed."

He might have forgotten that he wasn't using his regular phone, and I didn't know whether it was secure.

"They are light-years ahead of our best protocols, and I know them all, Nick. It's almost as if…" he took a breath, "it reminds me of the alien tech we saw back in the day."

Dammit, why'd he have to say that?

We had been told that the tech was a secret project the military was working on and that it wasn't alien, but we knew better. Still, it fell under the umbrella of classified info we were not supposed to talk about with anyone, including among ourselves.

I chuckled, just in case someone was listening. "That's funny, Ed. Good joke."

"Sure whatever. But I'm telling you—"

"And I'm telling you to stop right there. Some things are not supposed to be mentioned."

"You think I would call you from an unsecured line?" He scoffed. "What is this, amateur hour? Jeez, first their encryption humiliates me, and now you insult me?"

"No insult intended. Just an overabundance of caution. Besides, you know the protocol as well as I do."

"Yeah, yeah. You're right. E.T. didn't go home, and he might be listening."

I laughed. "I guess this means no hacking into the Perfect Match database."

"I'm not ready to give up yet, but I doubt I will find anything before your girl gets paired with someone. I suggest that you submit your questionnaire and hope for the best. I'm sorry that I couldn't help you in time."

"Maybe it wasn't meant to be." I shrugged. "But at least I don't have to share my questionnaire with you."

"Send it anyway."

"What for?"

"So I can give you pointers. If you're this hard up for a date, you've lost your game and need help."

I snorted out a laugh. "You're just being a nosy bastard. Thanks for your help, even if it doesn't pan out, keep me posted on the mystery. Maybe we can meet in person next time?"

"I haven't done anything up close and personal in years, man. I like my reclusive, shadowy life. But if I find anything useful, I'll call you."

"Thanks, but keep the classified information out of the conversation."

"Depends on what I find. Talk later, Nick." He hung up.

I took a breath and let it out slowly. With any luck, my questionnaire would be enough to match me with Jessica, and government helicopters would not land on my building with a custom-made head bag for me.

9

JESSICA

"*J*essica!" Phelps whined over everyone else on the floor.

Whenever he called me to his office, I heard the villain from *Jessica Jones* say my name.

Same insistent whine. Same tone. Same creepiness.

My desk neighbor John muttered, "Rather you than me."

I chuckled as I grabbed my portfolio and laptop. "Liar."

John smirked. "Good luck."

"I'm gonna need it."

I headed toward Phelps's office with tension in my spine and butterflies in my stomach. I wanted that damn promotion, so I had to bring my A-game. I'd worked on the library design for weeks and finally had the concept ready for presentation. A sudden dip in confidence and a wobbly gut would not wreck this for me.

"You're late," my boss said as I entered his office.

"I didn't see a meeting on the schedule—"

"No matter. I'm used to that. Women are just incapable of punctuality. You said you had something ready to show me, but I haven't seen anything yet."

He was such a jerk. When I'd told him I had the concept ready, he'd dismissed me with a wave and kept walking. And now he was blaming me for not bringing it to him?

I wanted to strangle the guy.

Instead, I plastered a smile on my face, laid out the renderings on the presentation table he kept in his office precisely for that purpose, and set up my laptop next to them.

Going over my ideas, I pointed to every unique detail that set my design apart. "...and here, we even have a VIP room for donors to the library. They have access to the Elegance Lounge, complete with leather armchairs, a few fireplaces, and a coffee bar. It's laid out like separate dens, giving the donors a sense of privacy. This level is only for the elite, of course. As this is one of the governor's legacies, I thought he would like to reward those who have helped make it possible."

Thanks for the idea, Nick.

For the first time since I'd known Phelps, he looked impressed. "You've put a lot into this."

"I have. Because I believe in this design. The governor has served our state better than most. He deserves something special."

For once, instead of staring at my cleavage he stared at my drawing. "Send me this in presentation form. I want to have it ready to go come Monday."

"You're going with my design?"

"That still remains to be seen." He looked up at me. At my eyes. A first. "But I'll say you are definitely the frontrunner, Jessica."

I tried to contain my excitement. "I'll send you the presentation as soon as I get back to my desk."

"Good. But don't mention it to the others. We must keep them on their toes."

I wasn't sure what to make of that. "Whatever you say, Mr. Phelps."

I gathered my things, caught him checking out my cleavage, which made the whole episode seem less surreal, and left his office feeling minimally gross and totally excited.

Frontrunner.

Phelps had never called me that, and I'd had some pretty good designs before, if I said so myself. I owed Nick for the den idea, which had to be what put my plan ahead of the pack.

A shame I haven't seen him in almost a week. I'd like to thank him. Vigorously.

I giggled and unloaded my things at my workstation.

John cocked an eyebrow my way. "Something must have gone right in there."

"Just thinking about...nothing." I couldn't tell John about Nick.

I liked John, but he was a gossip, and I did not intend to tell anyone about my crush.

Was it a crush? Had it gotten that far?

"Nothing? I have never seen you giddy like that. Did Phelps give you the gig?"

"No, relax. He's looking at everyone's work first." Technically, not a lie.

"Mm, hmm," he said suspiciously. "Then what has gotten you all glowy?"

"I'm not glowy."

"You're incandescent."

"Must be my new moisturizer."

His brown eyes narrowed on me. "I don't believe a word you're saying. Just letting you know that."

"Well, here's something you can trust. I need coffee. Excuse me."

I grabbed my mug and jetted for the break room. Whatever John thought he knew, I had no intention of confirming it accidentally, and he was very good at getting me to spill the beans.

The break room was deserted, save for Mavis, who rarely

left it. She was too old to fire, so they let her do whatever she wanted. Rumor had it she was Phelps's mom, but no one knew for sure, and when someone had asked, she laughed and said they were getting too personal.

She raised her coffee cup my way, then went back to watching her talk show.

I popped a pod in the machine, and as the coffee percolated, the telltale rumble of a rolling maintenance cart made my heart flutter.

It was silly—it wasn't like we had anything more than a flirty conversation a week ago—but still. I wanted to see Nick.

As I peeked out the open doorway, disappointment rolled by in the form of Angela, the janitor. I huffed and returned to my mug under the coffee machine.

"You think that's her actual hair color?" Mavis asked as she pointed to the screen.

"Not with three inches of dark roots showing."

"Didn't think so. My colorblindness makes it hard to tell sometimes."

I grabbed the cinnamon and shook an unreasonable amount into my coffee.

"Do you think he's cute?" she asked.

I checked the TV again. "Those are all women, Mavis."

"I meant the maintenance guy."

My cheeks flushed hot. "What are you talking about?"

"You jumped when you heard the cart, and I'm pretty sure you weren't looking for the janitor since she's a woman and you're divorced from a guy."

"I really have to get back to work. Excuse me—"

"He likes you, too."

I laughed nervously. "What are you talking about?"

"I saw him watching you. You kids think I don't pay attention. I know more than you think."

I was dying to hear what she knew, but if I asked, I would

admit that I was interested in Nick. "You have a wild imagination, Mavis. Have a nice day."

"Yeah, you too."

On the way back to my seat, I debated putting in a ticket for a phony maintenance problem, but it felt wrong. Or weird. Or something. I should just be straightforward. Tell him what I want.

Or I could say my coworker's chair needed more lube and see where things go.

I giggled again and opened up my email applications.

My heart did a somersault when I saw that I had mail from Perfect Match. Looking left and right, I made sure no one could see my screen and opened it.

I skipped over the congratulations, blah, blah, and went straight to where it said that my session was scheduled for Saturday at ten in the morning.

Oh my God, tomorrow?

But it would be the perfect way to celebrate my promotion. Perhaps the universe was finally smiling at me.

My mind raced, thinking of everything I'd said in the questionnaire. But as soon as I thought of Nick, all those details vanished.

For some reason, whenever I imagined my partner in the virtual adventure, I saw his face. Well, there was actually a very good reason for that. Nick had been my model for describing my perfect man. But there was no way he would be my match.

He couldn't afford it, and he'd been ghosting me for over a week.

Still, it was fun to think of him as my merman. I had to tell someone about it. I was too excited. I grabbed my cell and took the elevator to the roof where Mavis smoked. The view was decent enough, with lots of trees near the park, as long as I stayed on the south side of the building.

I dialed up my oldest friend. "Hey, Sarah, do you have a minute?"

"For you, I have ten."

I blabbed every detail of the past few weeks, everything from my work to Nick to Perfect Match. We both lost it when I got to Nick's mention of lubing the shaft. "...I could barely keep my shit together when he said it."

"He is definitely flirting with you. Get to the good part. How is he in bed?"

I sighed. "I don't know. I'm not...I haven't tried to move things past that night. I've been so focused on work, and now, with what Phelps said about being the frontrunner, I'm going to do the Perfect Match thing to celebrate."

"What does any of that have to do with Nick?"

"Nothing, technically—"

"To me, it sounds like excuses to avoid intimacy rooted in your commitment phobia issues."

I stared at my phone, baffled. "Who are you, and what have you done with Sarah?"

She laughed. "I know, I know. But I've been seeing a new therapist, and he's really got me pegged, I swear. It's like he knows me or something. Am I wrong about it, though?"

"Well, no, but—"

"Is it because he's a maintenance man?"

"No, I'm not a snob like my ex. But it makes me wonder what Nick and I could possibly have in common."

"Uh-mm." Sarah had a tone. "I have the perfect plan. Put in a ticket for something, and I will come tonight to your office to check him out. You know my good-guy radar is top-notch."

"Aren't you the one who dated the convicted armed robber?"

"How do you think I honed my radar? Thanks to Hold-up Harold, I know what to look out for now."

I snorted a laugh. "Thanks anyway, but I'm not bothering

Nick with fake issues until I finish Perfect Match. I can only handle one fantasy fling with no strings attached at a time."

"I support and envy your courage. Go. Have meaningless sex with a faceless hookup, and tell me all about it when you're done. If it's as good as the ads say, I'll give it a try too."

I giggled. "Bye, hon, thanks for listening."

"Anytime."

10

NICK

Friday night, Ed called. "Why aren't you at Hendrick's?"

"How do you even know about Hendrick's? It's a bar, and you don't go out."

He chuckled. "No, I don't, but according to your credit cards, you do. You go there most Friday nights, actually. And if you're feeling classier, Fig and Grape, or if not, Club Prana, or—"

"Yes, I go out a lot. Did I ever tell you that tracking your friends' credit cards is creepy? Because it is."

"How else would I know what my friends are up to?"

"You could ask."

He scoffed at the notion. "That's a waste of time when I can just go online and find out. So, why aren't you out tonight?"

"You don't know I'm not out. I'm on my cell."

"GPS tracking data says you're at home."

I blew out a long breath. "Ed. Speaking of creepy—"

I had no doubt that Ed wasn't the only one tracking me, or he might even be the one charged to do that, and this was his way of hinting at it, but I had nothing to hide. I was just enjoying my civilian life and staying out of trouble.

"Yeah, yeah. Whatever. So, how are things with your office girl?"

"What? You don't know?" I pretended dismay. "I thought that you knew everything."

"Very funny. So?"

"There is nothing to report. I've been avoiding her."

"Why?"

"Because I don't need complications. The only way I can hook up with her is virtually in Perfect Match Studios. Anonymously."

There was a moment of silence. "Did you hook up with anyone recently?"

"Not that it's any of your business, but other than my right hand, no."

"Oh, good. I wanted to tell you to do that so you won't go off like a rocket when you hook up with her. Your head might be in the virtual fantasy, but your body will be in a chair in the Perfect Match Studios, with a tech watching over you. That can get embarrassing."

"Yeah, you're right. I haven't considered that."

I also hadn't considered that I might be violating the terms of my honorable discharge by allowing Perfect Match access to my mind. I hoped it wouldn't be a problem because it was too late to back out.

Then again, if Ed had been hired to track me, he might have been obligated to disclose my activity, which might be why he was stonewalling me about Perfect Match.

"You're welcome," he said.

I rolled my eyes. "I'm sure you didn't call me to give me that piece of advice."

"I didn't. I have more bad news about Perfect Match."

Here it comes. He's going to tell me that I'm not allowed to do it.

"What is it?"

"I'll tell you in a moment, but first, I want you to tell me something."

I huffed. "What?"

"Why have you been avoiding your office girl?"

"I told you. I don't need the complications of having a fling with someone in my building. It's already awkward, and I have to sneak around like a thief not to bump into her. Now imagine how bad it would be if I hooked up with her in real life."

There was a long sigh. "I worry about you, man. You're one of the few good guys from our unit. Hell, you are one of the few who are still breathing. But you don't reach out to me or anyone else, and before you ask, I know that from looking over your cell phone records and email. You live by yourself. You work by yourself. You lie to your renters so they don't get too close to you. You sleep with random women only once, so they don't get attached. You are just as isolated as I am, and although that is how I like my life, you're not wired like me, Nick. You obviously want a connection with someone, or you wouldn't go out every weekend."

"I don't need a therapist. I had enough of shrinks in the service." He was undeniably a nosy bastard, but his assessment bothered me. "What's your point, Ed?"

"My point is, you started avoiding that girl because you like her. It's not healthy."

I laughed. "And I should take advice on what is healthy from a recluse?"

"I am not a good example. I'm terrible with women. Heck, I'm terrible with people, and I'm OK with that."

"Look—"

"If you like her, pursue it. In the real world."

Now I was convinced that Ed was working for our former bosses and was trying to persuade me not to do the Perfect Match thing without revealing why.

"I've already paid for a session, but if I accidentally let it slip that I booked it, Jessica might think I did it just to be paired with her, and if she's not into me, that could spook her."

"I didn't know good-looking guys like you got nervous with girls."

I didn't, but I didn't want to sound like a jackass.

"I am only human."

"No, you're a control freak."

"What are you trying to say, Ed? Just say it and save us this awkward dance." I braced for him to finally reveal who he was working for.

"Right, well, here's what I've dug up about Perfect Match. First, the bad news—I didn't find a way in. If the former owners have a backdoor, I couldn't find it, and the current owners have impenetrable shields around the data and the software. I'm still trying not to take it personally."

Should I be relieved? Or was it more stonewalling on Ed's part?

"Is there any good news?" I asked.

His tone quirked. "In a manner of speaking. The company appears to be not only legit but also good. As in, they do good things. The founders look to be precisely what their bios say they are—"

"Which is?"

"Two programmers with the best intentions and a lot of high-end tech. Barnes and Anderson had a friend who was in an accident and became a quadriplegic. The friend married, but he could no longer make love to his wife. The founders had experience in the virtual gaming world, so they came up with the idea of creating a place for the couple where their friend had a fully functional body and a way for them to be together like they had been before the accident. That was how they got their start. The new owners continue the charitable work, donating a huge chunk of their profits to help people with mobility issues."

"Huh. That makes me feel better about buying one of these obscenely expensive adventures."

I waited for Ed to drop the other shoe and tell me I couldn't participate.

"That is all I have been able to find," he said. "I'm still peeved about it, but I'll keep hacking away until I find an in."

"It's too late for me. I've already booked a session, and I'm just waiting for them to schedule it. At this point, it's up to Lady Luck whether I get paired with Jessica."

"This is not about you anymore, Nick."

I was so relieved that he wasn't telling me that I couldn't go that I snorted out a laugh. "You and your damned pride, man."

"In this life, what else do we have? Anyway, since you've already bought the service, what's the next step? How does it work?"

"I wait for them to schedule a session at a time that works for me and my Perfect Match lady. Then I go to one of their studios to get hooked into the system at the same time as my match, and we have three hours of a sexy adventure that could feel like days, weeks, or even months. If the service is as legit as you say, it should be a wild ride."

"Do you want me to hack into your office girl's calendar to see when she goes to the Perfect Match Studio? That way, you'll know if it's her."

"Oh, so you're asking my permission to stalk her, but not when you stalk me?"

Maybe he would finally fess up to his real part in my post-discharge life.

Ed laughed hard. "We're friends. I don't know her, so it's not right. And besides, it's not stalking. It's friendship with a shortcut."

I didn't want him anywhere near Jessica, in cyberspace or otherwise.

"Don't hack her calendar, Ed. Part of me doesn't want to know if it's her."

"How come? I thought that was the whole point of all of this."

"So did I, at first. But if we don't match, maybe it's not meant to be. I want to leave it up to fate."

His exaggerated gasp was audible. "The control freak wants to leave something up to chance?"

"Goodnight, Ed."

"Don't hang up just yet. There's one more thing."

"What's that?"

"I still think it's aliens."

"Goodnight, Ed." I hung up.

No way was I going down that rabbit hole with him.

I sat back in my leather armchair and stared at the crackling fireplace. He was right about one thing—it had been a while since I'd hooked up with anyone, and thinking about Jessica and her pouty lips was the best excuse to unzip.

Just thinking about her mouth on me was enough to make me rise to the occasion. My body ached, and I stretched out to get comfortable, but the moment my hand touched my zipper, my email notification dinged.

I wanted to ignore it, but then it occurred to me that it might be from Perfect Match.

With a groan, I rose to my feet and walked over to my desk.

The email was indeed from Perfect Match.

As I skimmed it for the important details, a flash of frisson gave me the chills. The appointment was scheduled for ten in the morning the next day, and I had to confirm before midnight that I could be there.

I didn't need any more time to think. I clicked the confirmation button and let out a breath.

Returning to my armchair, I sat down, put my hands behind my head, and grinned like a son of a bitch. The urge to jerk off was gone, and something felt lighter in my chest.

It was an unfamiliar fluttery feeling. The only time I had felt anything even close to this was as a kid on Christmas when I'd waited to open my presents and hoped one would be the gaming console I'd been pining for. I hadn't gotten the console then, but I had a feeling that this time I'd get precisely what I was after.

11

JESSICA

I arrived at the studio just before my appointment time. If the place was skeevy, I planned to leave. But as I opened the front door, I was relieved to see that the waiting room was classy and upscale.

It reminded me of the one time I'd visited an expensive plastic surgeon. It had been Charles's idea for me to consider getting, as he'd put it, "a little refresh."

He'd meant Botox and fillers, but I'd decided I was too young for all that.

Then a startling thought came to mind—what if Charles was the match?

He was one of the few guys I knew who could pay for something like this easily enough, and he had enough connections to find out when I would be here...

That's just paranoid, crazy talk. Enough of that.

I put him out of my mind and noted the potted plants and rock waterfall in the corner. Everything was lovely, and there was no reason to back out.

Other than my nerves.

As much as I wanted this, actually doing it was a different

story. Sarah had said that she supported and envied my courage, but I didn't feel courageous.

I was terrified.

"Good morning, Ms. Dare." The receptionist rose to her feet. "I'm Lisa, your adventure coordinator." She offered me her hand.

I didn't even know I had a coordinator, but then I hadn't read through the onboarding emails with attention to detail. I hadn't even read the instructions until this morning and had scrambled to wear something loose and comfortable but at the same time presentable enough to get out of the apartment.

"Nice to meet you." I shook the hand she offered.

Lisa smiled. "Are you ready to have the best adventure imaginable?"

She sounded excited for me, and I wondered whether it was genuine.

"I'm not sure," I admitted. "It's a little scary."

"Of course." She gave me a compassionate look. "I was scared my first time too. But after that, I couldn't wait to volunteer for more beta testing." She motioned for me to follow her.

"Which adventures did you try?"

"Oh, I tried most of them." She leaned toward me as if to tell me a secret. "It's addictive, and since I don't have to pay for it as long as an adventure is in beta, I get to experience it as many times as needed until it's perfected. The only downside is that I know I'm getting paired with other Perfect Match employees, which can get a little uncomfortable. We don't know who we are matched with, but there are only so many of us, you know. I just hope the guys I play with are from studios in other cities."

"Yeah. I can see how that can be a problem to do something so intimate with a coworker."

Was that why Nick had been avoiding me? We weren't coworkers, but what Lisa talked about also applied to us. It would be very uncomfortable to bump into someone who had shared my kinky fantasy in a virtual adventure.

She opened one of the doors. "Please, come in. Your technician is waiting for you."

"Thank you." I smiled at her, but my heart rate accelerated, and my palms got sweaty.

"I'll leave you in Chloe's capable hands. Enjoy." Lisa left the room and closed the door behind her.

Feeling abandoned, I turned to the smiling tech.

She offered me her hand. "Hello, Jessica. I'm Chloe, and I'll be taking care of you today and ensuring that your body is functioning optimally and your vitals are not spiking."

That was reassuring, but I hoped to get some excitement so at least some spiking was inevitable. "What happens if they do?"

"If you are in distress, I stop everything and wake you up." She patted my arm. "Don't worry about a thing. I've got you." She winked and gestured to the strangest chair I'd ever seen.

It was a combination of a movie theater recliner and a salon chair with one of those giant bubble helmets. The helmet was high above the chair, but I knew it was supposed to go over my head, and I wasn't sure what to think of that. But her welcoming smile did a lot to put me at ease. "Take a seat, and we will get started. I'm sure you read the instructions?"

"Yes, hence the yoga pants, t-shirt, and no makeup. But I have to ask. Have you tried this?"

"Several times. Everyone who works at Perfect Match gets to be part of the testing team, and let me tell you, it's addictive," she gushed the same way the coordinator had.

I sincerely hoped they were both telling the truth and weren't parroting rehearsed reassuring lines they had been trained to tell the customers.

I took a breath and sat on the weird chair. I tried not to expect what was coming, but it was impossible. "Um, this is probably crazy, but is there a way to guarantee that certain people cannot be my match?"

"What do you mean?"

"The service is pricey, and my ex-husband has the money for whatever he wants—"

She shook her head. "Unless people specifically request to be matched, we make sure that there is no prior legal connection." She smiled apologetically. "Naturally, that doesn't cover ex-boyfriends, which is why there is a section about people you specifically don't want to be matched with."

I must have somehow missed that section, or maybe I forgot about it. There had been hundreds of questions, and I'd been in a rush to complete the questionnaire.

"I hope I put Charles's name down, but frankly, I can't remember if I did."

"It came right after the section describing your perfect partner."

That made sense. I'd been so absorbed with thoughts about Nick that I hadn't noticed the questions about undesirable exes.

"A couple of things," Chloe said as she removed my shoes and put them under the chair that I left my purse on. "Your experience will be dreamlike in the sense that the perception of time will be very different from reality. It could feel like days or weeks."

I nodded. "I've read the description. That's part of the appeal. I hope to enjoy a nice vacation in the merpeople's beautiful underwater city."

Chloe put the blood pressure cuff on my arm. "Just so you know, the adventure is not precisely how you imagined it. Your partner's wishes influence it, and the artificial intelligence adds variables to make things interesting." She gave me a bright smile. "What would be the fun if everything was predictable, right?"

"Right." I swallowed what I really wanted to say.

I wasn't a big fan of surprises, and I kind of liked predictability.

"Your blood pressure is a little high. I might need to give you something to relax."

I shook my head. "It's just the intake jitters. I'll be fine."

She nodded. "Every detail will feel and look real. Your mind will trick your body into interpreting everything as real, so there can be physical manifestations of events. It's completely normal."

"Does that mean I could get injured for real?"

The tech shook her head. "You can get minor or superficial injuries in the fantasy, but nothing will happen to your body. There is no possibility of injury with our system. The only risk factor is overstimulation, but you are young, and your medical history doesn't indicate any heart problems. You'll be fine."

"Okay."

"There are many safeguards to guarantee our no-harm clause. You can't die. I monitor your stress levels, and if they go too high," she snapped her fingers, "the system will shut off even before I get to do it, but I'm here as an additional safety precaution. You have a safe word for freezing the system as well. You can either stop it completely or take a breather and continue. I'm here to assist you with that."

"Got it."

"Any questions?"

"I'm kind of blanking at the moment."

She smiled warmly. "I understand being nervous, but I promise it's completely safe. No ex-husbands will be involved, and you are in total control. This is all about you."

"Will I remember what happens in the virtual adventure?"

I already knew the answer to that, but I needed to hear Chloe say it. She inspired confidence, and I trusted her more than the Perfect Match brochure and other advertising materials.

"Yes. Your brain experiences everything as though it's real, so it stays in the memory just like any other event."

"I understand."

She checked my reflexes, asked if I had any loose teeth or fillings, and then turned to her laptop and started typing. "Your match was found pretty quickly, so we had to make a few shortcuts. Usually, we let you see your custom-created avatar before your session, but in your case, it's going to happen simultaneously. You can make last-minute changes, but since the avatar is a composite based on your and your partner's questionnaires, I don't recommend making too many changes. Women commonly go for bigger boobs, longer legs, and those kinds of things. For men, though, it's almost universal that they all want to be taller, have more muscles, more length—"

I chuckled. "That's silly. It's not the length or the girth that matters but what they do with it."

"Yeah. I agree, but I can't tell them that. It's more comfortable for women to be supervised by female techs and for men by male techs, so I don't get to interact with male clients." She turned her screen for me to see. "What do you think?"

"Wow. She's perfect."

"I know, right?" She turned it back and looked at my avatar approvingly. "They really did a good job with this one." She glanced at me. "Anything you wish to change?"

"No. As I said, she's perfect."

"Good. I hoped you would say that." Her expression turned serious. "Be prepared to forget who you are in real life for the duration of the adventure. That's the part that really messed with me the first time."

I frowned. "Yeah, I don't really understand how that's possible."

"That's how immersive the experience is. Did you ever have dreams where you were someone else?"

I nodded. "I once dreamt that I was a man. I still wonder whether it was a memory from a previous life or a mental connection with someone."

"Did you remember who you were in that dream?"

I shook my head. "I was someone else."

"That's how you will feel in the adventure. The person you picked will be your new identity. You'll have memories from your avatar's childhood, their complete life story down to the first time they scraped their knee as a kid. The programming is incredibly thorough, and to do that, we set your actual memories on mute, so you can hear your new inner voice. Again, it's like a dream."

"That is really fascinating but also really scary."

"If you'd like, I can give you a mild relaxant before you go in."

I shook my head. "I don't want it to interfere with the experience."

Chloe grinned. "You are absolutely correct. Do you need to use the bathroom? You don't want to have a messy accident." She winked.

I was so relieved. I was afraid they would put a catheter in.

"That's a good idea."

"The bathroom is right there." She pointed to the door.

I grabbed my purse and ducked into the bathroom. It was nicely appointed and even had a small shower, and I wondered if anyone needed to shower before or after an adventure.

I sat on the toilet and called Sarah. "I'm at Perfect Match and freaking out," I whispered.

"Stop freaking out and go get laid in a dream world!"

I laughed, and it echoed off the tile walls. Chloe had probably heard it, but what could she do? Get inside and tell me to end the call?

"You're right, I'm just... The whole thing is so weird. I asked if Charles might be the guy on the other end of this, and they guaranteed me it could not be him, but—"

"He is your ex-husband for a reason, and if their technology is half as good as they are charging for, then they could never match you with that asshole. Besides, the legal liability alone would be astronomical."

"I know, I'm just—"

"Freaking out, yeah, I caught that part. Jess, I know this thing is a little out of character for you, but my God, do you ever need it! When was the last time you even had sex?"

"With someone else?"

She snorted a laugh. "Yes, hon, with someone besides you and your shower massager."

I rolled my eyes. "Too long."

I hadn't been with anyone since Charles, and by the end of our marriage, we hadn't been cozy with each other.

"Exactly," Sarah said. "And now, you have the chance for the perfect hookup. Tailor-made to your tastes. You don't know who he is, so no strings attached. You cannot catch anything, so no antibiotics are needed after—"

"Ew."

"And zero chance of pregnancy. God, I think I'm talking myself into doing this."

"It's thirty-five hundred dollars per session."

"Never mind."

I laughed. "Like you said, it is perfect. We spent more than that on the girls' weekend we had in Vegas."

"Yeah, but that was real."

"And speaking of antibiotics—"

"Hey, I told you that in complete confidence! Where are you now?" She sounded worried.

"The bathroom inside my adventure suite at Perfect Match."

"Don't chicken out, Jess. You will hate yourself if you give up before you even try. Isn't that what you did by marrying Charles? You did the safe thing, and look how that turned out."

I huffed into the phone. "You are the only person I let call me out like this, you know that?"

"Yes, because you know I do it out of love. Now go get some virtual fun."

I giggled at her. "Thanks for the pep talk, coach."

"You got it."

We hung up, I finished my business in the bathroom, washed my hands, and went out.

"I'm ready."

Chloe didn't seem to mind the short break I had taken to talk to my bestie. "Let's do it." She started attaching sticky pads to my chest. "What is your avatar's name?"

"Princess Eveline, daughter of King Prosper III, and Queen Gwendolyn,"

"Siblings?" She attached more sticky pads to my arms and hands.

"A sister, Bernice. Fourteen." I'd always wanted a little sister.

"Perfect. Once the helmet is on, take a good look at your avatar and memorize her features."

"Okay." I nodded as the helmet lowered onto my head. Once it was in place, I hardly noticed it. Not cold, like I had expected. It was the same temperature as my face. The avatar looked a lot like me—the same cherry chocolate hair, my green eyes, and my lips.

I'd made her taller than me and smaller in the chest because my boobs were so big that they could impede a real adventure. I'd always wondered what it would be like to have an athletic build, so that was my pick. Eveline wasn't some shy office worker.

She was a badass.

NICK

"So, have you done this?" I asked my tech.

Shane smiled and nodded. "Everyone at Perfect Match has been through a virtual experience at least once. Most of us jump at every opportunity to do it again."

"How many times have you done it?"

Shane lifted his eyes to the ceiling as if the answer was there. "I lost count, but it's definitely over thirty. When they are testing new environments, they run us through the same adventure several times until it's perfected. But let me tell you, it's fun even on the first run. It's addictive."

It was reassuring to hear him say that. "Good."

After my phone call with Ed, I also didn't worry too much about the artificial intelligence plucking information from my head and selling it to the highest bidder or someone hacking into their servers and stealing it. According to Ed, their encryption was revolutionary, and they were doing good things for society. Not that having a charity indicated that the owners were good people. It was probably a tax shelter of some kind.

The fact that they had gone to so much trouble to obscure their identities didn't inspire confidence.

"I assume you read all the instructions and explanations," Shane said.

"I did." Several times.

The instructions called for comfortable clothing, but I'd decided against sweatpants. Once things got hot and heavy, I didn't want the tech to stare at the mast I would sport. Jeans were better at keeping things at least semi-discreet.

"Do you have any questions?"

"Probably, but I kinda just want to jump in."

He chuckled. "That's the right attitude."

"Oh, there is one thing." I lifted my left leg on top of the chair. "I've put it down in the questionnaire, and it's not a big deal, but there is something you need to be aware of." I pulled at my left pant leg. "You can't see it with my jeans on." I showed him my scars. "Sometimes when I sleep, this leg kicks because of the nerve damage, so I suggest staying clear of my left side when I'm in the simulation." I dropped the jeans back into place and lowered my leg.

"I got you." He smiled. "Some people do crazy things in the dream state, which is what the simulation approximates. I have been kicked and punched, and one guy tried to bite me."

"Are you kidding?"

He shook his head, chuckling. "When you're in the program, it's as real as things are right now, but most people are in a state similar to REM sleep, and they are immobile thanks to sleep paralysis. I can give you a muscle relaxant, but I don't recommend it." He leaned closer. "It might affect your experience, and we don't want that, right?"

"No, we don't, but I have a hell of a right hook, so you've been warned."

Shane grinned. "Thanks for the warning. I'll stay clear."

I looked at the strange chair that was part dentist chair, part salon chair, complete with over-padded reclining features, and a strange bubble helmet. Shane's chair and equipment panel were to my right, so he was safe from my leg but not from my punch.

"Alright then. Ready to begin?" he asked.

As I sat in the chair, Shane popped the armrests open and pulled out restraints.

"Whoa, wait." I lifted my hand. "There was nothing about restraints in the brochure."

"We used to restrain everyone, but now we only do it to people like you who are active during sleep." He handed me one cuff to examine. "You can break out of them with ease. They are more of a reminder to your body to stay still than actual restraints." He smiled apologetically. "I should have waited until you were in the simulation. You wouldn't have even known."

That would have been a colossal mistake. If I woke up and found myself tied to the chair, I would attack Shane before my mind cleared enough to realize I wasn't in enemy territory, about to be tortured for information.

"Don't put any on me. That will trigger my PTSD, and you really don't want that."

Shane blanched. "There was nothing in your questionnaire about PTSD."

"I use the term loosely. I don't have any disorders, but I was in the military for many years, and when I'm groggy and disoriented, my training might kick in."

Shane let out a breath. "Got you." He put the restraints back into the armrests. "What should I do if you get violent?"

"I don't expect that to happen, but in the event that my sleep paralysis is not activated, get out of the room, stop the simulation remotely, and don't come back without reinforcements and a tranquilizer."

The tech gave me an assessing look and then nodded.

"You're lucky you got me. Anyone else would have refused to continue."

"I appreciate that." My shoulder muscles, which had tensed a moment ago, started to loosen up. "One more question for which I couldn't find an answer online. If the adventure takes a salacious turn and I...."

He smiled professionally. "Your brain can experience an orgasm without emission. When you wake up, your pants will be as clean as they are now."

I'd had sexual dreams on more than one occasion, and I hadn't ejaculated in my sleep even once, but I hadn't reached full satisfaction either. I hoped this experience would be better.

"Thank you for the reassurance. Now I'm officially ready."

"Let's get started." Shane checked that my vitals were tracking and attached many sticky pads to my chest and arms. "What is your avatar's name?" he asked.

"Prince Nolan. It means champion. Cheesy, I know."

"People pick stranger names for worse reasons. No judgment from me." He typed into the computer. "And your family members?"

"King Oswald and Queen Annabella, my parents."

Shane asked, "Meaning?"

"Divine power and favored grace."

"Nice. Working this job, I have a thing about names, and with twins on the way, I'm always looking for something a little different."

"Congratulations."

"Thanks. Siblings?"

"No. Only a cousin, Theodore. I don't know the meaning, but I liked the chipmunk."

Shane smiled. "I always liked Alvin, myself."

Since all that information was in the questionnaire, I wondered why he was asking. Maybe to make sure that I remembered those names on some subconscious level?

"Now, let's move to the fun part. You get to see your avatar and make small adjustments if you want to. The software bases your avatar on the combined data from your and your match's questionnaire, so don't make too many changes."

"Got it." As the helmet lowered onto my head, I was surprised at how well it fit. "That's a great fit."

"We've recently updated the software to do that automatically, so the techs no longer need to make adjustments. The chair takes a 3D image of your head when you sit on it, so it can contour to its shape comfortably. Now open your eyes."

"How did you know they were closed?"

"Everyone does that when the helmet lowers over their heads. It's instinctive."

I opened my eyes and looked at my avatar. It had come out better than I expected. Trying to guess what Jessica's preferences were, I'd only given minimal instructions, and the programmers or the artificial intelligence had taken it from there.

"Your programmers did a good job. I like the crown."

"I know, right? If I was into guys, well...."

I was glad he didn't finish the sentence. He was talking about my alter ego, and I didn't want to hear him say he was attracted to me.

They'd given Nolan medium brown hair with lots of golden streaks that was a little longish and shaggy and would look great flowing in the water. He had aquamarine eyes like the sea, a powerful jaw, good cheekbones, and nicely shaped lips that looked a lot like mine. As for his body, he had good upper traps for swimming and a narrow waist, and as for the tail, they'd covered it in golden scales to complement his tan.

After all, Nolan was a prince, and gold indicated royalty.

I could see some of me in him, but I doubted my partner would be able to recognize me as him if she met me in the real world. Mainly, it was the expression in his eyes. If I met Nolan on the street or on the beach, as it might be, my impression would have been that he wasn't a showy peacock despite his good looks.

Now to find out if Jessica would take the bait.

"So, any changes?" Shane asked.

"Nope. He's perfect. Much better looking than I am."

Shane cocked a brow, and I expected the usual comment how I was good looking too, but instead, he put his hand on my shoulder. "Good. I'll start counting down from ten."

On seven, a door appeared, and when I touched the door-knob, my hand was tan.

"Bon voyage," I heard a voice in the distance.

13

NICK/PRINCE NOLAN

For a moment, I couldn't remember how I got so close to shore, but what I did remember clearly was that my cousin was waiting for me to plan our next trip, and I was late.

I took a big breath and dove in. My tail sprang into action, propelling me toward Poseidon City. It was a twenty-minute swim from the surface to the underwater dome, so I had no time to lose, but that didn't mean I could be careless. Most sea life didn't bother the Mer, but every once in a while a whale or a shark got adventurous, so I always kept an eye out for danger.

As the silver dome came into view a school of orange squid darted by, a sure sign that there was nothing threatening around.

I swam to a port, entered, and as soon as the hatch closed behind me, I took a deep breath.

Having been born in the city, it shouldn't impress me every time I returned to it, but Poseidon City was so marvelous compared to how the humans lived that I couldn't help the awe I felt at the ingenuity of our planners and engineers.

It was constructed like a spoked wheel, with tunnels connecting the spokes. Each spoke and connection was a waterway, intersecting in pools and ponds. Waterfalls were everywhere, feeding our streets and adding to the magical ambiance of the city.

As sea mammals, the Mer needed air to breathe, but they also needed their bodies to be in the water for at least four hours daily.

The longer the better.

Swimming past a residential neighborhood, I waved and smiled politely to those who curtsied or bowed. It slowed me down, but I had a duty to my people. As their crown prince, it was mainly smiling and waving for now, but one day I would have to take my father's throne, and the burden would become much heavier.

Until then, though, I planned to have as much fun as Theo and I could get away with.

I was swimming behind schedule, so I took less crowded side waterways.

The Gleaming City, as my home was also called, glittered in the late day sunlight. Golden towers beamed, and the jewel-encrusted roofs sparkled. It was my favorite time of day to be home.

Since I lived in Aureate Castle, my cousin's house was not as luxurious as mine, but it was still one of the fanciest. More importantly, it was private, so we could meet in relative secrecy and plot our adventures away from court and all those prying ears and eyes.

I knocked impatiently. "Open up, Theo."

The door lifted to reveal my smirking cousin. "You're late."

I swam past him, rolling my eyes. "Did you get the clothes?"

"Have I ever let you down?"

"Do you want me to answer that?"

"I got the clothes," he huffed. "Did you bring the bag?"

"Yes." I pulled my wet bag from my shoulders and opened it. Inside were two more bags, one inside the other to keep it dry.

He rolled our clothes and stuffed them into the bag. "It has been too long since we had a guys' night out at McCoy's."

Guys' night was code for meeting human girls, and we both knew it. McCoy's was our favorite human tavern, partly because it was near a beach that we had easy access to and because the ale was superb. "It has been a while. Do you think you're up to the challenge?"

He laughed. "Not like it's much of a challenge. All we can do is flirt and kiss, perhaps a little touching. Tell me what tavern girl is going to deny me that."

"There was McCoy's daughter—"

"That was a fluke, and you know it, you son of a bait. Lilian should have told me she was betrothed. I wouldn't have bought her all those drinks."

I smirked. "That might be why she didn't tell you."

"It was dastardly of her to use me for my money like that," he said, shaking his head. "Just so she could line her father's coffers. It's unseemly."

"No more unseemly than you trying to earn a kiss from her by getting her tipsy."

He laughed. "I love a girl who can hold her liquor. Too bad Lilian can drink me under the table."

"She grew up in a tavern. What did you expect?"

"Tonight, same bet as always?"

"First one to kiss a girl wins?"

He nodded. "It's a shame we can't go any further than that. We're royalty. You'd think we didn't have to live by the same rules as the rest of the merfolk."

"That's precisely why we have to live by the rules, Theo. We have to lead by example. Mer bond physically and spiritually with their chosen one on their wedding night. It's magic."

I couldn't wait to find the one who would complete me, but as the prince, I didn't have the luxury of choosing for myself. My mate would be chosen for me, and I could only hope my parents would select a sweet-natured princess. I couldn't stand the ones who thought their subjects were beneath them and existed only to serve them.

It was the other way around.

Rulers should serve their people.

"I've heard all the lectures before." Theo waved a dismissive hand. "Once we mate, we mate for life," he said in a singsong way to mock our tenet. "But some of those human girls are so damn enticing."

"Put that thought out of your mind for tonight. We will drink and make merry, and that is all. No sense in thinking about what you can't have."

"Right." Theo snorted. "As if I can think of anything else."

I knew precisely what he meant and commiserated inwardly.

We were healthy young males, and like any other forbidden fruit, the outlawed nature of premarital sex made it even more appealing. Fraternizing with humans was especially frowned upon, and that made it an even bigger temptation. "Keep it in your pants, Theo. Besides, isn't Princess Allura interested in you?"

"Pfft, Allura? I wouldn't touch her with a narwhal's horn. She's so annoying."

She was a bit of an airhead, and her nasal prattle could drive a saint mad, but she wasn't as bad as some of the others.

"Allura is pretty."

Theo shrugged. "Pretty might be good enough for you, but I want a mate I can talk to, not one that makes me wish for deafness when she opens her mouth."

"I wish for a mate that is both pretty and smart," I said. "I want a female I can connect with. One who gets me."

I could dream.

Giving me a pitying look, Theo looked out the window. "The sun is going down. Time to make our escape from Poseidon City."

14

JESSICA/EVELINE

"Y ou can't run away!" Bernice's voice came out as a squeak.

My little sister was not supposed to find out until after I was gone, but as usual, she'd burst into my bedroom uninvited and without knocking. I should have barricaded the door, but I'd been too upset to think straight.

"Watch me." I threw another simple garment into the bag.

Aghast, Bernice put a hand on her chest. "We are princesses! What is there to escape? And where would you even go?"

I straightened to look at her. "I'd rather be anywhere but here. You heard Father! He betrothed me to a buffoon!" Frantically, I kept packing my bag.

Despite the luxury, my bedroom was little more than a prison. Gilded mirrors, a four-poster bed with gauzy soft bedding, and paintings from all the faraway kingdoms. None of it mattered compared to what I was meant to endure.

"I know, Eveline, but look on the bright side." She sat on my bed and folded one leg under her.

"There's a bright side?"

"You don't have to marry his cousin."

I shot her a glare and continued to pack. "That is not a bright side. It's a threat. And to think that Eghurt means intelligence. Was he named that as a joke? At the party last night, he asked me if one twin closes their eyes, can the other twin still see?"

"Okay, so he's not the smartest."

I laughed. "Not the smartest? You're being too generous."

"But just because he isn't smart doesn't mean he's a bad person."

"He snapped his fingers at our servants. He yelled at Renda when she didn't get his drink fast enough for his liking. He—"

"Okay." Bernice lifted her hand. "I get it. He's awful. But think, Eveline." She folded her arms over her thin body. "No one else has asked for your hand, and you're not getting any younger."

"I would sooner marry a fish than marry Eghurt. No, a dog. A horse, a pig—"

"I understand—"

"No, you don't. I'd rather die, Bernice. Anything is better than being made to be that pompous ass's broodmare. And you know about his mother, Queen Verdona?"

"It's just a rumor."

"I saw her put something in Father's drink. I'm sure it was a potion that made him agree to the betrothal. She's a witch, and she is behind this fiasco of an arranged marriage."

"Come now," Bernice said patiently. "Father was frustrated with you long before the party last night. You're unladylike, willful, and opinionated. There's a reason he started calling you Princess Thorn."

"He thinks being ladylike means a woman does not speak her mind, so if that's the behavior he wants from me, he will never get it. I speak my mind, and I have no shame for it."

"Is that what you call publicly criticizing his alliance with Queen Verdona? Speaking your mind?"

"Yes. Don't you think the alliance is appalling?"

She huffed. "Of course, I do. But I'm not daft enough to say it in front of a room full of dignitaries."

"You've always been a better princess than me, Bernice. With me gone, Mother and Father can focus on finding you a proper husband."

Poor Bernice. Was I sentencing her to the same fate as mine?

Hopefully, she was smarter than me and would find a way to manipulate our parents to choose a husband she actually liked.

"Where will you go?" my sister said quietly. "What will you do? There are bandits. It's unsafe, and I don't think you'll escape them by speaking your mind."

"I'll—"

"This is going to completely ruin your already tarnished reputation. No one has asked for your hand in marriage because everyone has heard about your reputation, and if you run away, no one will ever marry you. You know what they will think."

"I don't care." I grabbed her thin shoulders to get her attention. "Bernice. I am going to the seaside village west of here, just over the border. I'll get a job at a tavern or something. And if there are bandits, I will fight them."

"Fight them?" She laughed. "With what? Your cunning wit?"

"When Renda gets here with my other supplies, my bag will be so heavy and stuffed with hard objects that it will be like swinging a flail. I'll be fine."

"And how will you sneak past the guards? It is not as though they will simply let you leave."

I snatched some of my plainer jewelry. Things to sell without too much suspicion of their being palace jewels. "Bribery works wonders on men who have never had fortune smile upon them."

Someone knocked in a pattern on my door.

"Come, Renda."

My handmaid entered, weighed down by her own bag. "I brought the dresses you requested—"

"Good, thank you, Renda."

"And also a cloak."

"Please unload your bag on the bed so I may see them."

"Begging your pardon, mistress, but I do not think you should do this."

I huffed. "The clothes, Renda. Please."

She frowned and poured the garments onto my bed. Plain, primarily brown. There were even tears and faint stains. "My Princess, this is unbecoming."

"It's perfect." Smiling at the ripped dress in my hand, I shoved it into my bag.

"Please, reconsider, my lady," Renda pleaded.

"Listen to your handmaid, Eveline," Bernice begged. "You are putting yourself in danger."

Renda nodded. "You don't know how men are outside of castles. They aren't genteel. You won't be treated like a princess out there."

"You mean to say I won't be treated like a captive or a piece of property to be traded? That's what I want. I know the two of you mean well, but I have had enough of this life. A life of balls and festivals and minding every word that comes out of my mouth. A life of putting on a brave face to make sure no one truly knows who I am. It is too much for me to bear. If I don't go, I'll die here."

Renda's pinched face squeezed tighter as she held her tongue. But Bernice's blue eyes sparkled with tears. "Even if you don't die, what do you think will happen when you return? Do you think Father will even try to arrange a marriage for you once you've sullied yourself?"

I took her hands in mine for what felt like the last time.

"Bernice, I don't mean to return. And if I do, I pray he never tries to arrange another marriage for me so long as I live."

"How will you have a family?"

I laughed and kissed her forehead. "I already have you. You're all the family I need."

"And you're leaving me behind," her voice cracked as she broke down in tears.

I held Bernice tightly, and it was the only time I doubted my ability to follow through with my plan. When she calmed down, I looked her in the eye. "Bernie, we will see each other again one day. I swear it. But for now, I must escape this marriage. I cannot be made to lie with Prince Eghurt. Never. If I fail...if this plan doesn't work, and I am forced back here...I would kill myself."

I turned to the window that was regrettably too narrow for me to squeeze through. I would have to jump from the roof.

"You won't," Bernice said. "You love life too much."

She was very perceptive for a fourteen-year-old.

Renda sighed. "Forgive my language, my ladies, but Prince Eghurt is a festering dung heap."

Bernice giggled, and it was nice to see her smile again.

I was sure that Renda had more colorful terms for Eghurt, and if I wanted to pass for a commoner, I needed to know how to speak like one. "Is that actually how commoners speak to one another, or are you being genteel for our innocent ears?"

She stared at the floor and muttered, "A commoner would say Eghurt is an asshole."

Bernice laughed, and her cheeks flushed pink. "Renda!"

"I thought so." I smirked. "The staff keeps that kind of language from us, don't they?"

"Of course, mistress. It is forbidden to speak so freely before you."

"Do you see what I mean, Bernie? We live in a bubble here. The castle is not the real world. Everything is so sanitized and constricting. Remember when the acting troupe came to put on that romantic play for our parents' anniversary jubilee last year?"

"What of it?"

"When we were watching the play, I thought about how the actors had to memorize the lines someone else wrote for them, then act out the story while saying those lines, and I thought about how that is exactly what life was like here. We're all made to memorize the lines Father wants us to say and act out the story how he wants it to play, and well, I just can't do that anymore."

Renda cleared her throat. "Begging your pardon, my lady, but since when have you ever done anything your father wanted of you?"

Bernice giggled. "She has a point."

"You both know what I mean. That is what they expect of me. And you. And everyone else here. We are supposed to do whatever Father wants and follow his orders and pretend we agree with him, and I cannot do it anymore. I can't live with those expectations. I want to be free. To live my life as I see fit. I refuse to live the life one man decided for me by selling me off to another."

Renda's lips pressed together tightly.

"What is it, Renda?"

"I am going to miss you, my lady."

I had known Renda for four years, and in all that time, she had washed my linens, brushed my hair, cleaned my chamber pot, and done all the other things a handmaid should do. She had also been my confidant on more than one occasion.

She was my friend, but although I was grateful for her service and thanked her often, I had never hugged her.

It just wasn't done. When Mother had seen other courts engaging with their servants in a friendly manner, she'd regarded it as inappropriate at best and uncouth at worst.

I hugged Renda. "Thank you for the dresses and for the years of perfect service. I wish I could leave you with some jewels, but I fear they would be found, and someone would accuse you of stealing them."

"Never you mind that, my lady. I am merely happy to have been of service. The guard shift change happens soon, so if you are doing this, now is the time."

"Right," I said, grabbing my loaded bag. It was heavier than I'd expected, but I managed. Either I bore the weight of the bag on my back or Eghurt's on my front. I shook the thought from my mind. "Until we meet again."

Bernice's lips wriggled, trying to hold back the tears. "Until then."

Renda only nodded, her eyes wet.

I took a breath and left for the adventure of a lifetime.

15

NOLAN

*T*he tunnel entrance was at the dome's edge and hidden behind a waterfall. The marketplace that occupied that section was closed for the evening, so Theo and I managed to get there without being stopped.

Only a select few of Poseidon City's citizens knew that this exit tunnel existed, and I was one of them. With unrestricted access to the royal library, I could retrieve the original city plans, which detailed everything from the materials used to construct the silver dome down to the sewer grid running under it and all its exit points. That was how I discovered this long-forgotten tunnel. There were four more old exits scattered around the dome's perimeter, but they were all more difficult to enter unnoticed.

As Theo and I slipped behind the waterfall and entered the tunnel, I let out a breath and turned on my glow stick. "That was surprisingly easy."

Getting up in my face, Theo scoffed, "You didn't even shave. How do you expect any tavern girls to kiss you with a baby urchin on your face? Besides, if either of your parents saw you like that, you would be admonished."

Grimacing, I ran a hand through my stubble. It would have taken a human male a couple of weeks to get such growth, but mine had grown that much since I shaved that morning.

Facial hair distinguished mated males from bachelors, which meant that I had to shave three times a day to maintain a clean-shaven look. It was an old custom from the days merpeople had gotten mated at eighteen, so keeping the growth under control had been manageable. Nowadays, mer no longer mated so young, and maintaining a clean-shaven face was a hassle.

As soon as I was king, I was going to change that stupid custom, and while I was at it, I would also abolish the prohibition on pre-mated sex, but that would be a much more difficult change to make than the facial hair.

The mer mated for life, and the belief was that the bond formed during the consummation of the mated vows.

"The court session dragged on longer than usual, and I didn't have time to shave. I had to rush to meet you."

"Oh, woe is me," Theo teased. "I'm just a lowly prince who must live an extravagant life of being waited on hand and foot."

I smacked his stomach with the back of my hand. "You're just jealous, but there is nothing to be jealous of. I'm forced to sit through tedious meetings that drag on forever, and the issues discussed were yawn-inducing. Today, I had to listen to a mussel farmer accused by his neighbor of coming too close to his eel herd's range. That discussion lasted for over an hour." I let out a sigh. "Let me tell you, Theodore. Matters of state are largely dull affairs."

"What I wouldn't give to be as bored as you, Nolan. My work is relentlessly demanding."

He was an artist, so his claim sounded like a joke.

I jumped onto a ledge and pulled my tail out of the water, letting it dry so it would turn into legs. Next to me, Theo did the same.

We didn't have towels to make the process quicker, and the tunnel was damp, so it took several minutes until the transformation happened. When it did, I stretched out my toes and wiggled them. "I love having feet, but I hate wearing shoes."

"I'm with you on that." Theo pulled two pairs of boots out of our pack. "But since we can't let our toes touch water, shoes are necessary."

Not to mention that we wouldn't be allowed to enter the tavern barefoot.

When we were both dressed, I lifted my glow stick, and Theo shouldered the pack.

"Before, when you said your work was relentlessly demanding, did you mean it?" I asked.

"Of course. I find beauty everywhere, and I must capture it to replicate it later. My mind is always busy with new inspirations for my creations. Sometimes, I even dream about my work." He sighed dramatically. "It's both a blessing and a curse. My only reprieves are our clandestine excursions and flirting with tavern girls."

"If you can find beauty in this tunnel, I will give you all the gold in Poseidon City."

It was a peculiar gray-green color and dark, with slime mold on the walls and floor and slippery hazards with every step, and my glow stick gave it a faintly ominous shimmer.

Theodore curled his lip in disgust. "There is no beauty here. This tunnel could serve as the inspiration for a series on the Underworld. I do not understand why we could not take your private hatch like last time. It is far better than this rank hole."

"Aye, but since we want to spend several hours at the tavern, I had to leave secretly and not where the servants would see me go. If we left much later, after the servants were gone for the night, we could have left through my private hatch."

"But if we went later, we would have missed the respectable girls."

I stopped in my tracks. "Since when are you interested in respectable girls?"

"They're the ones who are the most fun to get drunk."

"Oh, so you're looking for a challenge tonight?"

He grinned. "I am. Besides, if they're respectable, they won't go after you."

I cocked a brow. "But they'll go after you?"

"Which one of us remembered to shave?"

As I laughed, the sound echoed down the tunnel. "Shit," I said quietly.

"Yeah. You don't want the mer patrol above to hear us."

"They are scheduled to pass by the marketplace at seven. By then, we will be far away from here."

"Don't count on that." Theo lengthened his steps. "They don't always patrol in the same order. They might decide to start at the market and continue from there."

It was true. The new head of security had introduced new patterns so the patrols would be less predictable for trouble-makers like us.

We walked faster, but each step was perilous because of the slippery mold.

Theo groused, "This is like walking on ice."

"I know, just be careful, and please stop pulling on my jacket, or you'll take us both down—"

His feet slipped from under him, and he fell, yanking me down. Luckily, I landed on top of him. Unluckily, he let out a whoop as he fell.

He grumbled, "Sorry, I—"

"Who goes there?" a guard shouted at the mouth of the tunnel.

Damn. They'd heard my laugh and come to investigate.

"We should run," Theo whispered.

"We're not running," I mumbled, smiling politely and waving toward the guard approaching us.

There were two kinds of patrols; one did its rounds on foot, and the other did it in the water, swimming through the channels. Regrettably, those guarding the perimeter of the dome were usually on foot.

"If we don't run—"

"We're doing no such thing," I hissed, straightening my coat to look presentable.

Theo huffed. "The tunnels are forbidden. Do I need to remind you—"

"Let me handle this," I murmured. Smiling broadly, I stepped into the light the guard's glow stick was emitting. "Good evening. Gerald, isn't it?"

When he saw me, his eyes bugged out, and he kneeled. "My prince, I did not recognize you in these clothes. Have you gotten lost? I will be proud to escort you back to the castle."

"I am not lost. Please rise."

He stood and wore a canny expression. "Are you heading toward land, my prince?"

"Yes, I am."

He looked worried. "It is not safe out there, my prince. I strongly advise against it."

I put a hand on his shoulder. "It's not our first time, and we know how to handle ourselves. We are going on a secret reconnaissance mission, and I would appreciate my best guard monitoring this tunnel to ensure that we are not followed. I handsomely reward those in my employ for their discretion." I took his hand and snuck a gold coin into his palm. "Once I become king, I will remember all who served me well as prince and reward them with more than this small token of appreciation."

He shook his head and handed me back the coin. "I can't take this. You have my loyalty, my prince."

Behind him, I noticed a shadow at the mouth of the tunnel,

and a moment later, a feminine silhouette was backlit before vanishing to the other side.

So that was why Gerald was there. He'd planned to do precisely what Theo and I were about to, but instead of taking a friend or a cousin, he was taking his paramour on an adventurous excursion.

Lucky mer.

"Please. It makes me feel better to compensate you for the task I burdened you with." I pressed the coin into his hand. "Buy yourself a tankard on me."

"As you wish, my lord."

"I am curious about something, Gerald."

"Yes, my prince?"

I smiled again. "Are you even on patrol tonight?"

The guard laughed nervously. "Truth be told, I, um, well—"

"Your lady should have stayed better hidden." I fished out a few more gold coins. "Here. Take this. This is not a suitable place for a date, and you shouldn't take her to the land of humans either." I leaned closer to him. "If you think it's not safe for Theodore and me, two strapping males, it's definitely not safe for your future mate."

He shook his head. "I cannot take your money, my prince."

"Take the money and give your future family a better story than, 'I took your mother through a grimy tunnel to show her how the humans lived.' Take your lady to a nice restaurant or to see a performance. Lucinda is performing tomorrow night, and I heard tickets are still available for the show."

Gerald's eyes sparkled. "My Ronella loves Lucinda. She will be thrilled." He closed his hand around the coins. "I thank you for your generosity, my prince."

"Good. Theodore and I will be on our way, and you should send Ronella home so you can watch the entrance to the tunnel. I don't want us to be followed on our way out or stopped on our way back in. Tomorrow, I'll speak with the head of the guard to give you the afternoon off so you can attend the show."

"You are too generous, my prince."

Theodore huffed. "I dare say I agree with Gerald."

"My gift to you and your future family," I assured the guard. "Go on."

"Thank you, my prince." Gerald bowed and turned back the way he'd come.

Theo shook his head. "You cannot run a kingdom that way. You can't buy loyalty with money."

"That's true, but I'm not running a kingdom tonight, am I? I had to do something to save our tails. Come on."

"What if he turns us in?"

"He won't."

"But what if—"

I rolled my eyes. "Why are you so worried? It's not as if anyone will care if you're caught here. I'm the one with something to lose."

His lips twisted in a grimace. "Thanks for reminding me how unimportant I am, Nolan."

Damn. I forgot how touchy my cousin was about the subject of royal succession. "I didn't mean it that way, and you know it. You are very important to a lot of people."

He closed his eyes and huffed. "I know you don't mean to offend me. I just don't need your royalty shoved in my face repeatedly."

"You're a royal too."

"You are the crown prince. I am the son of the disgraced and disowned Prince Osiris. I might as well be a commoner."

"Don't say that."

"Whatever." He let out a breath and affected a smile. "Tonight is not about royal politics. Tonight is about girls and ale."

I grinned and clapped him on his back. "That's the spirit, cousin."

16

EVELINE

*H*aving changed clothes in a closet near the ground floor kitchens, I heard the chatter among the palace staff. They cursed and used coarse language, and I marveled at every syllable. It wasn't the first time I'd heard such words, but it was the first time I'd heard them all together.

I loved how they used distinct tones to convey vitriol or affection, even though the same words could have meant either emotion. The context was so layered. Reading such things in the forbidden books I had snuck out of the library was no match for hearing how ordinary people spoke.

If I was to pretend to be a commoner, then I would have to speak like them.

Renda had said the guard change was happening soon, which meant it was nearly time for the dayshift of the palace staff to leave for the day, and my plan was to use them as my cover.

I pulled my hair down, letting it fall in loose waves around my shoulders, and lifted the hood of my cloak to further conceal myself. I dirtied up my hem with soot from some of the cleaning rags in the closet and smudged a bit on my cheek,

If Father could see me now.

When I heard the staff shuffling past the kitchen en masse, I took a deep breath and, heart in my throat, I ducked out of the closet. Following the crowd of forty or so, I listened to them talk about their day and gripe about other members of the staff, specifically their supervisors.

Every word fascinated me until one asked, "You get chimney duty, girly?"

I coughed viciously, covering my mouth with one hand and holding up the other. "Sorry. Think I'm coming down with something."

"Oof, stay back. I cannot afford to get sick meself." The woman turned back to her friends who, upon hearing the cough, had all rushed to distance themselves from me.

It was just as I had planned, and as we shuffled out of the castle and into the courtyard, I lagged behind the group.

It was exhilarating to leave the castle and be in the courtyard.

I used to watch the staff leave from my room, staring down at them, jealous that they could come and go as they pleased while I was a prisoner in the castle.

The trees were so much taller up close, and the flowers prettier. It would be worth the effort even if I were caught on the grounds. But then the crowd passed through the gate, and I slipped out with them.

No one stopped me.

I was free.

My stomach sank, and my heart soared. I wanted to sprint, bound, and dance in the streets, but I had to lay low and keep pretending that I was a tired maid going home for the evening.

Outside the castle walls, the staff parted into two prongs, each heading toward one of the nearby villages. One part walked toward Poppy Crossing, a farming community, and the other headed toward Tranquility Post, a foresting outpost.

The third nearby village was a fishing community aptly named Seaside, and that was where I was going. Despite being walking distance from the castle, it didn't belong to our kingdom.

I asked a young boy in the crowd, "How far to Seaside?"

He frowned. "Why do you want to go there?"

"I'm meeting some friends." One thing I knew from the books was to never let a stranger know your true plans.

"It's a long walk, miss. It's half an hour to Poppy Crossing and another two hours from there to Seaside."

"Thank you." I had never walked such a distance before, but I was sure I would manage just fine.

With my father's patrols keeping the roads near the castle safe, I didn't fear the journey, but I was in the real world now, and the truth was that I knew very little about it. As eager as I was to escape marriage to Eghurt the Awful, I was keenly aware that there were worse fates than that for a lone young woman.

I had to be careful.

Going through Poppy Crossing, I was disappointed to find that its few shops were closed for the night. Only the inn was still open, and music poured out of a candlelit window. I was tempted to linger and listen, but I still had a long walk ahead of me.

The group of palace staff dwindled as residents peeled off for their homes, and as I followed behind those who lived on the outskirts of the village, an old man spied me. "Do I know you, lass?"

"I'm from Seaside. I'm new."

"And they got you working chimney duty? Who did you piss off to get that?"

I chuckled, then coughed loudly again. "Sorry, I'm under the weather."

"No mind to me," he shrugged off my concern, "I'm old, lass.

I won't see next winter. Might as well die from talking to a pretty girl."

I giggled and coughed again. "I think you might be the death of me."

"That is a nasty cough. When you get to Seaside, have a stop at McCoy's Tavern. They'll fix you up a toddy that will knock that cough right out of your lungs. Until then, save your voice so you can order it." He tipped his hat at me and caught up with his friends.

What a nice man.

If I ever returned to the palace and resumed my duties, I would reward him for his kindness and ask Doctor Fulmort to take a look at him.

The man wasn't old enough to contemplate death by next winter.

Except, I wouldn't be back, and there was nothing I could do for him. A twinge of guilt gnawed at me for neglecting my duty to my people, but I reminded myself that my first duty was to myself, and I had to escape marriage to Eghurt.

As I passed the last house on the street, I smelled the family's supper through the open window and stopped to take a peek. They sat together, laughing and drinking over a supper of stew and bread, and I couldn't help the envy I felt.

It wasn't for the deliciously fragrant stew but for the sense of family, which I had never enjoyed in the palace despite dining with my parents and sister every evening.

Our suppers were formal affairs, and Bernice and I were supposed to sit with our backs straight and nibble at our food because princesses weren't supposed to gorge themselves like commoners.

I often left the table hungry and ate in my room stuff that Renda had brought me from the kitchens earlier.

Tonight, they were having supper at the castle in honor of a visiting dignitary, and hopefully, Bernice would cover for me as we'd agreed, saying that I was under the weather and had to stay in my room.

I trusted that Renda and my sister would hold out as long as they could, but Father was a bear of a man when he was angry, and when he discovered my escape, he would roar his fury. He'd counted on my marriage to Eghurt to secure the alliance with Verdona.

As much as I would have liked to believe that my father had been tricked into agreeing to such a union, I knew better. Marrying me off to an asshole like Eghurt was in character for him.

My father didn't approve of me because I was outspoken and unladylike, and I didn't approve of him because he was too traditional and selfish. I had always assumed that I would be the one to make the first step, but I had underestimated my father's lack of care for me.

In my heart of hearts, I naively hoped that he loved me and wanted the best for me, but I should have known better.

Huffing out a sardonic sigh, I wiped a tear from my eye and looked around to reorient myself.

I'd been so lost in thought that I had reached a border of our kingdom. The demarcation was a barely noticeable line of rocks embedded in the dirt path and a small wooden sign, but a whole new world awaited me on the other side.

Once I crossed that line, I would be out of my father's grasp.

I leaped over it and landed with a happy squeal.

With a new spring in my step, I walked along the path at a steady, unhurried pace, but as soon as I smelled the ocean and the salty air filled my lungs, I ran the rest of the way to the beach.

The sea at night was magical, with the moon glittering on the water and the waves crashing gently to shore. Finding a rock to sit on, I put my heavy sack next to me and watched the beauty before me.

As the waves lapped at the shore, a faint sound of music reached my ears, and I hoped it was coming from the tavern, the one that the old man had suggested I should get a toddy at. I didn't know what a toddy was, only that it was supposed to knock the cough right out of my lungs.

Not that I needed a cough remedy. What I needed was a job. Heaving the bag onto my other shoulder, I followed the sound of music.

I didn't make it more than fifty paces when half a dozen men emerged from behind a clutch of trees, and from the looks they gave me, they were up to no good.

The tallest one said, "Look what we have 'ere, boys."

Oh hell.

Curtly, I said, "You have nothing. Good evening." I tried to hurry past them, but they circled me.

"Now, now, no need to be rude, girly," the shortest one taunted.

"Bet she's pret'y under all that," another one said.

"Let's see." The tall man reached for my cloak, but I batted his hand away.

"Do not touch me, sir!"

"Oh, we got a fighter," a man said behind me. He yanked the hood of my cloak back. "An' she's real pretty."

A dark look in his eyes, the tall one cracked his knuckles. "I get her first. I'll teach her some respect."

Another one grabbed my bag, but I yanked it from him and swung it in a circle at them all. "Back away."

The short one laughed. "Not a chance, little lamb. Tonight, the wolves feast."

NOLAN

*T*he tunnel's exit hatch was a giant oyster shell covered by rocks with barnacles adhered to ensure it was well hidden. The palms surrounding it were densely packed together, providing further camouflaging and a small area just big enough to serve as our changing room.

"The ale best be cold when we get there." Theo brushed the sand off his black breeches.

"The ale will be cold, the girls will be warm, and the music will be loud. That's why we go to McCoy's." I smiled as I pulled my coat over the fancy human clothes I'd gotten for us.

Obtaining the latest fashions had been a challenge, but it was well worth it. The more money the girls thought we had, the nicer they were to us. My newest coat was aquamarine blue, like my eyes.

"What do you think?" I asked my cousin.

"I think you look too flashy in that."

"I got you the newest fashion, so you stand a chance with the girls even though you are walking in with me," I teased.

He laughed. "How generous of you." Theo held up his new coat, admiring the black brocade stitches on the forest green fabric. "Alright, I'll give it to you. This is really nice." He pulled it on. "How do I look?"

I refused to tell him he looked handsome, although he did. In fact, dressed so lavishly, he cut a more impressive figure than I did. "You look like a wealthy human."

"Perfect." He grinned.

As we trod across the beach toward the lights of Seaside, I asked, "How is your father doing? I have not heard from Uncle Osiris in a while."

"He has been traveling a lot lately to take his mind off things."

We both knew what things he meant. Osiris had disgraced himself by stealing our grandmother's diadem to use as a proposal to a princess of a foreign kingdom. Our grandmother had left it for me to use in a proposal, so when the thievery was discovered, they cast him out of the royal court.

I couldn't understand why he had done a stupid thing like that, but then I'd never been in love. Perhaps my uncle's desire for the princess had addled his otherwise exceptionally sharp brain.

According to mer law, Osiris's royal status couldn't be revoked, but he was no longer in the court, so I saw him less often. It was such a shame, too. We'd been close before he had fallen from grace.

"I hope his travels find him well."

Theo arched a brow. "Do you?"

"I do. I know things are strained between him and the family right now, but I hope he will be forgiven in time. Osiris just made a stupid mistake. Everyone makes at least one in their lifetime."

"Aye, but not everyone gets banished."

"He wasn't formally banished, Theo. He—"

A woman's scream cut me off. And as we both turned our

heads in that direction, Theo put his hand on my forearm. "Don't. We shouldn't get involved."

He was right. Mer were forbidden from interfering in human affairs, but I couldn't just ignore a woman in trouble.

"You can stay here. I'm going to help her." I pulled out of his grip and rushed in the direction the scream had come from.

"Don't be an idiot, Nolan." I heard Theo's boots crush the sand behind me. "At least let's assess the situation first."

"Fine." I slowed down as we reached a grouping of trees that provided cover while affording us a view of the drama unfolding ahead.

A young woman was swinging her pack at a group of hoodlums surrounding her like a pack of vultures. "Back off, now!" she snapped.

The men kept grabbing at her and laughing.

One said, "Now, now, that's not how you make friends."

"Leave me alone!"

"Let's show her how to make friends, boys." He kept her distracted by coming closer. She backed away from him, only to be caught by the man behind her. He and another grabbed her arms while another stole her bag.

As I lunged forward, Theo snatched my arm and said, "Nolan! We cannot intervene in human matters. You kill them, and you will lose the crown!"

"I'm not going to kill them." I wanted to, but I couldn't break the law. "I could use your help, though."

He grunted in annoyance. "It's been a while since my last brawl, and I'm out of practice, which makes it more of a fair fight for them."

As we ran at them, the tall one shoved the woman into the sand, but just as he reached for the tie of his breeches, she kicked him in the groin and sent him yelping.

I grinned, but then one of the others kicked her in the ribs and the red haze that had cleared from my vision a moment before returned with a vengeance.

I ran up behind him and punched him in the kidneys. He grunted as he fell forward onto the sand. It was then that the others noticed us.

Theodore tapped one on the shoulder and said, "Hello," just before punching him in the face.

He had knocked the bandit out cold. Two down.

Another came at me, swinging wildly. Clearly, he had no combat training whatsoever. As he punched, he left himself wide open. I hooked my fist and swiftly jammed it under his jaw. He stumbled backward and shook his head in confusion. I hit him again, and the second time, his head knocked against a palm trunk as he fell. His head lolled to the side, unconscious. Three down.

As I watch the first guy I knocked down recover and getting up to rejoin the frey, someone grabbed me from behind, their forearm around my throat. They held a dagger in front of my eyes. "You think you're some kinda 'ero, eh? Comin' to save a whor—"

I flipped him over my shoulder and swiped his dagger as he fell. "Truly appalling manners, even for scum like you." I broke the dagger from its hilt and threw both pieces in the sand beside him. "Your dagger is a toy."

"How...how did you—"

I kicked his face, knocking him out.

Still three down, but we were getting there.

"A little help?" Theodore choked.

I spun in the sand to see two men holding his arms out to the sides while the tall one was punching him in the gut. Left to her own devices, the woman had somehow gotten up after that kick and was even trying to pry away one of the men holding Theodore.

Respect welled in my chest. She was so brave.

In one smooth move, I picked up the blade of the cheap dagger and flung it into the man's shoulder. He yelped and released Theo to pull the blade out, but I'd landed it just out of his reach. With him out of the way, Theo dropped to his knees, bringing his captors down with him. He climbed on top of one while the other turned his attention to the woman.

As the scumbag raised his hand to strike her, I caught it and used it to punch him in the face a few times until he had a nice welt. Then I grabbed a fistful of his hair and smashed his face into my knee. He fell over.

Four down.

Theo sat atop his bandit's chest, ready to strike, when he looked up. "Behind you!"

I spun, but it was too late. The tall one landed a punch, and I turned around just in time to take it in the gut instead of my back. It knocked the wind out of me—he was stronger than he looked. But I held my stomach tight and punched him in the jaw to ring his bell. He staggered back some distance but kept his eyes on me.

Pure rage shone from those beady eyes, and I knew he would not go down easy.

Neither would I.

I braced my feet in the sand, readying for his attack. He ran at me, fists balled. Just as he leaped to swing with all his might, a large bag came into view, knocking him against a palm tree to my left. He howled in pain as the dagger blade dug into him from the tree. The woman stood there, panting and angry. "That's what you get!"

That little thing knocked a two-hundred-pound man all the way over there?

Respect.

He snarled, "I'll have you yet, harlot!"

"Not on my watch," I said just before pounding him.

He went down, but I stayed on him and beat his face bloody. Someone grabbed my shoulder.

"It's over, Nolan," Theodore said.

I paused my assault just in time to realize the tall one was out. I climbed off him and checked. Theo's assailant was also motionless. "Yours still alive?"

"Aye."

I swallowed against a dry throat. "Good."

"We should kill them." Theo surprised me.

"I would love to, and it was difficult to hold back, knowing what they were. But as you said, killing people comes with complications we wish to avoid."

I could not say more in front of the woman, but Theo understood my meaning.

"They will harm others. You know this. It can stay among the three of us."

With a groan, I brushed my fingers through my hair.

I wanted them dead, but it wasn't in me to commit a crime and keep secrets that big. If I did that, I would confess and lose the crown.

I turned to the woman. "They attacked you. What would you have us do with them?"

She hesitated. "I would throw them in prison and sentence them to forced labor to atone for the crimes they committed, but I don't have the authority here, and I don't know who has in these parts. Maybe the people in the tavern can tell us who enforces the law around here."

The woman sounded well educated and authoritative, but she was dressed like a commoner, and her dress was in tatters, though that was probably not its state before the fight. Perhaps she was a lady's maid, and that was how she'd learned to speak like that.

Theo sighed. "Let us wash up and get to McCoy's. Your first round is on me for saving my scales back there."

"McCoy's?" she asked. "That's where I'm going to find work. Your ale is on me. It's the least I can do to repay your gallantry." She stepped into the moonlight, and I had my first real glimpse of her.

Beautiful and brave.

Any other maiden would have collapsed in tears by now, but she stood tall and proud, with her chin up and her emerald green eyes simmering with fierce fire.

Her dark auburn hair fell in messy waves past her shoulders, tangled from the fighting she'd been through, and her beautiful, delicate face was bruised, weakening my resolve to leave the slime alive.

I distracted myself by focusing on the anomaly of her.

I had to find out who she was.

"Pay for our ale?" I laughed. "You saved me from that brute with your bag. I owe you a pint."

She smiled, and her teeth were gleaming white and even. "Uh, I think you were in the middle of saving me, so—"

Not a commoner. I was sure of that. This was a high-born lady, and I had to find out what she was doing all alone on the beach, dressed in a commoner's garb.

"I don't care who pays," Theo interrupted. "I am parched and going to McCoy's." He marched ahead.

"That rude man is my cousin, Theodore. I am Nolan."

She smiled again, setting my heart alight. "I'm Eva. Eva Trovalia. Pleased to meet you." She curtsied better than any princess I had ever known, and as she rose, her eyes met my lips. "I didn't know I'd find a gentleman here."

"I believe our night will be full of surprises. After you." I gestured to the path, and as she passed me, the scent of vanilla and lilacs captured me.

EVELINE

"*L*et me carry your bag," Nolan offered as we started toward the tavern.

"That's okay. It's not that heavy." That was a blatant lie, but I didn't want to appear weak.

It was enough that Nolan had to rescue me from the bandits, and he was banged up worse than I was.

"I insist." He stopped walking and extended his hand. "You've been through enough this evening. It's the least I can do."

I wanted to resist, but the truth was that my side still ached from where the bandit had kicked me. Surprisingly, though, I wasn't as shaken by the incident as I should be. Tonight would have ended very differently if Nolan and his cousin hadn't shown up at the right place and time.

I would have been raped by those slime worms and probably murdered as well.

Perhaps I was still in shock, or maybe it was the misplaced confidence that nothing could really happen to a princess. Except, I didn't feel distressed, and I wasn't naive enough to believe that those slimes would have left me alone if I had told them who I really was and what fate awaited them if they dared to harm me.

The truth was that before tonight, I hadn't been a big believer in providence, but I couldn't shake the strong sense that fate had intervened by sending Nolan to my rescue and that everything had happened according to its plan.

"Thank you." I handed him the heavy bag and tried not to wince while holding it out to him.

He smiled, taking my breath away.

God, the man was handsome. Tall, broad-shouldered, with sandy brown hair, perfectly shaped kissable lips, and eyes the color of the sea on a calm day.

I had difficulty taking my eyes off him and watching where I was going.

If I stumbled and fell, having Nolan save me again would be embarrassing. I'm sure he'd had enough for tonight. Then again, if I fell, he would need to catch me, and I really wanted to feel those muscular arms around me.

Something must be very wrong with my head to entertain such thoughts after what had almost happened. Had I gotten hit harder than I remembered?

When Nolan caught me staring at him, I quickly added, "Thank you for saving my life."

"I'm grateful to fate for bringing me to this spot tonight." He shivered. "I don't want to think what would have happened if Theo and I had arrived a few minutes earlier or later."

I shivered for a whole different reason.

Evidently, I wasn't the only one who had a feeling that our encounter had been fated.

"Indeed. I should offer a prayer to providence for your timely arrival."

Nodding, he hoisted the bag onto his thick shoulder and frowned. "How did you manage the weight of this? It must be heavier than the whole of you."

I lifted my chin. "I'm stronger than I look."

He gave me an appreciative look over that had none of the leering undertones I'd been accustomed to at court.

He was either a gentleman or just didn't find me attractive.

How disappointing. But then, what did I expect? I was wearing a dirty, torn dress, my hair was probably all messed up, and I wouldn't be surprised if I had bruises on my face and arms.

"I wondered how you could clobber the large one into the tree with your bag. It was an impressive move. Where did you learn it?"

Bernice and I had been taking lessons in self-defense from the former head of our father's guard, and the old guy had shown us no mercy. He didn't care that we were princesses or even that we were girls. He'd worked us as hard as he'd worked his soldiers before retiring.

Well, that might be a slight exaggeration or even a gross one. After all, Bernice and I trained for one hour four times a week, while the soldiers trained all day long, six days a week.

Still, I couldn't tell Nolan any of that without blowing my cover.

"My father believes that girls should know how to protect themselves, and he trained my sister and me. The strong muscles are from work, though."

Nolan nodded. "Your father is a smart man."

At that comment, I barely managed to stifle a grimace and nodded noncommittally.

"So," Nolan's cousin drawled as he sidled up to me. "You said that you're going to the tavern for work, but those bandits said that you're a harlot. Are you changing careers, or—"

Nolan cut him off by slugging his shoulder. "Forgive his manners, Miss Trovalia. Theodore's mouth is sometimes disconnected from his brain."

I smirked at them both. "I must disappoint you, Theodore,

but I am not a harlot." I turned to Nolan. "And please, call me Eva. I'll not stand on ceremony with the men who saved my life."

"Disappoint me?" Theodore scoffed. "Why would I be disappointed that you're not a harlot?"

"Because you cannot purchase my affections, and given your lack of manners, I imagine you are accustomed to paying for female company. But let me give you a pointer. Even a harlot is a lady, and you should address her as such."

Nolan's shoulders shook with stifled laughter. "You're very perceptive, Eva."

Hearing my fake name coming from his lips felt like a gentle caress, and I melted a little inside. On the outside, I kept my tough-girl expression.

Theodore scowled at me. "You have been through a traumatic event this evening, so I won't take offense," he said with a stiff upper lip. "For your information, I'm saving myself for my future bride, and I will never pay for female company."

That was very unusual and admirable.

Young men were not held to the same standards as young women, and the fact that Theodore was saving himself for the marital bed impressed me.

It also explained his lack of decorum. He just didn't know that calling a woman a harlot was offensive, even when it was correct. Some things were just not done.

I dipped my head. "My apologies. I shouldn't have been hasty with my judgment of you."

He smiled smugly at Nolan as he put his arm around my shoulders. "Now that we got things settled, I'm curious about something. If I were looking for paid female company, and you were in the business of providing it, how much coin would it take for you to spend time with me? Five coppers?"

He was just teasing, but it was tasteless and crude nonetheless.

As I elbowed him in the gut, he coughed, and Nolan grinned proudly at me.

"You think you can buy someone like me for five coppers?" I put my hands on my hips. "I would command a far greater purse. But since my company is not for sale, it's a moot point."

Theodore rubbed a hand over the side I'd elbowed. "I don't mind haggling over the price. While saving the whole of me for my future bride, I'm still allowed to enjoy some sweet kisses from pretty lasses."

Ugh, the guy was insufferable. How could Nolan stand his cousin?

"Don't make her knock you into a tree, Theo," Nolan advised.

"I was only jesting," he said. "I've never had to pay for company, and I never will."

Nolan rolled his eyes. "As you say." He turned his attention to me. "What sort of work are you looking for?"

"Why? Are you hiring?"

He arched a brow. "What do you think I do?"

I panned my gaze over the both of them. "You wear more fashionable clothes than most men and conduct yourselves well." I cast a sidelong glance at Theo. "Mostly well, anyways." I turned back to Nolan. "By your clothes and your posture, I would guess that you are merchants and doing well for yourselves. Perhaps you're even trading with royals."

Theodore opened his mouth to say something, but Nolan cut him off again. "You have a keen eye, Eva. We indeed trade with royals quite often."

EVELINE

*A*s the tavern came into view, it was a more welcoming sight than I had expected. The building was two stories tall and well-kept, with clean windows and a freshly thatched roof, but what made me smile was the light, raucous music, and laughter spilling from its interior.

That was precisely what had been missing from my stifling palace life.

Theodore opened the door and bowed, waving his hand in an exaggerated motion that made a mockery of a courtier. "After you, my lady."

"Let me get you a drink," Nolan offered as we entered. "You can inquire about a job after you have some ale in your belly."

"Okay." I didn't argue.

I was nervous about asking for a job for the first time in my life and worried about someone recognizing me.

Nolan led me to a corner table and motioned to the bench. "A lesson in self-preservation. Always sit with your back against the wall, facing the front door. That way, you will not be taken by surprise."

"Good advice." I slid all the way to the corner and kept my hood on.

"I'll get the ale," Theodore volunteered.

"Get us something to eat as well," Nolan called after his cousin as he sat beside me.

He was so close that his muscular thigh was touching mine, and I reveled at the contact. He smelled of sea breeze and clean male, and I couldn't get enough of it.

Why couldn't someone like him ask for my hand?

Not that Nolan could have done that, even if he was so inclined. As the crown princess, I had to marry another royal, and Nolan was just a merchant, tall, gallant, handsome, and evidently successful, but with not a drop of royal blood in him.

I sighed.

"Missing Theodore already?" he teased.

"Not particularly." I smiled up at him. He was so tall that even sitting down, he towered over me. "I'm rather happy with my current company."

Nolan's brows lifted in pleasant surprise. "So, Eva, what work were you doing before coming here?"

"A maid," I blurted. "I was a palace maid."

"Is that so?" He pretended to be impressed. "I cannot imagine why you would leave such a fine job."

I shrugged. "I was well paid, but it was dreadfully dull. Every day was the same as the day before." I ran through my maid's daily tasks. "Empty their chamber pots, put their dresses back in the closets, clean their rooms, and so on."

"They who?" He leaned closer to me. "Did you serve the royal family?"

Damn. I should have come up with a different employment history, but then it would have been even more difficult to describe what I had done in my previous job.

"I was Princess Bernice's chambermaid."

Nolan smiled, flashing me his perfectly straight, white

teeth. "I've heard good things about her. People say that she's as lovely as she is kind. "

"Oh, Bernie is a sweetheart." My heart ached, thinking of my sister.

"I heard less complimentary things about her older sister. Princess Eveline."

I bet he had.

"What kind of things?"

"That she's basically a thorn in her father's side and that no one makes her an offer of marriage because she's a shrew."

I felt my ears catch fire, not because I was embarrassed but because I was angry. If I were a male, they wouldn't have called me names.

"Don't believe everything you hear."

"So, she was nice to you?"

I nodded. "Princess Eveline was always polite to the staff. It was the snooty and opinionated court advisors and other syco-phants she couldn't stand."

"So the princesses treated you well, and you were paid handsomely for your services. Did someone else mistreat you? Was that why you felt you had to leave?"

Yeah, and that someone had been my own father, who had sold me to be a broodmare for a horrible man. But I couldn't tell Nolan that.

"I wasn't mistreated, but I felt stifled. Look around us. This place is so full of warmth and life. People are dancing, laughing, and saying things that no one at the palace would have dared to say. It's so free. There are no rules, no guards telling you what you can and cannot do."

"I see. You're a freethinker, then?"

I smiled. "You could say that."

He nodded sagely. "It must have been difficult for you to work in a regimented place like the palace."

I arched a brow. "You sound as if you are personally familiar with palace life. Have you lived in one?"

His eyes darted toward Theodore, who was still waiting for our drinks. "I didn't, but we sell our wares to several palaces, and they struck me as too formal and restricting, so I get what you are saying about feeling stifled. Sometimes it's challenging to keep my opinions to myself."

My heart leaped in my throat. We had so much in common. "Precisely! For instance, when the king recently made an alliance with a despicable queen, it was all I could do to keep my mouth shut." I didn't, but he didn't need to know that.

He nodded knowingly. "And I don't imagine that the king was interested in the opinion of his daughter's maid."

I laughed sharply. "He has no interest in anyone's opinion, not even his advisors'. I don't know why he keeps them on. Not that they are better than him. They are a bunch of sniveling sycophants."

Nolan narrowed his eyes at me. "Were you fired for speaking your mind? Was the king cruel to you?"

Yes.

"The king doesn't even know I exist, let alone care about my opinion."

I doubted he knew my or Bernice's maid's names or even those of his own.

Theodore returned with our ales and a couple of shepherd's pies. "Now, if you'll excuse me, that lovely blonde at the bar awaits my return." He jetted off to the girl with her eyes on him.

"That was fast," I said.

The ale was ice cold and frothy, a refreshing relief after our night. Glancing at the pie, I remembered my mother's admonitions about eating like a princess and pushed it away.

Nolan didn't touch his either, but I doubted it was for the

same reason. "Of your king's alliance, what bothered you so?" he asked.

"Queen Verdona is rumored to be a witch. I would have dismissed that as silly gossip, but I watched her during her visit, and I heard the princesses talk about her." The truth was that I had known that from the reports our ambassador had sent, but a maid would not have had access to them. "She's greedy and manipulative and seeks only to increase her holdings while her people starve. An alliance with her is tacit approval of her poor behavior."

He chuckled, his aquamarine eyes full of surprise. "I wouldn't have expected a maid to know so much about politics."

Oh hell. "Hard to avoid when tending to the princess. She has many opinions on the matter, and I agree with her. We spoke at length on the matter many times."

"She sought your counsel?"

"Is it so hard to believe a maid could give valued advice to a princess?"

"Forgive me. I've not known many princesses who were wise enough to listen to their maids."

He had a point.

"I guess I was more fortunate than most in that regard." I sighed, then shrugged. "The best part of palace life is the gossip."

"Not the food?"

"Why would it be the food?"

"Most commoners don't have access to such exclusive fare as that which they serve in a palace."

Right. "It was good, to be sure, but the gossip was where it was at. The palace is a bland dish, but the staff supplies the spice." I leaned closer to whisper. "I heard about a maid who was caught on her knees in a closet with a guard, and let me tell you, she was not praying."

It was such a scandalous piece of gossip that I would have never shared it as Princess Eveline, but doing so as Eva the maid felt daring and liberating. Nevertheless, my cheeks must have looked like ripe tomatoes with how hot they felt.

As Nolan choked on his ale. I patted his back until he could breathe again. It felt as though his muscles had muscles of their own, and I kept patting them long after he'd stopped wheezing.

"Eva!" He laughed. "That is scandalous!"

I giggled. "I told you that the gossip was the best part."

"And yet you said that life in the palace was dull, and that's why you left."

I sighed dramatically. "Juicy gossip was a rare treat. Most of the time, it was about stupid things like who offended whom and why or who had been neglecting their chores and having others pick up the slack. Most days, I was bored out of my mind."

He smiled. "How about your talks with the princess?"

"Those were fun but too few and far between."

I hadn't discussed politics with my maid, but I had done so with Bernice, and it had been stimulating.

My sister was ten years younger than me, but she was very smart. Thinking about her made my heart ache and filled me with doubt. I'd only been gone for a few hours, and I already missed her fiercely. I was also worried about her.

Had I left my old life in a rush without giving it proper thought?

I felt selfish for choosing my freedom over the well-being of my sister, and I would probably always feel guilty for abandoning her, but I had no choice.

Life as Eghurt's wife would have been worse than death.

My first night of freedom had been more eventful than I would have liked, but it had all ended well, and I was in the company of the most attractive and pleasant man I'd ever encountered, so things were looking up.

"Enough about me, Nolan. Tell me about yourself. What is a merchant's life like? You must have heard thousands of fascinating stories during your travels."

He smiled, sending my heart aflutter. "Not really. The life of a merchant is boring. I'd rather hear more scandalous palace stories if you don't mind. I could listen to you all night long."

Until now, no man had ever been interested in what I had to say. All the men I knew were royals or their sycophants, which made them snooty, entitled pricks.

I didn't know whether Nolan had been serious about wanting to listen to my stories or if he'd just said that to seduce me. My experience with men was limited, but Renda had told me that a man would say just about anything to get into a woman's panties.

I regarded Nolan from under lowered lashes. "If you are ready to listen to me all night, I can certainly oblige you. Are you sure you're up to that?"

He grinned. "I cannot think of a better way to spend my night."

20

NOLAN

*A*s Eva regaled me with tales of the palace, I could not help but become distracted by the curve of her lips. They were tilted upward, always ready to smile or laugh, and her eyes lit up as she went on about Princess Bernice. She had such a strong affection for the girl that I doubted Eva had left her position voluntarily.

Figuring that it was too embarrassing for her to admit that she'd been dismissed, I didn't press her on the subject again.

"The queen is a little stiff and formal," she said. "But she's a good person."

"But Princess Bernice is your favorite. I see it in your eyes when you speak of her."

"Yeah." She sighed. "You are so easy to talk to, Nolan. I don't think I've talked with anyone for so long in ages. I enjoy talking to you."

"I enjoy talking to you, too, Eva."

"You've hardly said a word," she teased. "Why is that?"

"It is a rare treat that I get to spend so much time getting to know a smart woman."

"Are all your female acquaintances dumb?"

"Not at all." I laughed nervously as I thought about my mother and how terribly she would have been offended if she had heard me say a thing like that. "I did not mean for it to come out that way. It's just that I spend most of my time with men, in meetings, or while traveling."

"Traveling for work, I assume."

"Yes," I lied, "A merchant's life is on the road, so a female's company is a rare treat for me, especially one as intelligent and well-versed in worldly affairs as you are."

I wanted to add beautiful, alluring, fascinating, and a hundred other flattering descriptive words, but I didn't want Eva to think that I was saying those things just to seduce her.

Well, seducing her was precisely what I wanted to do, but I wasn't going to, not with flattery or in any other way.

"What about the men you spent your time with?" She glanced at Theodore, who was laughing at something his companion for the evening had said.

"Theo is clever, but most of the men on my ships are less than intellectually stimulating, so spending time with someone of your caliber of intelligence is unusual. That makes you an anomaly, and I intend to enjoy the night with you for as long as I can."

She smiled from the flattery but then frowned. "I really should speak to the barkeep about a job, though. I don't have much coin."

"Then allow me to buy you another round of ale."

"That won't get me a job," she said with a smirk.

"Barkeeps like it when their barmaids encourage patrons to drink, so consider this a tryout for your job."

"That is a thin excuse to keep me all to yourself."

"I suppose it is transparent," I teased. "Come up with a boring tale for me by the time I return. It'll be my punishment." I winked, then left for the bar.

Theodore was still preoccupied with his blonde companion,

chatting her up, and I had no wish to disturb his efforts or for him to disturb mine.

When the barkeep came to take my order, I scooted two gold coins across the ale-stained bar top.

He eyed the gold and then looked up at me. "How much ale do you want to buy?"

"Two tankards, but the money is for something else. See the brunette in the corner?"

"Aye."

"I'd like you to give her a job here as a barmaid."

The old man frowned at the coins. "I'm happy to take on anyone willing to work with this crowd, but I won't refuse your gold." He took the coins. "Is there anything more you want in exchange for it?"

"I also want you to give her a safe place to sleep and to treat her right. Eva's had a rough night dealing with some bandits on the beach. She is a good woman, smart and hard-working, and you won't regret hiring her. But please, do not tell her I talked to you about her. I don't want her to know I spoke on her behalf."

"Did Brover and his boys cause her trouble?"

"I didn't get a name. There were six of them, one taller than the rest. A nasty fellow that should be put away behind bars."

"That's them, alright." He clucked his tongue in disgust. "Nasty boys. I'll speak to the sheriff in the morning. Did they harm her?"

I knew what he meant by that and shook my head. "Roughed her up some, scared her. But she's spirited. She fought back until my cousin and I arrived. We took care of them for her, but they should have come around by now and could stagger into town any minute. Let your sheriff know before they can harm another defenseless woman."

The barkeep spat on the floor with disgust. "The sheriff knows about them, and he's not doing anything about it. I think it's time for the townsfolk to step in." He glanced at Eva. "I'll take care of your lady friend. Us decent folk need to stick together." He passed me the two ales. "The lass looks like she needs something sweet to cheer her up. I'll send some dessert over."

"I appreciate that. Thank you." I handed over several coppers to cover the ales.

"After you younglings finish chatting, send her my way. She can share a room with Annie or Rosemary and start working tomorrow."

"Thank you, sir."

I carted the ales back to Eva and smiled. "So, have you come up with a dull tale for my punishment?"

"Your travels must be full of truly boring men if you're willing to listen to my dull stories."

"Hello, you two," Theodore said, his arm around the blonde woman as he walked up. "This is Genevieve. Genevieve, this is my wretched cousin, Nolan."

"Hey!" Nolan protested.

"And this is the delightful woman we met on the beach. The one I told you about."

Genevieve's eyes widened. "Did you really fight off six bandits all by yourself?"

Eva laughed. "I did my best, but if not for these two gentlemen, I would have been robbed or worse. Truly, Nolan and Theodore are heroes. Especially Theodore. He took out four of them himself."

Perturbed by the erroneous depiction, I shot Eva a look.

Genevieve gasped, "Is that right?"

Eva nodded enthusiastically, but there was a gleam in her eye when she glanced at me. Then she told Genevieve, "He even threw a blade into the back of one of them from twenty paces away. I've never seen such skill."

I laughed disdainfully, but then she gave my thigh a squeeze under the table, and as her touch sent a thrill through me, my ire instantly subsided.

Genevieve put her hand on Theodore's chest. "You must be quite the warrior."

He grinned. "So, you like warriors, eh?"

"Oh yes. I find them fascinating."

Eva said, "I'm sure Theo can tell you all about it. Privately. He's so humble—telling the story here would be like bragging."

"That is a splendid idea," Genevieve gushed. "Would you like to go for a moonlight walk with me, Theodore?"

"I would love to." He took her hand, and the pair left to walk outside.

Eva smirked. "My apologies for hijacking your gallantry like that, but I thought Theo could use some help getting a kiss from Genevieve."

Her subterfuge impressed me. "I cannot believe you did that. Stealing my gallantry to get my cousin a kiss from that woman. It's the work of a scoundrel."

She giggled heartily and drank her ale. "I made them leave us alone, didn't I?"

When she leaned closer, I was awash in her scent again. She smelled better than any commoner girl I had ever met.

"Well, in that case, I suppose I can allow this infraction to slide."

More giggles and each one was music to my ears.

"I couldn't come up with a boring story to punish you, Nolan. So, I decided that your punishment would be telling me a story."

"Oh, hell." I laughed at the thought. All my stories had mermaids in them. *What am I going to tell her about?* But then I realized I had more than fish tales to speak of. "When Theo and I come to shore, we often stop at local taverns to learn about the people, their...fashions, the language, local politics. Whatever we need to know when we are to sell our wares. And usually, there is a bet."

"A bet for what?"

"Whoever gets a kiss from a girl first wins."

She gasped in mock shock. "Nolan! How disgraceful!"

"It was something foolish we did in our youth, and now it is a tradition. We must amuse ourselves somehow. Days in the sea are long."

"Well, I hope I'm not a bet."

I shook my head. "Certainly not. Since we've met you, the word bet hasn't crossed my or Theo's lips."

She faked wiping her brow in relief. "Phew. I can't let it be known my virtue was at stake over a bet."

My mouth went dry. "Is your virtue at stake?"

She giggled. "No. Not yet."

That *yet* caught my ear. I gulped down my ale before continuing, "On an excursion to this very bar, Theodore and I met a lovely woman. She was funny, charming, and quite attractive."

"But you're here with me, so what was wrong with her?"

"She seemed to have eyes for Theodore, so I backed off and let them keep chatting while I made merry with a few of the barmaids."

"A few?"

"We only sang and danced, nothing too rowdy. But back to the woman. She strung Theo along for hours, getting him quite drunk."

Eva's eyes burned with excitement. "Was she a lady bandit?"

"Would that please you?"

"A woman must make a living somehow."

I laughed. "Not a bandit, but certainly not what she appeared to be. Once Theo was out of gold for the evening and tried for a kiss, she refused him."

"But why? He's rather handsome."

"Oh, is he now?"

"Not as handsome as you, though."

I fought the heat of her words. "I thank you, Eva. As it turned out, she was McCoy's daughter."

"So she grew up in a tavern?" she said with a laugh. "No wonder she could outdrink Theo and get him to spend all his money."

"She was betrothed."

"Oh, my." Eva laughed again, harder and full-bodied. "Poor Theo."

She was utterly different from every woman I had ever known. No games, no coyness. She was simply herself—open and honest. I could not get enough of her.

"Aye. Despite that, he had a good time that night."

"Are you?"

"What about me?"

For once, she sounded nervous. "Are you having a good time tonight? With me?"

"Oh, yes. Are you?"

She smiled and nodded, then finished her ale with her eyes on me. Some of the foam clung to her lip, and I longed to lick it off.

But that would have been forward, and after being set upon by bandits, I was unsure if she was open to such things. "You have a bit of ale foam right there."

Eva wiped her mouth clean and smiled again. "Better?"

"Yes."

21

EVELINE

*N*olan kept me talking for hours, just as he'd promised. We stayed long after the minstrels had left, and all too soon, the barkeep hollered, "Last call!"

He smiled sadly. "Regrettably, this has to end. I could have listened to you until morning."

I took a long sip of the ale. "I doubt I could have continued. My throat is sore, and I had so much ale that I'm slurring my words."

To Nolan's credit, he hadn't tried to take advantage of the situation and steal a kiss from me.

How disappointing.

"I hadn't noticed. You sounded perfectly fine to me."

I chuckled. "I didn't take you for a flatterer."

"I'm serious—"

I didn't know whether that was all he wanted to say or he'd stopped because Theodore walked into the tavern alone and looking despondent.

"Did Genevieve run off after seeing you clearly under a streetlight?" Nolan teased.

His cousin scooted next to me. "I walked her home, but

before I could get my kiss goodnight, her father showed up with a hammer and a nasty attitude. I had to run for my life."

"Oh, poor Theo," I taunted.

He made a face, then rolled his eyes. "Well, at least I had a nice walk with a pretty girl in the fresh air. You two were stuck here."

"We weren't stuck," Nolan said with a sly smile. "We had a great time."

"Whatever." Theodore eyed Nolan's tankard. "I could use a drink."

"The barkeep just announced the last call."

Theo threw his hands in the air. "I cannot catch a break."

"Hey," I jumped in, "I thought I threw you a break with that little story."

He laughed. "Yes, you certainly did. In fact, had I not been with Genevieve already, I might have fallen in love with you for that ploy. Thank you."

Nolan sighed. "We should be going. They're just waiting for everyone to leave so they can close the place for the night."

Since I needed to see about a job, I only followed them as far as the front porch. "Tonight has been eventful, to put it mildly." I smiled at Nolan. "Thank you for saving me from those bandits. If not for you and Theo, I'd most likely be dead. You have my eternal gratitude." I leaned up and kissed Nolan's cheek.

Standing proud and tall, he stammered a quick thank you.

Theodore bent down and offered his cheek as well, but I didn't kiss it. I offered him a handshake instead.

He scoffed at my hand. "Oh, come now, I don't get a kiss?"

I arched a brow. "I offer you my hand, and you sneer at it?"

"It is a perfectly lovely hand but not what I'm looking for tonight."

I shrugged.

Theo's smirk was a warning that he was planning a witty

comeback or some other mischief. "Fine, be like that. It's obvious that Nolan is your favorite, and you don't have a kiss for me, but you can at least give Nolan a proper one."

Nolan nudged his shoulder. "Theo, that's rude."

He would not look my way at all. In fact, he was suddenly bashful.

It was precious.

He was such a handsome man, and I was willing to bet he'd gotten kisses aplenty and probably more than that.

Heck, I was a princess, and I wouldn't say no to him.

Theodore thought it was hilarious that his confident cousin was suddenly feeling uncomfortable. "What has gotten into you, Nolan? Since when were you shy?"

"I'm not." Nolan took my hand and pointed at Theo with the other. "Leave us alone."

As he pulled me toward a darker corner of the porch, my heart started hammering in my chest. Was he going to kiss me now? A proper kiss like the ones I'd seen my maid share with a soldier?

It had been so arousing that I'd fantasized about it for weeks. Now I was finally going to do it myself.

Not getting a clue, Theo followed us. "Why should I go?"

As Nolan huffed in irritation, I decided to take matters into my own hands. Neither Theo nor anyone else was going to deprive me of this kiss. A fire could start in the tavern for all I cared.

Wrapping my hands behind Nolan's neck, I pulled him to me for the kiss I craved more than my next breath.

When his lips brushed mine, a thrill shot through me, unlike any I'd experienced before. My heart raced, and I grew dizzy. I didn't want the kiss to ever end, and I wanted more.

Theodore huffed. "I'll leave you to it, then."

As his footsteps faded fast, Nolan took me in his arms and held me tight as he took over the kiss. His body was so hard all over, and his stubble brushed against my face in the most delectable way. When he groaned in my mouth, it was so primal, sending another bolt of lightning straight through me. When his tongue slipped into my mouth, massaging my own, I nearly fainted from the bliss.

I had never been kissed like that before, and my body told me I'd been missing out. I needed this. I needed Nolan.

He pushed me against the wall as he kissed me, and I wanted everything he had to give me. My body was tight and hot with yearning, every kiss leading to another until my lips were raw. It was as though we were devouring one another but were left starving for more.

When he pulled back, we stared into each other's eyes, panting.

My mother and my governesses had warned me against allowing a man to take liberties with me. They'd told me that I would lose myself in the moment.

I had long scoffed at such notions.

No man could hold sway over me in such a way. But Nolan did. At that moment, I would have done anything he wanted.

He was dangerous to me, and I wanted to throw caution to the wind.

Except, Nolan had more self-control than I did, and he pulled away first. Clearing his throat, he stood upright and straightened his coat.

I was lost for words, staring at him with doe eyes, but before I could come up with something to say to him, he took my hand and pressed his lips to the back of it with his eyes still on me. "Eva, I would like to call on you again. If you are open to—"

"I am."

He smiled warmly. "Then I will call on you tomorrow."

"I'd like that. Where are you staying?"

"With friends in the area. They are private people. I will meet you here. Is seven okay?"

I nodded, still flushed with his heat. "Then…I will meet you. Here. Tomorrow. Seven." He had turned me into a stammering airhead.

"I will count the hours until then. Goodnight, Eva Trovalia."

I sighed and smiled. "Goodnight, Nolan." I watched as he and his cousin walked up to the beach until I could no longer see them, my heart fluttering all the while. It was then that I realized I did not know their last name.

Oh well. I'll ask when I see him again.

22

EVELINE

I practically skipped back inside and up to the bar.

Smiling, the old barkeep said, "We're closed, lass."

"Aye, sir. I was hoping you had an opening for a new barmaid."

"I do." He put down the rag he'd been cleaning the bar with. "Do you also need a place to stay?"

"Yes." I frowned. "How did you know?"

When he grinned, his mustache wiggled. "I know everyone in this village, but I don't know you, which means you have just arrived and have nowhere to stay."

I could have been visiting family or friends, but perhaps he knew everyone in town so well that he also knew none of them had been expecting visitors.

"That makes sense. I don't have money for a room, though."

"I'll deduct room and board from your pay, but the first three nights are on me. Consider it a trial for both of us. You will have a chance to check out the room upstairs and see if you have what it takes to be a barmaid." He looked me over with a critical eye. "You seem like a nice girl from a good home, and some of the men who come to this tavern have no manners. You will need to be tough to ward off unwanted advances."

"I know. I can be tough when I want to." *Just ask my father, and he'll tell you what a disappointment I am to him. Useless.*

"Good." He chuckled. "If you can keep the wealthiest patrons of the night entertained like you did earlier, I'm sure you can handle the others. Rich men are the hardest to please."

"I have often found that to be true myself."

"You'll share the room with Rosemary." He nodded to a barmaid who was cleaning tables. "And if you don't get along, you can stay with Annie." He pointed to the barmaid with the broom. "It's not much, but it's safe, and no one will bother you upstairs. Customers are not allowed up there."

"Thank you. I promise you won't regret hiring me." I extended my hand.

He shook it. "I'm sure I won't. Go see what Rosemary needs help with."

"Right away." I darted to the girl and introduced myself.

"You can 'elp Annie wit' the spilled ale there. The mop's in the corner."

Having never touched a mop in my whole life, I was out of my depth. The ragged ends just pushed the ale around. But after several swipes, it eventually soaked into the mop. My hands hurt from the wooden handle, but I had done it.

Proudly, I asked, "What's next?"

"Bed. Come on."

I followed Rosemary to our room, which was just large enough for two child-sized mattresses with less than a foot of space between them. The only illumination came from the moonlight shining through a tiny window.

When Rosemary lit a small candle, it didn't improve things much.

The linens looked clean, most likely because I couldn't see well enough to inspect them.

"When is the bath filled?" I asked.

She laughed. "What bath?"

"The tub. When do they fill it so we can clean up?"

"There ain't no bath here."

"How do you clean up before sleep?"

Another laugh. "If I'm not dead on my feet by the time I reach me bed, I wipe down with a bar cloth in the restroom we all share with Albert and his family. Tonight, I'm too tired to bother. Goodnight." She took her apron and dress off, blew out the candle, and crawled under the blanket in her chemise.

I, however, could not.

I rushed to the restroom, but there were no spare cloths in there. Hopefully, the barkeep wouldn't mind if I borrowed one. I pilfered the cloth and cleaned up with the only thing they had —cold water and a wedge of hand soap. It wasn't much, but it would have to do.

I had heard that cold baths were the thing for rampant, unquenched desire, so I hoped my cold scrub-down would do that for me. My whole body still tingled with excitement from the kiss I'd shared with Nolan, and I was antsy for something I couldn't define.

More kisses, perhaps?

When I returned to the bedroom after my cold wash, Rose-mary was already snoring.

I folded my dress and tucked it under the lumpy mattress before climbing into the narrow bed. After a few minutes of wiggling around the lumps and making the mattress squeak, Rosemary grunted in her sleep, "Too loud."

"Sorry," I whispered.

I tried to hold still after that, but it was difficult, given all the bruises I'd sustained earlier in the fight with the bandits.

A cold cloth bath and a lumpy mattress were not what my dreams were made of, but for now, they would have to do. A commoner's life wasn't easy, and I had known that when I escaped. Besides, all the discomfort would keep me from thinking about Nolan.

I swooned, just saying his name in my head.

He was simply perfect in every way.

He'd saved me, listened to me for hours, loved every story and commentary that had left my mouth, and kept his attention on me the entire time. Not once had he glanced at Rosemary or Annie, and they were both pretty girls with nice curves on them.

Nolan only had eyes for me.

And that kiss—

God, that kiss.

It was a dream come true.

23

NOLAN

*A*s Theo and I stopped at the end of the tunnel to change out of our human clothing into what was acceptable attire in Poseidon City, he groused, "I can't believe you won the bet. I was so sure that Genevieve would give me a kiss. What a disappointment that was."

"We didn't officially put down bets," I reminded him.

"Well, I believe I helped you win, so we can call it a draw."

I laughed. "You're the glorious hero of the night. Thank you."

Missing the sarcasm in my tone, he chuckled and shook his head. "Actually, I think that was Eva."

"She was very brave, but I'm surprised to hear you say that."

"Since she altered the story of the beach fight and made me sound like a mighty warrior to Genevieve, she became my hero. I wasn't kidding when I said I was a bit in love with her for that."

I chuckled. "As long as it's platonic love, be my guest."

"Oh, I see. So it's like that."

"Like what?"

"You are into her."

I didn't want to get into that sort of discussion with my cousin. Sometimes it seemed to me that Theo was living vicariously through me. He always wanted to know every detail of my escapades and badgered me relentlessly until I told him everything.

Tonight, though, he wasn't going to succeed.

"Goodnight, Theodore." I tucked the human clothes into my bag and slung it over my shoulders. "I'll see you tomorrow."

"Oh, come on. You can't leave me hanging like that. You always tell me everything. What gives?"

"I need to get some sleep, Theo. Goodnight."

I dove past the waterfall into the canal and swam toward my private entrance to the palace.

I couldn't stop thinking of Eva the entire time. Luckily, the canals were deserted at this late hour, so no one spotted me where I should not have been. Sneaking past the night guard was not much of a feat either, and I made a mental note that our patrols were still too predictable despite the changes the new commander of the guard had implemented.

Waiting around the corner as the guards changed positions, I plastered myself against the wall before dropping behind a clump of coral that hid my secret hatch. It was intended for emergencies, such as invasions or riots, but neither had happened in hundreds of years.

The hatch opened to a wet tunnel that dipped low into the palace's basement before going up and becoming dry and ending in my room. It wasn't a U but more of J.

As it rose through the palace walls, a stone stairwell led to my bedroom hatch, which was hidden behind a bookshelf.

I'd tied a length of rope to the back of the bookshelf and fed the rope through a hole in my room hatch lid, so I could pull the bookshelf into place after I left. It was perfect on the way out, but on the way back in, I had to carefully shove the hatch, or the books would fall, and the noise would alert the guards.

I sat on the staircase and pulled my tail out of the water, letting it dry, so it turned into legs again. I had planned on leaving a towel there to hasten the process, but I had forgotten in my rush to get out of the palace.

Once the transformation was complete, I ran up the stairs and carefully got back into my room. I quietly shoved the bookshelf back into place and stripped down for the night.

My quarters were nearly as extravagant as my parents', with a private pool for lounging and bathing and a magnificent view of the resplendent city and the glittering dome. Servants were available at my beck and call, though I tried not to be a bother to them. I had every luxury known to mer and men, and despite that, I felt like something was lacking.

I wasn't happy, and the reason for my melancholy was quite obvious.

I missed Eva.

I lay naked on my oversized bed and looked at the teeming sea life above. The ceiling was part of the dome and made of glass. It was a skylight of sorts—except I saw the sky through a hundred or so feet of water.

That left my room rather dark unless I used a bioluminescent lamp, but if Eva was with me, she would light up the room with her smile.

She was so full of life, so vibrant.

If I didn't see her again, that smile of hers would haunt me for the rest of my days, but I wouldn't let that happen. I was going to see her tomorrow, and the day after that, and every other chance I would get to sneak out of the palace.

Eva Trovalia. Even her name sounded like music to my ears.

Thinking about her laugh led to thoughts of how she looked when she laughed—so free, so joyful.

I closed my eyes and thought about the dirty stories she'd

told me. Especially the one about the maid in the closet with the guard.

On her knees.

Fates, what a visual.

In my mind, I pictured Eva as the maid and me as the guard, her lips closing around my shaft...

I reached for a jar of oil and slicked myself up. There would be no sleep for me if I didn't release the pressure.

The image in my mind faded, becoming her lips as we kissed. Her soft moans. That tight grip on my neck as she melted against me. Her slight whimper when I pinned her to the wall of the tavern. What would it be like to touch her? To make her squirm on my hand.

Or on my erection.

I conjured images of her on top of me, her breasts bouncing as she rode me, then I pictured rolling her over and pressing myself into her wet body. I imagined kissing every inch of her skin. Memorizing her taste. The way she looked into my eyes when I entered her.

It always felt strange that I, a virgin, could imagine the act so vividly and viscerally as if I'd done it hundreds of times with hundreds of different females.

Maybe my subconscious contained memories from a previous life, or perhaps all males were born with carnal knowledge, a genetic memory transferred from father to son, and that was how I knew precisely how each touch would feel and how the woman I was pleasuring would react down to the sounds she would make.

Not just any woman.

I wanted only Eva.

Each naughty thought made my body ache for her. Her lips parted as she gasped, telling me she was going to come. The way she said my name...I had to hear her say it as she fell apart in my arms. I needed to feel her writhe under me and on top of me.

I would be gentle.

The first time.

But after that, we could explore each other's wishes. Dark desires. Fantasies.

To make her mine, I would give her whatever she wanted. As my body throbbed closer to my climax, a tug pulled at my heart.

That was it.

I had to make Eva mine.

We would lace our fingers together as we peaked as one. As we breathed each other's names in ecstasy. As her soft moans filled my memory again, I climaxed in an explosion unlike any I had ever experienced.

I lay back, panting, spent, but the tug on my heart was still there. The moment I had turned to leave her, I had felt something unravel deep inside of me. As though every step away from Eva made the fibers of my heart come apart.

My soul tried to redirect me back to her.

Could she be my mate?

I laughed without mirth while cleaning myself.

Eva could not be my mate. It was a ridiculous thought. She was human. I was not. I could not live in her world. If it rained, or there was even a heavy fog, my legs would transform, bonding and becoming a tail. And she certainly could not live in my underwater world. Not to mention that humans did not know mer existed, and we were all sworn to keep it that way.

Even if I combined the populations of all the mer cities, the number of mer would still be only a tiny fraction of the number of humans. If they ever discovered that we were more than a myth, we would be hunted into extinction.

My heart aching, I shook my head and lay back down.

Sweet, joyful Eva could never be my mate. But when I

thought of the word, that pull in my heart yanked harder. Perhaps I just needed a good night's sleep. As I drifted off, her lips came to mind again, and my shaft tried to spring to life.

"Go to sleep," I grumbled.

Unsurprisingly, he didn't listen to me.

24

NOLAN

*B*y morning, I knew with unwavering certainty that Eva was my mate.

I had dreamt of her all night, and our lore claimed that only happened between mates. I was convinced that she'd dreamt of me too.

Perhaps she had some mer blood in her. There had been many instances of mer breaking the rules and coupling with humans. The offspring could have been born looking entirely human, and their legs never transformed into tails, but they had enough mer blood to make them possible mates.

In my case, though, it wasn't enough. My mate needed to have mer royal blood. No one else would do for the crown prince of Poseidon City, the most powerful and prosperous of all mer communities.

My first stop of the day was Theo's.

When he opened the door, he was less than pleased to see me. "Why are you here so early? I was out into the wee hours of the morning because some thoughtless bastard was busy having a good time with a random human."

"Shush." I put a finger on his lips. "The servants might hear you."

He rolled his eyes. "We have only two. One is in the kitchen, and the other is nearly deaf."

"Eva isn't random, Theo. I think she's my mate."

He frowned, then laughed. "Get in here."

"No. Get dressed. We're going to the Oracle."

His mouth dropped open. "Are you serious?"

"Hurry. Go, go, go." I gave him a shove.

"This is a really bad idea, Nolan." He sighed heavily and turned around to get dressed.

The Oracle was tricky, and she demanded a stiff price for her predictions. I knew that, but it wasn't going to stop me.

"I can go by myself."

"Fine. I'll accompany you to the Oracle's home." He grunted, "But I'm coming under duress."

When we reached the Oracle's modest house, I knocked on the door.

With what she was charging for her predictions, she could live like a queen and employ an army of servants, but the crone was stingy.

"The crone sleeps late. We should turn around."

"It'll be fine." I knocked again. "I'm the prince. What is she going to do? Kick me out?"

Theo grimaced. "It's good to be a prince."

When the Oracle flung the door open, her eyes flashed daggers at us, and she barked in her nasal voice, "Who is fool enough to—oh. My Prince." Her eyes widened with recognition, and she curtsied arthritically. "My apologies. I didn't know it was you. Please, come in."

The Oracle's home was in disarray—books and baubles and thingamajigs on every surface, some stacked on one another. Though disorganized, she was the one we all relied upon for matters of the heart and the future.

She tightened her black robe around her as if she was cold. "Do you need a reading, my Prince?"

"Yes. On the matter of my mate."

A smile bloomed on her old face. "Ah, the matters of the heart. My favorite." She reached for my hand, examining the bruises first. "You two tussle?"

"Something like that," Theo said, covering for the fight.

"Boys," she said with an eye roll. She gave Theo a knowing glance, and I wondered if she knew where we had been last night. "My Prince, your mate is a beautiful dark-haired maiden who will make you very happy."

"Where should I search for her? Is she far away? Is she of royal blood?"

She stared at my palm. "All I can say is, aside from her beauty, she is unique in every way."

"Thank you, Oracle." I had hoped for more answers. "If anything else comes to you, please, call on me at the palace."

"Of course, my Prince."

"Since I'm here," Theo said, "what can you see for me?"

She read his palm. "There are great things in your future. You will rise above many others."

He frowned. "I thought you would give me guidance."

"I can only give what the lines tell me. Yours have less to say because you speak too much."

I snorted a laugh. "She's right."

"Thank you, oh mighty Oracle, for your vast wisdom," Theodore sniped as we left.

"You are lucky to be royals whom I cannot turn away at this early hour. My advice to you, Theodore, son of Osiris, is to be careful of your tongue, or your luck may run out."

25

EVELINE

"*D*on't be a lazy git." Rosemary nudged my ribs with her foot before leaving our room.

Her foot had landed right where the bandit had kicked me the night before, so I was wide awake and grunting when she slammed the door.

Thoughts of Nolan had kept me up late, and I had hardly slept a wink on the lumpy mattress. But I had a job to do.

After I cleaned up and dressed, I came downstairs and looked around the tavern.

This early in the morning, only a few customers sat at the bar, and a girl I didn't see the night before was serving them drinks.

I walked up to her. "Hi, I'm Eva, the new girl." I offered her my hand.

"I'm Anna." She wiped her hand on her apron before shaking mine. "Get an apron from the kitchen."

"Yes, ma'am."

So there was an Annie and an Anna. I would try to remember who was who.

She tittered. "Don't call me ma'am. You make me sound old."

She gave me a once-over. "I'm probably younger than you. How old are you anyway?"

"Twenty-four," I murmured.

At my age, I should have been married with at least two kids.

"I'm nineteen." She took my arm. "Come on, I'll introduce you to Cook." She led me to the kitchen.

It was hot and steamy, with pots boiling, bread baking, and dishes being washed.

The cook grunted a greeting my way and pointed to the row of aprons hanging by the door.

"Don't mind him. He's not much of a talker." Anna pulled down one of the aprons and handed it to me. "Just follow my lead and try not to spill anything. Albert gets mad if we waste his ale."

As the morning flew by in a flurry of half-explained procedures and dirty single-entendres between Anna and the cook, more patrons slowly trickled in.

By noon, I was waiting tables and sore all over.

The life of a commoner was far more challenging than I had expected, and as the patrons ran me ragged, I tried to hang on to thoughts of Nolan.

He was unlike any other man I'd ever met, and I got dizzy each time I thought of him and that incredible kiss, which did not help matters when I carried several pitchers of ale and tried to balance them so I wouldn't spill a drop and get a dirty look from the boss.

He'd said he would come over today, but it was a long time until seven, and I wasn't sure I'd survive until then.

I was preoccupied with thoughts of Nolan when someone bumped into me, spilling ale down my dress. "Watch yourself, new girl!" Rosemary grumbled. "Ain't no standing still when you're a barmaid. Go on, clean yourself up."

I huffed indignantly before going upstairs to clean up in the restroom.

My back was cold, but the rest of me was hot from all the work I'd done since waking up. But I trudged on, looking forward to when the tavern closed for a couple of hours in the afternoon.

I would go to my room, take off my boots, and rest my aching feet. I was sure they were covered in blisters.

After tidying up as best as I could, I returned downstairs, only to stop in my tracks and take a step back.

The sight of two new patrons chilled my blood.

Palace guards.

I knew them, and if I walked into the tavern's main room, there was no way I could avoid them, but if I didn't, I would lose my job.

Panic gripped me.

They were going to drag me back to the palace before I could see Nolan again. He wouldn't even know what had happened to me, and I would never find him again.

My throat went dry.

Was there a chance they wouldn't recognize me without my finery? I'd just get their order without making eye contact, and I'd mimic Rosemary's commoner's drawl.

"We got mutton stew for lunch today. Two bowls and two ales?"

But they both smiled at me knowingly, and the older one said, "That sounds mighty fine, miss."

The second man laughed.

"Coming right up." I dashed to the kitchen and placed their order.

"Take this." Cook shoved a tray with another order into my hands. "Table four."

I balanced the tray on my palm as Rosemary had taught me when Anna shot into the kitchen.

"What is the story with those palace guards?" she asked.

"What do you mean?" I pretended innocence.

"They keep staring at you, but not in the leering way men usually do. And when I asked what I could get them, they ignored me."

I frowned. "They're in my section, not yours."

She put her hands on her hips. "Aye, but you're slow. Are those guards friends of yours?"

"No," I grumbled before returning to the tavern with my tray.

After I dropped it off and fetched their ale from the bar, I darted back into the kitchen for relief from the guards' eyes.

There was no doubt in my mind that they knew who I was, and I couldn't understand why they were playing these games instead of grabbing me and dragging me back to the palace. Something was afoot.

I couldn't do my job like this. I had to confront them.

When I delivered their stew and ales, I couldn't keep quiet. "Do ye think ye know me or something? Why do ye keep watching me?"

The older one—Thomas, I recalled too late—looked at me with thinly veiled amusement. "I have known you since you were a babe. I would bow, but we were instructed not to."

"I dunno know what you talking about. Who sent you?"

"The king. I believe you call him—Father."

I rolled my eyes. Quietly, I said, "Fine, the jig is up. Why haven't you taken me with you to the palace yet?"

"We were sent to watch over you, my lady—"

I lifted my hand to shush him. "Do not call me that here."

He ate a spoon of stew and smiled smugly. "What do you want me to call you?"

"Eva."

"Well, Eva," he taunted, "your father wants us to watch over you so we might report back to him on your toils."

I took a quick look around to see if anyone was paying attention to my conversation with the guards, but the tavern was so full by now that all the barmaids were busy serving clients, and thankfully, it was noisy enough so the words we exchanged were drawn into the chatter.

"He didn't order you to take me back?"

The other one laughed. "He has decided your punishment for running away like a spoiled brat was to live and work as a commoner for a month. I bet you won't last even a week before you'll come begging to marry whomever he chooses for you."

"You'll return and do your duty to your country," Thomas said. "As you should. Your behavior is unbecoming of your station, and you're lucky your father didn't declare you a traitor. You know that we need the alliance your marriage will secure."

He was awfully opinionated for a simple guard, and he didn't know my father as well as he thought he did.

"Whose idea was it to let me work here for a month?" I asked.

They exchanged a glance. Thomas shrugged. "Queen Verdona."

I should have known.

"If she thinks that I'll come running into the open arms of her son, she's delusional."

They both smirked.

"Better Eghurt's arms than a bandit's, don't you think?"

A cold chill slithered down my spine, and this time, it wasn't because of spilled ale.

Had Verdona sent those bandits to harass me?

"How do you know about the bandits?"

Thomas's companion, whose name I couldn't remember, shrugged. "The local sheriff notified the border guards to watch out for those troublemakers."

That still didn't explain how they had known that the bandits had attacked me.

"This is humiliating," Thomas said under his breath. "Your father knows how stubborn you can be, but he knows you cannot take this for long."

"He believes I'm humbled by working here?"

"You're a prince—"

"Don't say that word!"

He huffed. "A seedy tavern is no place for a lady of your station."

"You know what, Thomas? I would rather scrub chamber pots or lick the floor clean in this tavern than marry Eghurt. There is nothing that will make me marry that worm."

"You're shirking your responsibility to your people," the other one griped. "How can you turn your back on them like this?"

"My people? Who exactly are my people, sir? Anyone who would see me in a miserable marriage to improve their own lot in life is not my people. I will not acquiesce, so you might as well march back to the palace and tell my father to either call off the marriage or forget that he has an older daughter."

"You think you're the first girl to be married off to someone she doesn't approve of?" he scoffed. "Your father knows what's best for you and our country, and you should obey his wishes."

I was willing to bet that my father had the guards memorize those statements verbatim because they parroted the exact words that he'd said to me before I ran away.

Thomas waved a hand in dismissal. "She'll give up when it gets too hard."

"Don't count on it. You should leave."

Thomas chuckled. "We will go when our shift ends, not a minute before it. Until then, Miss Eva, keep us in brown bread and stew." He seemed overly happy to order me around.

Back in the palace, neither of them would have dared to talk to me like that.

I forced a smile and grabbed their half-eaten bowls. "In the past five minutes, the two of you have called me a spoiled brat, stubborn, and a quitter. I have a long memory, gentlemen. Best pray I don't return to become your queen. It would be a shame if I were in charge of your continued employment. The thought alone is almost worth the price of marrying Eghurt."

I zipped into the kitchen, a renewed vigor fueling every step. Not the sweet passion I felt for Nolan but an inferno of rage in the shape of my father.

What would Father do after the month was up?

Would he order the guards to take me back?

How would I see Nolan?

How would I taste freedom again?

I couldn't marry Eghurt, no matter the cost.

A plan coalesced in a flash. Nolan and Theodore could take me with them on their ship. We could sail away, never to return.

But would they do that for a woman they'd just met?

They probably needed a maid on their merchant ship to clean up after them.

As Cook ladled more stew into the bowls, I said, "Feel free to spit in those bowls."

"Gettin' too friendly, eh? Wha'd they do? Grab ya or some such?"

"Some such."

"I got in trouble the last time I spat in the food. But I won't tell if you do."

NOLAN

*O*ur greatest poets wrote about the effect finding one's true mate had on a mer. Our bodies would call out to each other, emitting sounds only fated mates could hear.

I'd never put much credence in that myth, but as my body hummed in anticipation of seeing Eva again, I knew it to be true.

The problem was that my mate wasn't the only one who could hear the music.

Whales could hear it, too.

The first thing I had seen upon opening my eyes that morning was a blue whale watching me from above through the glass ceiling of my room. The creature had blocked the sun, casting a huge shade over the palace before drifting away.

Needless to say, it had caused quite a stir among the servants. Blue whales were rare in these parts.

Then came the dolphins, troublesome scamps one and all. They were playful creatures, but sometimes they got confused and turned their amorous attention to merpeople. When there were no mer to bother, they played with urchins from the seafloor, bouncing them back and forth to one another.

Once the dolphins departed, a pod of narwhals drifted above the city dome, at first hovering over my ceiling and then following me along the dome as I traversed the palace.

In the throne room, a guard approached my father. "Would you like us to chase them off, your Majesty?"

"Leave them be." My father looked up. "They are not hostile."

They could be, though.

Their helical horns held powers of their own, and in theory, they could damage the magic of our dome.

Thankfully, my father didn't suspect that any of that was on my account, and as I heard the guards placing bets on who had found their mate, my name hadn't been mentioned.

Nevertheless, it was only a matter of time, and I had to get out of there and see Eva as soon as possible so the humming would stop.

I held on for a couple more hours and then excused myself and headed to Theodore's home, and from there we used the same route we had the day before.

Frankly, I would have preferred to go alone, but Theodore knew about my plans to see Eva, and if I hadn't invited him, he would have been offended.

When we entered the tavern, I scanned for my mate, my senses homing in on her right away. My heart leaped at the sight of her, and my vision clouded at the edges. The noisy tavern patrons faded away, and the inner hum that had been driving me crazy all day long stopped. With my mate within reach, my soul was at ease.

Theo smacked my chest with the back of his hand. "Snap out of it, Nolan."

"Hmm?"

"You're in a trance. I'm starting to think that Eva might be a siren."

"What are you talking about?"

He chuckled. "Thought that would get your attention. I'm getting us ale." He marched up to the bar.

As soon as Eva noticed me, a beautiful smile bloomed on her face, and she walked up to me. "Good evening, Nolan."

Hearing her say my name took my breath away, and I needed a beat to compose myself. "Hello, Eva."

Her gaze darted nervously around, and then she looked at me from under lowered lashes. "Can you come with me outside for a few moments? I need to talk to you."

I prayed to Poseidon that talk was a code word for something else. The memory of the kiss we'd shared was still as vivid in my mind as if it had happened moments ago, and I couldn't wait to taste her again.

"Of course." I offered her my arm.

She didn't take it. "Can you wait for me outside? I need to tell Anna that I'm leaving for a few minutes."

Perhaps she didn't want people to know that she was leaving with me. "I'll wait for you on the front porch."

"Thank you." She smiled and darted away.

I stopped at the bar on my way out. "I'm getting some fresh air," I told Theo.

"Huh, so that's what it's called today. Fresh air." He clapped my back. "Enjoy."

As I waited for Eva in the same dark corner of the porch where we'd kissed the night before, I hoped to do precisely that.

When she joined me, I took her hand and brought it to my lips for a kiss. "What did you want to talk to me about?"

"I need a favor."

That wasn't what I had expected, but I would do anything for her. "Name it."

She smiled bashfully. "I'm not sure how to ask this."

"You can ask me anything."

"It's just that this is a really big favor."

"Then it might cost you," I teased.

She looked worried. "I don't have a lot of money, but you can have all of it."

"I was thinking about a kiss."

Her shoulders relaxed a little. "I need to get out of here. Can you and Theodore help me escape?"

My gut clenched.

How could I do that?

I needed to stall for time to figure out what to do. "Why do you need to get away? You've just gotten here."

She gulped. "My father is a harsh man. He and I have been at odds for a long time, and he betrothed me to a despicable man who is the son of an even more awful woman. I cannot marry into that family. It's like a death sentence."

I couldn't imagine a father treating his daughter like that. My father and I had our disagreements from time to time, but I had no doubt that he always had my best interests at heart. He would have never married me off to a shrew just to get back at me or because it was politically advantageous.

But no matter the quality of the betrothed, the thought of Eva married to someone else infuriated me. It tapped into a fiery core of anger I didn't know existed within me, and as it erupted, it was nearly blinding in its intensity.

For a long moment, I was lost for words as I battled the haze.

This had never happened to me before, but then no one had ever threatened to take my mate away from me either.

"You cannot marry a man you despise," I finally managed to say.

She let out a relieved breath. "Thank you for understanding. That is why I left my old job at the palace. I needed to escape my father. But he discovered where I was and sent men to watch over me. It's only a matter of time before he tells them to drag me back. These men are the reason I asked you to wait for me out here. I can't be seen talking to you, or they would suspect that I'm plotting my escape." She hesitated for a moment. "My father won't be able to find me on your ship. I can work for my keep, clean and launder and serve food, and I don't need much space, a cot will do—"

"Shh, shh," I said before brushing her hair back. "Everything will be okay."

As distraught as Eva was, she leaned into my palm for comfort, responding to my touch as a mate would. She must have mer blood in her, or this powerful bond between us wouldn't have been possible.

But where could I take her? I had no land contacts.

Could I sneak her into Poseidon City?

We would use the tunnel, which was dry land most of the way, and she wouldn't have to spend more than a few minutes underwater, during which I could share my breaths with her.

But where would I hide her? My room?

I stifled a snort.

Bringing a human into Poseidon City would be a serious transgression. To my knowledge, no one had ever done that, and the notion was so ridiculous that no law existed to prohibit it.

Perhaps I could use that to my advantage? I wouldn't be breaking any laws, so even if I got caught, I would only get a stern admonition, but I wouldn't lose the crown like my uncle had.

Besides, didn't the Oracle say my mate would be unique in every way?

Clarity was required, and being a mer in love, I could not think clearly.

"I need to consult with my cousin."

"Of course. After all, it's his ship, too, right?"

I smiled. "I'll be right back." I kissed the back of her hand before dashing inside the tavern.

After I hurriedly explained the situation to Theo, I asked in a whisper, "So, what do you think?"

He snorted a laugh so hard that ale foam shot from his nose. His eyes watered, and he had to take a moment to collect himself. "You've lost your mind, cousin."

"Not at all. She's my mate. You know what that means."

Theo leaned closer to whisper in my ear. "You have to realize that bringing a human to our city—even if she's your mate—would probably cost you the crown."

"I am not sure it would. We have no laws against it. But even if it does, the crown no longer matters to me. I found my truelove mate. You know what would happen to me if I deny the call."

He blinked. "Do you really believe in that myth?"

"Yes."

A mer who refused the gift of a truelove mate or got rejected by their one and only would turn into sea foam.

"To truelove." He raised a pint in my direction. "I still think it's a foolhardy idea. The stupid sea foam myth is just a cautionary tale, and after you pull this stunt, your father will create a law prohibiting mer from bringing humans into the city."

"I'm just going to hide her for a few days until her father's men give up the chase. Then I'll help her settle somewhere safe. Everything is going to be fine."

Theo laughed. "If you say so."

I didn't believe a word I'd said. Unless Eva didn't return my love, I would keep her with me forever.

27

EVELINE

I had known Nolan for a day, and I was trusting him with my life.

Was I mad?

It would seem so, but my gut told me that I could trust him. He'd saved me when he could've turned away, and he'd been nothing but kind to me since.

I trusted his cousin less, but I knew I had nothing to worry about from Theo as long as Nolan was around.

All I needed was for them to hide me long enough for the betrothal to be called off. Then I could go back home and deal with my father.

The trick would be evading the two guards who had replaced the first pair. Percival and Tristan were not nice men, groping the other barmaids and allowing themselves liberties in the way they spoke to me. Once I returned to the palace, I was going to make sure that they were dismissed.

When Nolan returned, his smile told me his answer. "We have an idea."

"Oh, thank God."

"Do you think that a month would suffice for the betrothal to be called off?"

I wasn't sure, but a month was better than nothing, and maybe I could persuade Nolan to extend the time. "That could work. But my father's henchmen are in the tavern right now, and sneaking away will be tricky."

"Show them to me."

We walked to a window, and I subtly pointed them out. "Those two miscreants there."

"Shall I dispatch them now?"

Did he mean that he wanted to kill them?

My sweet Nolan couldn't be a murderer. Besides, there was a chance he would get hurt, and I didn't want that.

"I don't want anyone hurt."

"How will we deal with them, then?"

As he said it, Percival began looking around, presumably for me.

"I will have to get back inside soon, or they'll come out to look for me. We will have to wait until the tavern closes for the night. It will be easier for me to sneak out then."

Nolan smiled. "I am excited to bring you with me."

"Is it a large ship?"

His eyes flickered for a flash. "Sort of."

"I've been on open water before. I loved it."

"Did you?"

I smiled and nodded. "The sea calls to me. It always has. My father hated the voyage, though. He was terribly seasick the whole time and swore he'd never step foot on deck again. But my mother and sister loved it just as much as I did. If I could, I'd spend every day at sea."

"You have no idea how happy I am to hear that. The sea is very special to me."

It was awkward to ask, but I needed to know what I was in for. "Your ship, will I be safe there? I don't mean to doubt you or your crew, but ships do not have the best reputation with women."

He took me in his arms, and it was such a comfort to be there. As I breathed him in, he smelled of the sea. I imagined that a lifetime on the water would do that.

"No harm will ever come to you. Not with me around, and I don't plan to leave you alone if I can help it."

"Making promises you can't keep, I see," Theo said as he joined us. "You have work to do, cousin, and you can't bring Eva with you while you're at it."

I smiled and rolled my eyes at him. "Well, I trust Nolan to keep me safe. And as dastardly as you imagine yourself to be, Theodore, I have a sneaking suspicion I'd be safe with you as well."

He grabbed at his chest in mock pain. "Oh, you're killing me, Eva. Safe? Do you think a man wants to be called safe? Dangerous, daring, handsome, sexy, a monsoon in the sheets, yes. But safe? Absolutely not."

Nolan chortled. "When a woman wants safety, and you can provide it for her, safe is the highest compliment she can give you, Theo."

"You misunderstood," I said with a sly smile. "I said that you would keep me safe. I don't think for one moment that either of you is safe." I pretended to fan myself with my hand. "Two handsome men like you—"

I stopped mid-sentence as Percival grabbed Tristan's arm and gestured toward the three of us at the window.

The guards rose to their feet and started for the door.

"I have to get back inside right now. Will you be here later tonight?"

"You have my word." Nolan put a hand over his heart.

I ran back inside and stopped the guards. "Where do you think you are going? You need to pay for your ale before you leave."

Tristan laughed. "You seem very chummy with those men. Your father will be very disappointed to hear about your misconduct."

I put my hands on my hips. "They are merchants, and I was inquiring about goods for the tavern."

Percival sneered. "I didn't like the cut of their jib. Too fanciful. What business could you have with a pair of low-rent merchants?"

I had no answer at the ready, so I jutted out my chin and looked down my nose at him. "That is none of your business." I walked away.

But Percival snatched my wrist. "Actually, it is very much my business."

I shook him off. "What do you mean?"

"If you don't want your secret revealed, I suggest we continue our talk over there." He pointed to a corner table.

"Fine." I huffed and followed them there.

It wouldn't be long before Anne or Rosemary scolded me for neglecting my duties, but I had no choice but to hear Percival out.

As we sat down, I crossed my arms over my chest. "I'm listening."

"Your father knows what kind of place this is, what type of men come here, and what they are looking for." Percival waved his hand at the men sitting at the other tables. "If you fall for some sweet talker and forfeit your pristine condition..." He trailed off as if I was supposed to understand what he'd meant by that.

"What do you mean?" I asked.

Tristan scoffed. "Your father is worried that you'll screw the first guy who tells you you're pretty, and then you won't be suitable to marry Prince Eghurt."

My cheeks heated. "That's what he's worried about? That I wouldn't be a virgin for Eghurt?"

"Aye." Percival nodded.

All the more reason to escape with Nolan and get naked with him.

I smiled, tight-lipped. "Well. Neither of you needs to worry about that."

"Oh, you're right," Percival said confidently. "We rented a room in the tavern so we can keep an eye on you at all times. Until you give up this foolish pursuit, no man will be able to get close to you, let alone take what belongs to Prince Eghurt."

This was a nightmare.

How would I sneak out?

"How clever of you. Why don't you two go back to your table, and I'll have Cook make something extra special for you?"

Maybe I'll bribe the cook to put poison in their food, and if not that, a sleeping potion.

They exchanged a look, and Tristan shrugged. "I'd like some more of that stew. After all, your father is paying for our meals, so I'd better take advantage of that." He patted his protruding belly.

I smiled with daggers in my eyes. "Coming right up."

When I left the table for the kitchen, I snuck out the back door and found Nolan and Theodore. They were standing in the dark corner where Nolan and I had kissed.

"What happened?" Nolan asked.

I tried not to cry. "The guards are staying overnight." I told them what Percival and Tristan had said to me. "What am I going to do now?"

But Nolan was calm and collected. He brushed my cheek with his fingers and cupped the back of my head in his hand. "Do not fret over this, Eva. I have it under control." He sweetly kissed me, and the tension inside of me eased.

"How?"

"I will take care of the men, and then Theo and I will come for you."

Despite my thoughts earlier, I didn't want the guards dead. They were despicable, but they had families.

"Please, don't hurt them."

"I won't. I'll just make them fall asleep."

How was he going to do that? I needed details.

"Do you intend to get them drunk? Play a drinking game with them or something?"

"Something like that. I give you my word that no harm will come to them."

I was relieved. "Thank you, Nolan. And you too, Theodore. I have to get back now."

We parted ways, Nolan and Theo heading for the front door of the tavern and I for the kitchen entrance. I slogged through there to get to my room. No longer concerned with my work reputation at the tavern, I had one thing on my mind, and it was not Tristan's meal. For all I cared, he could wait until death for his stew.

I took out a slip of paper and a pencil and wrote a note to my parents. Presumably, the guards would take it to them. I didn't say much, only that I would return upon hearing news of my betrothal nullification.

28

NOLAN

*T*heo and I left the tavern a few minutes before closing time and hid in some bushes nearby.

Watching through the wide windows, I was jealous of Eva's co-workers for interacting with her.

I was only a hundred feet or so away from my mate, yet my body hummed for her again.

"You still have time to reconsider," Theodore said.

"There is nothing to reconsider. We are doing this."

"Tell me something. Would you do anything for your mate?"

"Of course. Anything at all."

He paused. "Even leaving her?"

"What the devil are you talking about?"

"Your plan, Nolan. You intend to take her to our city, but did you consider that she might not survive the trip?"

"We are using the tunnel, so there will be very little underwater time involved, and I can share my breaths with her."

"She will panic."

"I will thrall her to sleep."

"Genius," he said mockingly. "You are postponing the freakout for when she wakes up."

"Why would she freak out?"

"Because you're a damned merman, Nolan. As is everyone else there."

Nothing could dissuade me. "Eva is the least judgmental person I have ever met. It will be a bit of a surprise—"

He laughed sharply. "A bit?"

"She will understand. The fates are not cruel. They would not entwine our destinies without reason."

He drew a long breath. "The fates are known to be mischievous. They are not always looking out for your best interest. They might be toying with you for their own amusement, or they might be testing you."

"Aye. They are testing to see what I will do for my truelove mate. If I'm not willing to do everything I can to be with her, I don't deserve her."

Theodore's stern expression vanished, and he smiled. "Good answer."

"Was that a test?"

He shrugged. "My job is to be the voice of reason in the back of your head because you have none. But since you have such a strong conviction about this, I'm willing to suspend disbelief."

"That's so gracious of you," I said sarcastically.

"Thank you." He grinned at me.

As the lights went out in the tavern, I put a hand on Theo's arm. "Let's wait a few more minutes. When everyone is in bed, we move."

"Why not just thrall all of them and be done with waiting?" Theo asked. "I'm getting eaten alive by bugs out here." He smacked his neck and showed me the bug he'd squashed.

"I am not a strong thraller like my father. I can put up to five people at a time under my thrall and be sure that it holds until morning. If I waste my energy on thralling everyone sleeping in the tavern, it won't hold for long. I'd rather save my power for the two men I need to neutralize."

Theo smacked his neck again. "What a pity that I did not inherit my father's gifts of magic. I would have thralled the bugs to leave me alone, and I wouldn't be covered in bites."

"You have the ability to thrall, but it's limited. If you practice, it will improve."

To be honest, I wasn't sure if that was true. The ability to thrall was not a muscle to be worked out. It was a gift of the fates, and mer were endowed with different gifts or none at all.

Regrettably, our society was built like a pyramid, with those at the bottom having only the most basic magic, enabling them to transform from bi-pedals to mer and back. At the top of the pyramid were the royals who possessed the strongest magic, but that didn't make them the best or the smartest of mer.

That was why I believed our society needed to change the way it valued its members.

When I ascended the throne, I would get blessed with more magical abilities, my thralling would improve, and so would my strength and speed.

I could also change things for the better.

The question was whether I would still qualify for the job with Eva in my life. I didn't know what my future would look like, but I didn't care if she cost me the throne.

Well, that wasn't true.

I cared.

There were so many things I planned on doing once I was king, and it would be disheartening to give my dreams up, but my mate came first because, without her, I would literally become nothing.

Or at least that was the myth surrounding truelove mates.

Did I really believe in it?

Part of me did, and another part didn't. No one had seen a

mer turn into sea foam during my lifetime, but more than a few mer had been lost at sea, so it was possible that some of them had suffered that terrible fate.

29

NOLAN

*W*hen all the lights in the tavern had been extinguished except for one, Theo and I walked up to the door where the guard stood, smoking a pipe.

"It's closed." He pointed to the sign on the door.

"We know." I lowered my voice to the register of my thrall and said, "Sleep now."

As the words were spoken, my breath shimmered in the moonlight, and the man's eyes rolled back in his head. As he started to fall, I caught him to stop him from hitting the cobblestones. Gently, we laid him there under the tavern's awning in case of rain.

One down, and only one left to go.

"After you," Theo said.

The door squeaked when I opened it, but fortunately the main room of the tavern was vacant. We crept up the stairs to where the barkeep, his family, the barmaids, and the occasional paying patrons slept.

The hallway was dark and long, lined with doors, and I cursed my oversight in not asking Eva which door was hers or where the guards slept.

Fortunately, mer had excellent night vision.

Cracking the first door open, I heard a feminine voice ask groggily, "Who goes there?"

I peeked inside, but neither of the two women in the room was Eva.

"Sleep now," I thralled her in a whisper.

A moment later, the only sound coming out of that room was heavy breathing.

As I closed the door, Theo shook his head. "You should have asked her which room was Eva's."

"I know." *Poseidon, help me.* I turned the knob and opened the next door.

A man asked, "Princess, is that you?"

Theo stifled a laugh, and I barely managed to lower my voice to the correct frequency for thralling. "Sleep now."

The man started snoring in an instant.

I shut the door.

"From now on, I'm calling you Princess," Theo teased.

"Be quiet." The third door loomed before me. I'd thralled four people by now, which meant that I was nearly tapped out.

I had to preserve my magic.

"Poseidon, if I have ever had your favor, now is the time." I opened the door.

"Eva, that you?" Eva's roommate asked sleepily.

Hades, what if Eva was in there?

Should I thrall them both and carry Eva out?

"Sleep now." I closed her door.

As my mate came out a door at the end of the hall, I poked my head into the bedroom and commanded, "Sleep now."

It didn't matter if her roommate got the leftovers of my thrall. All I needed was for her to fall asleep, and her exhaustion from a long day at work would take care of the rest.

Eva smiled and rushed to us with her bag slung over her shoulder.

"This way," she whispered and led us down the stairs. "Cook is still cleaning in the back. I told Rosemary I had to wash my things, hoping she would fall asleep before you came."

"Smart." I took the bag from her.

As we reached the front door, footsteps alerted us to someone approaching, and a moment later a portly man in a stained apron intercepted us with an impressive glare.

"Are you going with these men willingly, Eva?"

Thankfully, he kept his voice down.

"Yes, Cook. I am. Can you pretend like you didn't see us?"

As I thought of using the dregs of my thrall on the man, Theo shook his head, warning me not to do it in front of Eva.

The cook smiled. "You kids have fun. Just be careful." He winked at Eva. "I didn't see nothin." Then, he toddled back to the kitchen.

"Can we trust him?" I asked her.

"I think we can."

"Then let's get out of here."

We rushed out the front door, went past the sleeping guard, and continued toward the beach.

"Is this the way to your ship?" Eva asked.

"This is the way to freedom," I promised.

She took my hand in hers, and we walked briskly until we reached the palm cluster where our hatch entrance was hidden.

"I can't see your ship." She squinted in the dark. "Where is it?"

"I'm taking you to it." I dropped my voice and thralled, "Sleep now."

As her eyes rolled back in her head, she fell into my arms, and Theo pressed his palm to the rock covering the hatch.

Only a royal palm print could open it, but since he was my cousin, he could open it as well.

I had to rely on his help to lower Eva's limp, sleeping body down the hatch and into the tunnel, but once there I took her from him and carried her myself.

With how slimy its floor was, we couldn't go as quickly as I would have liked, but we covered the distance in good time and stopped behind the waterfall.

I laid her carefully on the ground, rolled her over onto her stomach, and started unlacing her bodice.

Theo looked appalled. "What in the name of Hades are you doing?"

"Her dress will get wet and heavy, and she will be much more difficult to carry. We can put it in our dry bag."

Theo had been carrying both bags, and Eva's was quite heavy, but my cousin was a strong swimmer despite spending his days holding small paintbrushes.

"She will give you hell when she wakes up naked."

"She is wearing a slip beneath her dress. I'll leave it on."

He shook his head. "That's a really bad way to start a relationship. Just saying."

I tugged the sleeves down her arms. "Eva is my mate. She will understand once I explain to her why it was necessary to remove her dress."

"You have an awful lot of faith in the mated bond."

"I do."

I pulled the rest of the dress off her, revealing the thin ivory slip beneath, then passed the dress to Theodore. He shoved it into the dry bag, and we prepared for the trip into the tunnel.

"You realize she will be frozen to the bone by the time you get her to your room."

"I'll keep her warm."

"I bet you will."

After we both undressed, changing into our mer attire, I sat on the ledge with Eva in my arms and Theodore splashed water over my legs. Once the transformation happened, I didn't dive through the waterfall as I usually did, sliding carefully into the canal on the other side instead.

From there, we swam to my private hatch entrance, dodging the guards on the way and making sure that Eva's head remained above water.

The trickiest part was the J-shaped hatch because the bottom of the J was submerged.

When we reached it, I pinched Eva's nose to prevent her from breathing in water, swallowed as much air as possible, and dove into the hatch behind Theo.

He led the way, so he could help bring her up if needed. It was dark in the tunnel to my room—had I left a light on, it would have attracted attention. The cold, wet darkness was familiar to me, but I prayed Eva did not wake and panic. I'd thralled so many people earlier that I was worried I wouldn't have enough magic left for her.

Pressing my mouth to hers, I gave her as much air as I could.

When we emerged, I released my hold on her nose, and when she breathed in just fine, I thanked Poseidon and carried her to my room. Laying her on my bed, I whispered to my cousin, "Vow to me you'll tell no one of this. Vow it to me as your future king."

"You don't have to ask. You know that I would never betray you."

"I need your vow, Theodore. I trust you, but I need the magic of a vow to ensure that no one can trick you into spilling the pearls or threaten you with repercussions if you insist on keeping your mouth shut."

He sighed. "Fine. I vow to my future king that I will tell no one about Eva or the events of this night." His breath shimmered, indicating that his words were bound by magic.

"Thank you."

"You're welcome."

He cast a quick glance at Eva, and something indecipherable passed through his eyes. "Good night, Nolan." He left through my secret hatch.

I drew closed the window curtains and the canopy over my bed to block the sight of my bed from the glass ceiling. The water around the palace was restricted, but guards patrolled it several times a day, and I couldn't risk a guard peeking into my bedroom and seeing a human female in there.

Lying next to Eva, I watched her sleep, and my worries faded away. I knew it was just a temporary reprieve and that come morning, the real battle would begin, but for now I was at peace, perhaps for the first time ever.

30

EVELINE

J stretched out on the bed that was far too warm and comfortable to leave.

Soon, though, Rosemary would be on my case for being a lazy git, whatever that meant.

What happened to the lumps, though? Why was I so comfortable?

I opened my eyes, and instead of a grimy bedroom that was smaller than my old closet, I found myself in a room that was far grander than the one I'd occupied in the palace, in a bed that was far bigger than any bed had a right to be, and lying next to a sleeping man who had no business being in there with me.

Nolan.

I fought a gasp.

He was on top of the covers, his muscular chest and arms on display, and the only thing covering his unmentionables was a sarong kind of garment that I was sure would reveal more than I was prepared to see as soon as he moved.

As I lifted the fluffy blanket, I saw that I was only wearing my slip.

Had I done something I wasn't supposed to the night before?

Why couldn't I remember anything other than looking out to sea and searching for Nolan's ship?

Taking another look around the room, I was confused. There was a small pool in the middle of his cavernous bedchamber, and I never would have even imagined such extravagance in a castle, let alone on a ship.

Nolan had to be much wealthier than I'd imagined.

Somehow, I had gotten lucky with a highly successful merchant as my benefactor.

Merchants were the only people who could live better than royals. They could come and go as they pleased, and some of them had larger purses than the treasuries of many small kingdoms. But at the same time, they did not have the responsibilities of managing a population and dealing with politics and court intrigue, and all the other things royals had to contend with.

Given the splendor of his ship, Nolan was one of the best.

Aside from the pool, his bedchamber was lined with bookcases, and I wondered how he kept the books from falling off the shelves during a storm.

Magnets, perhaps?

I turned to him, dying to talk about all the trinkets and the books and that pool.

Touching his beautiful face, I sighed contentedly.

I felt safe.

In his sleep, my benefactor looked so much more peaceful and content than he was when awake. I hadn't realized how tense he'd been before seeing him like that.

His stubble had grown a shade darker than his hair, and it suited him. As I memorized his handsome face, the striking jaw, the regal nose, his lips lifted in a smile, he opened his luminous aquamarine eyes.

"Good morning, Eva," he murmured.

"Good morning, Nolan."

"How long have you been awake?"

"Only a few minutes. You must tell me, how come your ship's cabin is so extravagant? I've never seen anything like it on land, let alone on a ship."

He took a beat as though debating sharing the answer. "We are not on a ship."

"We are not? Where are we?"

The curtains were drawn, so I couldn't see what was outside the cabin.

"We are underwater."

I laughed at his absurd joke, but he did not. In fact, he looked quite serious. "What's going on, Nolan? Where have you taken me? And how come I can't remember anything after we stopped at the beach?"

Pushing up on the stack of fluffy pillows, Nolan let out a sigh.

"This is going to be a bit of a shock to you, but I want to assure you that you are perfectly safe, and there is no way your father or his men can ever find you here."

"That's good to know, but why do you think I'll be shocked?"

"You can't remember anything because I thralled you to fall asleep, and then I carried you through a series of tunnels, some air-filled and some water-filled. I shared my breath with you to keep you from drowning and then carried you here. To my room, which is in an underwater city." He smiled. "Welcome to Poseidon City, Eva."

I laughed again and nudged his muscular shoulder. "You're toying with me because you know I've not seen much of the world. That's not fair, Nolan. Don't play with me like that."

"I'm not toying with you." He slid out of bed, somehow managing to do it without his sarong parting and revealing those unmentionables that I was very curious about. "I'm going to show you something extraordinary, but I need you not to scream."

Fear-laced confusion clenched my gut. "Why would I scream?"

Without another word, Nolan parted the curtains and retracted the canopy over his bed.

The wall window framed a strange city with canals serving as streets, and above us was the ocean, teeming with sea life.

"I must be dreaming." I rubbed my eyes, but the scenes didn't change.

The city appeared to be surrounded by a dome that kept the rest of the ocean at bay. A few people walked on the sidewalks, and some were swimming in the water canals. It was early in the morning, and the light, which filtered through the water, was dim. Normally, I loved the early morning. But at the moment, it was all I could do not to panic.

"Nolan, what is this?"

"Poseidon City. My home."

This was a dream. It couldn't be anything else. I had fallen asleep in my lumpy bed at the tavern while waiting for Nolan to come for me.

When he woke me up, hopefully with a kiss, I would tell him about my strange dream, and we would laugh about it.

Since this was a dream, though, I might as well enjoy it.

Bemusement replaced panic. "Could you take me on a tour of your city?"

He arched a brow. "Don't you have a hundred questions for me? Aren't you mad that I lied to you about taking you to a ship?"

"This is so much better. My father will never find me in an underwater city, and while I'm here, I might as well enjoy myself, right?"

He chuckled. "Well, that's true. I can't believe how open-minded and accepting you are."

"I have one question." I lifted a finger. "How does that dome keep the water out?"

"It's part ingenious engineering and part magic."

"Ah, of course. Magic. What else?"

Yup, it was a dream. I was impressed by what my mind could conjure. I hadn't known that I had such an incredible imagination.

Nolan frowned. "How do you know about magic? Few humans do."

"The mother of my so-called intended is rumored to be a witch, and she's a terrible person, so I thought that all magic was bad. But since it can do all this, I'm inclined to change my mind." Looking out the window, I noticed that one of the women swimming in the canal had a gorgeous, shimmery tail. "What is that?" I pointed.

"A mermaid."

Definitely a dream. "Are you a mermaid?"

He chuckled. "I am a merman."

"Oh, of course, you are. What was I thinking?" I was having so much fun in this dream that I never wanted to wake up. "So, how about a tour?"

"I guess we could go to...." He raked his fingers through his sun-kissed hair. "But we will have to keep to the less affluent neighborhoods, where we might pass unnoticed. You are the first human to ever visit Poseidon City, and we need to keep your humanity a secret." He glanced at my exposed legs. "You will also have to stay far away from the water so you won't get accidentally splashed."

It was a reminder that I was wearing a nearly see-through camisole, but since this was a dream, I could be shameless.

"Why not?" I tucked the blanket around my legs.

"Because your secret will be outed. As soon as water

189

touches a mer's legs, they transform into a tail, and yours will not."

This dream was becoming more interesting and imaginative by the minute.

"So, if you were to get splashed while you were on dry land, your legs would turn into a tail?"

Nolan nodded.

"How fascinating." I smiled, thinking what a scandal that would have been. "I guess I will have to be careful and stay dry."

If any of this were real, Nolan would have been taking a huge risk by visiting the tavern.

"There aren't a lot of us, and most people know each other, but if we keep to the poorer neighborhoods, people there will assume you're a noble, slumming it for the first time. We will have to keep things short, though. Mer dip in water frequently. It's a ubiquitous part of our culture, so if you stay dry for too long that will draw attention as well."

It seemed that even dreams had rules, but I didn't mind. This was still the best dream I'd ever had.

"You're the boss here, Nolan. I will follow your lead."

"One more thing." He winced. "After the month is over, I will have to thrall you to forget what you have seen. I haven't sorted out all the details of how we are going to keep you hidden here to save you from having to marry that vile man, but I'll figure it out. I vow that you will never have to marry anyone against your will." With his last words, the air shimmered silver near his mouth.

I smiled. This was such a vivid and beautifully detailed dream, and I couldn't wait to see it unfold. "Thank you. I understand the need to thrall me. After all, if I told anyone about this underwater city that is home to merfolk, I'd get locked away in a convent far away, or worse, in an asylum. And if anyone believed me, they would try to get down here to find your city."

Nolan smiled. "I told Theo that you would understand. You are an incredible woman, Eva."

I dipped my head in thanks. "I'm curious about something." I glanced at the sarong he was wearing. "How does the tail thing work? Do you take off your sarong before dipping in the water, or does it stay on once your legs turn into a tail?"

"They come on and off easily, and they dry quickly. Some prefer to leave them on and others to take them off before a swim."

What have I been thinking about that my mind has created such an elaborate fantasy?

"I have another question. What do mer eat?"

"The usual. Fish, shrimp, seaweed, the occasional clam or urchin."

"All that, but no octopus?"

He shuddered at the thought. "No one eats octopuses. They are pets."

NOLAN

I knew Eva would be accepting of the extraordinary, but I had not expected the ease with which she had done so. "Are you sure you're okay?"

She tilted her head with a smile. "Why wouldn't I be? This is marvelous."

"Frankly, I expected at least a little freak-out."

"Do you want me to pretend that I'm scared? I can scream or hit you or—"

"No, nothing like that." I laughed. The girl was hilarious. "We've always assumed that humans could not handle the mer's existence. I had faith you would not hate me for not being fully human, but I did not expect you to accept my dual nature so easily either."

"You are the most incredible man I have ever met, and you were kinder to me than most." She kissed the end of my nose, which made me laugh. "Show me your world, Nolan."

Such sweet words. "Alright then. Let's start with my quarters. These doors lead to my wardrobe. That door goes to my bathroom, and—"

"You have your own bathroom?"

"Aye." I opened the door for her. "And it has running water. You can take a bath and use the shower for a waterfall effect."

She peeked inside. "I don't understand. What do you mean by running water? Do your servants run with the buckets to fill up that enormous bathtub? And what is that bowl with the seat?"

I smiled and reached over to the tub to turn on the shower head.

She jumped, having not expected the water to fall from the jets. "The water is brought in through pipes, and you can adjust the temperature to your liking. This is the cold water faucet, and this one is for the hot." I pointed to the jets. "This is called a shower, and the bowl with the seat is a toilet. It's like a chamber pot, but with water to wash things away."

She gasped, "No way!"

"Yes. It's rather convenient."

"Can I try it?"

I laughed. "Of course."

"Okay, get out." She waved me away.

"Sure." I chuckled and stepped out, closing the door behind me to give her privacy.

I went to the wardrobe to find sarongs—one for me and two for her.

Usually, I slept in the nude, but I had worn one to bed on her account. Now I changed into a more formal sarong, a dark blue with black trim.

The two I selected for Eva had a pattern of pale blue and white flowers on them. They had been gifts from a visiting mer dignitary and were exquisitely soft. Too feminine for my taste, but I'd kept them for some reason.

Perhaps fate had told me not to give them away because one day, my mate could make good use of them. I smiled at the thought.

When Eva emerged from the bathroom nearly half an hour

later wrapped in a towel, she gushed, "I could get used to this. I feel like a new woman after washing up in your bathroom. Your shampoo smells divine."

My chest clenched around my heart, and I prayed to Poseidon that I would be able to realize our shared wish. But then I noticed her staring at me. "What is it?"

She gulped audibly. "You're um…you look very handsome in that sarong."

"Thank you. Now, if you'll excuse me, I must use the bathroom. Take a dip in my pool if you wish."

She clutched the towel. "I don't have a bathing suit."

"I'll knock before I step out of the bathroom, so you can cover yourself with a towel."

I smiled and left her to her imagination. Not that I thought she would be nude when I returned, but a man can dream.

After I finished my morning routine, I knocked on the door. "Can I come out?"

"Yes, you can."

I found her in the pool, sadly wearing a towel in the water, but she looked happy, which was really what I was hoping for. "Enjoying yourself?"

She sighed contentedly. "Very much. Every bedroom should have running water and a pool."

"I'm inclined to agree. But if you still want that tour, we should leave soon before the city wakes up."

"If I'm to blend in, what do I wear?"

I held up the sarongs for her.

She blinked several times. "That's tiny. It's not going to cover anything."

"It's what everyone wears here."

"Oh."

She stepped out of the pool and wrapped another towel around the wet one before taking the sarongs.

As our hands brushed against each other, she stared into my

eyes, and the hand which clutched the towel over her breasts shook a little.

Would she drop it?

My heart stopped. Her cheeks flushed red. The air in the room became heavy, and I couldn't stop staring at her lips. Slowly, I leaned forward for a kiss.

But she leaned away from me. "I'll... I'll change in the bathroom." She darted away faster than a triggerfish.

What was that? I knew she liked me, and she'd kissed me before.

Why had she pulled away?

Perhaps because she was almost naked?

Humans were not accustomed to seeing so much exposed skin. It was normal for the mer, but it probably seemed scandalous to those poor, repressed land dwellers.

The bathroom door cracked open, and her voice was quiet when she called out, "Um, Nolan? I could use some help."

When the door opened fully, and I saw her, I could not move. She wore one pale blue sarong around her hips and the other curving upward, crisscrossing over her breasts. Her nearly bare back was to me, and she held the ends of the sarong at the back of her neck.

I was stunned speechless by her beauty.

"I can't seem to get the tie right, and I really do not want to flash your neighbors. Help?"

"Uh, of course." I stepped forward, eager to touch her. She lifted her long dark hair out of the way, and I breathed her in as I tied the sarong. It was all I could do not to untie it. "Comfortable?"

"I think so. I'm just... I'm practically naked."

"Not yet." I couldn't believe I said that.

It was like a different male had used my vocal cords to speak.

She was my mate, but she didn't know that yet, and unless

she accepted me as her one and only, I couldn't complete the bond with her.

She giggled. "Is that your plan?"

"There is nothing I wouldn't give to see you in your naked glory."

She bit her bottom lip as she looked at me from under lowered lashes. "Since this is a dream, I can be as scandalous as I want, but I'm still a little shy."

So that was why Eva seemed so accepting. She thought she was dreaming.

Perhaps I should let her think that for a little while longer. It would ease her into her new reality.

"Come here." I took her hand and led her to the full-length mirror in my wardrobe. I stood behind her and watched her eyes as she looked at herself there. "You're perfect."

"I cannot believe I'm going to be where other people can see me like this. What about shoes?"

I chuckled. "No shoes."

"Really?"

"We don't have much use for them when we are in our mer form."

She smiled and nestled backward against me. "Since I'll be dressed like everyone else, it should be okay. I just need to get used to it."

"Mm, hmm." I kissed her bare shoulder.

I needed to touch her, to kiss her, and as she further relaxed into me, her body fit mine with such precision that it was as though we were made for each other.

Without warning, reality came crashing down.

Eva didn't know that I was a prince. How was I going to sneak her out of the palace without her learning who I was?

Perhaps I should tell her?

But what if she treated me differently?

What if she stopped being so friendly and sweet toward me?

My gut churned at the thought.

Royalty was all about formality, and I could not stand it if she were to become formal with me. I wanted to be honest with her. I yearned for a sincere and open relationship with my mate. But she'd had enough shocking news for one day.

"We have to be discreet when we step out of my quarters. No one can know who you are."

She smiled. "You worry too much."

"Some would say that it is my lot in life to worry."

"Well, I am dressed, I saw a mermaid, and I think I am about as ready as I can be for whatever I'll see out there." She lifted her hand. "Wait, do people walk their octopuses on leashes the way humans do with their dogs?"

Chuckling, I shook my head. "No, that would be silly. We hold their tentacle when we walk them."

She raised an eyebrow at that.

"Just kidding."

"Oh, you're terrible!" She batted at my chest playfully.

"Octopuses stay at home in their tanks."

"That makes more sense."

"Unless it's a baby octopus. Then you might see them riding on someone's shoulder."

"Are you messing with me again?"

"No, actually. It helps them to bond with their owner when they're young."

Eva narrowed her eyes at me. "You're toying with me."

"I'm not. I swear. Keep an eye out for them. They're adorable."

"You're serious right now?"

I nodded. She didn't need to know I was teasing. It was cute to see what she might believe.

"Huh. This place is quite a fantasy."

"You call it a fantasy, but I call it home." I shrugged. "Ready?"

"Yes." She tugged on her sarong, trying to cover more of her legs. "I'll be quiet as a church mouse."

Opening the door, I peeked out carefully. "The coast is clear."

EVELINE

*S*neaking through the luxurious building, we found our way to an exit.

Once outside, I breathed the salty air and relaxed down to my toes. The dome was a marvel created by my mind, as was the entire city, and I was proud of myself for having such a wonderful imagination.

I just hoped to remember all this when I woke up.

The buildings gleamed in the morning light, and they looked more organic than anything I'd ever seen on land. Soft edges and curves replaced harsh angles, and some even had round windows. The colors were light, and the shapes reminiscent of sandcastles formed by hand, except these ones were decorated with metal plates and jewels.

I glanced back at Nolan's building. It was the most glorious of them all. "Your quarters must cost a fortune."

He smirked. "You could say that."

Poseidon City glistened. Between the watery dome and the random pools here and there, everything had a wet component to it, and I hoped I would be able to remain dry. On the water streets, large eels pulled the occasional cart.

"Don't they bite?" I asked.

Nolan chuckled. "Why would they? We feed them well."

"Oh."

He held my hand as we walked along the paths leading from his building into the deeper parts of the city. "The area we are heading to is not as affluent as my neighborhood, but I will keep you safe."

"Are you joking?"

He frowned. "What do you mean?"

"You've done nothing but keep me safe, Nolan. I asked if you were joking because it never would occur to me to doubt you."

He smiled warmly. "Oh." Then we continued our walk.

I didn't notice much difference between the buildings in what he called a less affluent neighborhood to the one we came from, save for the fact that his building was the largest I'd seen in the entire city and had more jewels embedded in its walls.

To me, they all looked of a similar quality.

The strangest sight was not the buildings or the occasional eel cart, though. It was seeing people bow to Nolan. Did they bow to wealthy merchants in Poseidon City?

I had to ask, "Are you a lord?"

"I don't like to bring it up. I don't like being treated differently. Is that okay?"

"I know exactly what you mean," I said with a sigh.

Dammit. I shouldn't have said that.

"You do?"

I chuckled as I scrambled for a way to cover my slipup. "My roommate at McCoy's hated me because I used to work in the palace. She thought I felt superior, which was silly."

He smiled and nodded. "People are too preoccupied with status symbols and wealth instead of treating each other based on the merit of their personalities and the qualities of their character. Who you are born to and where you come from shouldn't make a difference."

"Exactly. I'm no better than anyone else. But when I tried to tell her that, she wouldn't listen."

"I was fortunate." He squeezed my hand.

"How so?"

"When I told you that I was a merman, you didn't freak out."

"We all have our secrets, Nolan. Some bigger than others."

"That we do," he said before he looked away.

His profile was so regal, so handsome, and he was so perfect in every way.

Well, his legs turned into a tail when they got wet, but that was in the dream world. In the real world, Nolan was just as handsome and regal but had no tail.

Since this was a dream, though, perhaps I should tell him the truth about who I was?

I hadn't treated him differently after he confessed to being a merman. Maybe he wouldn't treat me differently for being a princess?

But what if he decided that Eveline the princess was too dangerous to hide in Poseidon City? She could mean much more trouble to the mer than Eva the maid.

I didn't want the dream to end, and if I introduced a new variable, I might inadvertently eject myself from this world. I wanted to stay here forever, but that was a silly thought.

At some point, I would wake up, but hopefully with the real Nolan by my side.

"What are you thinking about?" he asked.

I touched his cheek. Smooth until I reached the soft hair of his beard. "That I want to stay in this dream forever."

"Do you still think this is a dream?"

"Mermen don't exist."

He lifted my hand and kissed my palm. "They do. I'm right here."

I smiled up at him. "I enjoy having you here with me, and I take solace in the thought that when I wake up, I will find the real Nolan next to me."

He looked at me for a long time. "How is this Nolan different from the real one?"

I laughed. "The real one doesn't have a tail, and he doesn't live in an underwater city. All the rest is the same. Both Nolan's are exquisitely handsome, brave, kind, and generous."

He smiled. "You really think so?"

"I know so." I lifted on my toes and kissed his cheek.

"I think that the real Eva and the dream Eva are one and the same, and she is perfect in every way. Beautiful, smart, joyful, and full of life."

I liked the way he looked at me as if I was the most important person in the world to him, but then it got too intense, and I averted my eyes. "I'm a little hungry. Is there anywhere we can get a bite to eat?"

"There's a great place for breakfast just up ahead."

33

EVELINE

*T*he restaurant was small, with only eight seats along a bar.

A man in a tall hat bowed to Nolan. "The usual, my—"

"Yes, please," Nolan answered hastily.

The man smiled and nodded. "As you wish. Who is your lady friend?"

"This is Lady Eva. She's visiting from Selkie Springs."

"Oh? Don't know if I've met anyone from there."

I smiled, trying to play along. "We don't often travel so far from home."

"I would think not. Don't you have to return to the spring every night?"

Nolan's eyes bugged out as though he'd forgotten that detail.

I tried to think fast. "That's just a myth, sir. Designed by our elders to keep the young folk from venturing out into the world."

"Huh," he said as he finished cutting the fish and put two plates of raw fish in front of us, adding several small bowls with dipping sauces.

I wasn't sure I could eat uncooked fish, but Nolan dug right in, and as I watched him dipping the pieces of fish into the dark sauce and putting them in his mouth, I decided I could do it.

Since this was a dream, I could imagine that it tasted good, and it would. I followed Nolan's lead and tried a bite. "That's not bad."

He smiled. "I was hoping you'd like it." We ended up polishing off two more plates of the raw fish before heading back.

When we snuck in as quietly as we had left, I asked Nolan why he was being so cautious.

"My neighbors are terrible gossips, and having a woman in my quarters would be frowned upon."

"I can understand that. A couple shouldn't cohabit before marriage, and evidently, the rules stayed firm in the dream world."

How disappointing.

"What now?" I asked as he closed the door.

"I've been out of the water for too long, and I need to dip in. Would you like to join me in the pool? You can leave your sarongs on if you want."

"Is it normal to leave them on?"

"When in company, ladies usually leave their tops on, though not always."

I was nervous about submerging myself wearing the thin sarongs, but I was also dying to finally see his tail. "I would love to join you."

"Ladies first." He motioned for me to get in.

I stepped into the water, quickly sitting down on the ledge and crossing my arms over my chest. I was sure that once the material got wet, I'd look naked.

Surprising me, Nolan leaped into the air and dove into the water in a perfect arc. Suddenly, a shimmering golden tail encompassed his lower body, and when he came up for air, he tossed the sarong to the edge of the pool.

"So. Thoughts?" He sat on the ledge next to me, spreading his arms on the pool's lip.

I gaped at his tail. "It's so pretty."

He laughed hard. "I would prefer masculine or even intimidating."

"Can I touch it?"

"Go ahead." He leaned back and flipped his tail toward me.

Just like a fish's tail, the golden scales glittered in the light, and the end was feathery and thin, with blue, nearly transparent membranes. Faint bones gave it structure. It was beautiful.

When I ran my finger along the feathery edge, Nolan shivered.

"I'm sorry."

"Don't be. It just tickles."

Next, I touched the scale part. "What about here?"

"It feels the same as if you were touching my leg."

"Huh. I cannot get over the detail in this dream," I mumbled, my eyes still stuck on his tail, "I thought of everything."

"What was that?"

I shook my head. "It's gorgeous. What's it like to swim with a tail?"

"It's different from swimming with legs. You kick when you swim, but," he dipped under the water and swam for me, then popped back up, "I glide like a wave, up and down."

I nodded. "You're so agile in the water."

"I'd better be," he said, chuckling.

"Have you ever seen a shark?"

"Of course."

"Did it bite you? They look so fierce."

"They're really just like dogs."

I laughed hard. "What? With all those teeth? I've heard they kill fishermen every year."

"Mostly, they're just curious. Unfortunately, the only thing they have to explore with is their teeth, and they don't know their own strength. Some who live near here are enormous—they can blot out the sun. But the big ones don't even have teeth. They suck their food in, and it's only tiny shrimp and anchovy."

"If that's all they eat, how do they get that big?"

"They eat a lot."

I chuckled. "That's incredible."

"It's rare for sharks to bother us, but they are plentiful. When you're on my bed, if you watch long enough overhead, you'll see them."

"Oh, I'd love that." But then I thought of what he had said. "Wait, are you trying to get me into your bed again?"

He smirked. "Picked up on that, huh?"

I giggled and wanted to kiss him. But I worried kissing would lead to something more.

This was a dream, so what did it matter? I could do whatever I wanted.

I bit my lip, thinking of the most salacious thing I could. "Nolan?"

"Yes?"

"When we were kissing at McCoy's that first night, and you pressed me against the building, I—"

"Was that alright?"

I nodded vigorously. "I liked it. A lot. But I felt you…there, hard and pressing against my hip, and thought that meant you liked it, too."

He swallowed hard. "Of course, I liked it."

"But you're a merman."

"So?"

"So, um, right now, when you are in your mer form, where's your, you know, your unmentionable?"

34

NOLAN

"*U*nmentionable?"

She blushed furiously. "Don't make me say it. I already feel like a loose woman for just bringing it up."

I could tease her until she called my manhood by its proper name, but even the silly word she'd used was enough to make me harden, and I had to cover that part of me with my hands.

The woman was going to be the death of me. I cleared my throat. "It's hidden in a secret pocket."

She scooted closer, and with every inch that closed between us, my heart sped up until I thought I would pass out.

Her breasts were nearly visible through the sarong, and her nipples pebbled, poking the fabric. It took tremendous effort to keep my eyes on her face. I couldn't think straight. My desire for Eva drove me mad, and only my will kept me from taking her in my arms.

"Are you shy, Nolan?" she asked gently.

"Not generally."

"Then why are you covering yourself?"

"I..." I laughed nervously. "I don't want to scare or offend you."

She smiled, making me ache for the touch of her lips. "After everything you've shown me today, I can handle another new experience. You won't scare or offend me."

"But my body, I cannot seem to control it with you."

"Are you hard right now?"

My mouth became a desert. "Yes."

"Can I see it? Please?"

How could I deny her? I took a breath and let my hands fall away, letting my erection slip out of my tail slit.

To my relief, she appeared fascinated. Not disgusted. Not scared. I intrigued her. Perhaps even aroused her? I couldn't tell.

Whatever her thoughts, Eva's eyes were glued to me there, widening by the moment. "It's so big."

I smirked proudly.

Wasn't that what every man wanted to hear?

Wait, what did she base her comparison on?

Perhaps it was none of my business, but jealousy consumed me, and I could not hold my tongue. "Have you seen others?"

She blushed and giggled. "I've not seen any on a man, human or otherwise. Just horses and other animals."

"Gods, I hope you don't think that I am as big as a horse."

She huffed. "Don't make fun of my inexperience, Nolan."

As she turned away, I took her slender wrist in my hand to stop her. "I'm just as inexperienced as you are, Eva."

She didn't pull her wrist out of my grip. Instead, she scooted even closer, but her eyes lost their sweet expression.

Something bothered her. "Of all the things you've told me since I woke up in your bed, this is the least believable."

"It's true. I have never been with a woman. Have you ever been with a man?"

"No." She bit her bottom lip and resumed staring at my erection under the water. "How come you've never been with a woman? You're so handsome, Nolan. And such a good kisser. It's just hard to believe."

"Oh, I've kissed plenty of women. I just never allowed it to go further than that."

"Who were they?"

I smiled. It seemed jealousy ran through her heart as well. "I told you about my bets with Theo."

"Oh, right. You did."

"Besides, you're a wonderful kisser, too."

Her cheeks flushed pink. "Thank you."

"So, how many and who have you been kissing?"

She giggled. "Not as many as you, and never the kind of kiss I shared with you."

"What do you mean?"

"I've never opened my mouth for anyone. The most I have done was a quick kiss on the lips."

It might be selfish of me, but I was glad that she was even more inexperienced than I was.

I rubbed my thumb over her pulse. "The reason I have never been with a woman is that merfolk are supposed to bed only their one mate. Since we get only one during our lifetime, it is a transgression to bed anyone else. Those who transgress with their future mating bond risk losing the chance to properly bond with the one mate fated for them."

"It's different for humans. Women are expected to be virgins on their wedding night, but men can do whatever they want prior to marriage, and some continue even after promising loyalty to their wives."

"I know, and I find it appalling. Either both are allowed, or both are prohibited from having premarital sex."

She nodded. "I've always thought so."

I sighed. "In that respect, mer society is more egalitarian than human society."

"I'm inclined to agree."

"Eva?"

"Yes?"

"You still haven't stopped looking at me there, and it's a little odd."

My male anatomy was precisely the same as that of a human male, and other than the pocket it resided in when I was in my mer form, there was nothing unusual about it.

She blushed and turned away. "I'm so sorry. I hate it when men stare at my cleavage when talking to me, and here I am doing the same to you. I didn't mean to converse with just that part of you."

I tucked myself back into place as best I could, but proximity to Eva made it hard. Literally. "All covered up."

"Maybe we should get out of the pool," she suggested.

"Why?"

Eva looked me in the eye. "Because being here with you… like this, talking about these things…I'm not clearheaded."

"I can relate," I said with a chuckle. "But I enjoy being here with you. Like this. Talking about whatever we want to talk about. It's rare that I get to have such a candid conversation with someone so…" I struggled with the right word for her.

"Female?"

I shook my head. "Astounding. Breathtaking. Sensual."

As she looked down between us, her voice grew quiet. "Is that how you see me?"

"You are the most magnificent creature I have ever seen."

A nervous laugh escaped her lips. "Surely you've seen some who were more magnificent than me just by virtue of living down here."

"I have traveled to other underwater kingdoms and seen travelers from every pond around the world's oceans. I've visited shores far and wide, but I can confidently say there is no one in the water or on land that is more magnificent than you.

Eva stepped closer, pressing herself to my body. "Nolan, kiss me."

I took her in my arms and brushed my lips over hers. Soft, supple. Her mouth yielded to me as we kissed. When she moaned in my mouth, my shaft emerged from my slit once more. I couldn't hold back, and I didn't want to. Kissing my mate made the world stop spinning, and my heart soar. Nothing else mattered.

Her small hands clasped the nape of my neck, and she held on tight as she wrapped her legs around my waist. I cupped her bottom to support her. With only her sarong between us, her warmth enticed my erection to sink into her, but alas, that damned fabric was in the way. She wriggled herself against me, working her hips back and forth, and with every pass, she let out another moan.

My head spun with every sensation.

Gripping her bottom, feeling her body on me, it was all too much and yet not enough. I murmured her name in her ear as I kissed down her neck.

It was then that she went stiff.

Eva pushed back and panted. I could not read her expression—something between awe and a frown.

Softly, I asked, "What is wrong?"

"It's just...let me down."

I set her to her feet, wondering what I'd done wrong. "Have I offended you?"

"No. Remember when I said I wasn't thinking clearly?"

I nodded.

"This whole thing, Nolan...my head is foggy with you."

I gulped as disappointment sank in. We had to stop. She was right to stop us. We weren't wed. I didn't even know if she cared for me or if she understood we were mates. I took a breath and tried to cool off. "I understand, Eva."

"How can you?"

"What do you mean?"

She shook her head and stepped back, looking away. "This is all so confusing."

"Can I help to clear it up?"

"No." She huffed and folded her arms around herself. "Nolan, I'm trying to maintain a level head, and I'm not good at it. You make things hazy inside of me—"

"I don't mean to. You do the same to me."

"I feel this strange pull toward you. Like there's no one else for me in the world."

My heart swelled with her words. She felt the mating bond. She just didn't know what it was. "I know what you mean."

"You do?"

I smiled and nodded, then took her hands in mine. "Eva, we're—"

But she shook her head and took her hands away from me. "I don't…Nolan, I want you so much. Too much."

I was on the edge of a knife. Every time she came near, I was elated. Every time she pulled away, my heart was wounded. I would do anything for her to stop this dance and bring her back into my arms. "How is it too much? What can I do?"

"I don't know what there is to do about it. But I like touching you. And kissing you. I don't want this day to end." She came close once more and stroked my cheek.

I kissed her palm, then held her hand on my chest over my heart. "Neither do I."

35

EVELINE

*T*his was torture.

I had never cared about keeping my virtue for some prince my father decided to marry me to. Such a thing sounded repugnant to me. But I couldn't do this to Nolan.

If I were the reason his mating bond withered, or if I were the reason he couldn't find love, then I would hate myself forever. No matter how much I wanted him, I could not doom Nolan to a lifetime without the love of his mate.

And there was no way I could be her.

This no longer seemed like a dream. I was in an underwater city with a merman, and I was falling in love with him.

Except, I was not a mermaid, and one day, I'd have to go back to the surface.

Even if he followed me, he couldn't stay for long without people finding out his secret. No matter what I felt for Nolan in my soul, I was certain there was no way we could be fated to be together.

Fate would not be so cruel.

Then, there was the fact that he didn't even know my real name or who I was. When he had ecstatically whispered my fake name in my ear, that looming detail became so glaring I could no longer gloss over it.

He called me Eva. Not Eveline. Not Princess. How could I take away his future when he didn't even know the most basic thing about me?

But what if this wasn't real?

It couldn't be, right?

This was only a dream.

It was the most detailed dream I'd ever had, and I was falling in love with my dream merman, but merfolk were not real, underwater cities were not real, and none of that other stuff mattered. The mating bond, marriage, hell, and even pregnancy was not a risk. It was all just a fantasy.

Why not enjoy it?

I smiled up at Nolan. "So, merfolk are only supposed to ever be with their mate, right?"

"Yes."

"Then let's pretend we are fated for one another, and this is our wedding night."

He gulped. "Do you mean that?"

"Unless you don't want me—"

"I want you more than my next breath. More than life itself." He ran his fingers through his damp hair. "But what about you? When you go back home in a month, what will happen?"

"I don't want to think about that right now. I just want to be with you."

A nervous smile flicked the corner of his mouth. "I want that too."

If any of this was real, I'd worry. Being married off to some pompous prince while being pregnant with a merbaby would ruin my life. But I wasn't going to be pregnant with a merbaby because they weren't real, and if I had my druthers, I'd never marry some prince.

My heart lurched in my chest every time Nolan came near

me. I needed him in a way that I didn't understand, but it made perfect sense in the dream.

Each time we touched, something inside of me stilled and caught fire.

If only I could marry the merman of my dreams…

I kissed him, but he gently pushed me back.

"What's wrong?" I asked.

"If we do this, there could be consequences. Serious ones. For you and for me."

"But this is a dream. There are no consequences."

He softly chuckled. "You are unlike anyone I have ever known. Unique in every way…."

"Same goes for you."

"I'm not just a normal kid from Poseidon City," he said.

"You do not know how exotic that sounds."

He chuckled. "You're just as different to me as I am to you."

I pressed myself against him, staring into those luminous blue eyes. He was hard at my hip again, and I longed to touch him there. To feel what it was like. "I don't care about the consequences right now. Do you?"

He looked pained. "I don't want to care about them, but I don't know how to stop."

I gulped, trying not to sound disappointed. "Alright then. We stop."

He smashed his lips against mine, kissing me roughly, and I couldn't help myself. I reached down and touched his arousal.

The smooth, warm skin was a surprise like silk on hard steel. When I stroked him there, he groaned in my mouth and pulled back from our kiss to breathe deeply.

"Gods…" His voice was raspy.

Was I taking advantage of him?

What if he didn't want it?

"We don't have to do anything you don't want to do, Nolan." Saying that while my hand was wrapped around his erection seemed like a contradiction, but I couldn't stop touching him.

His hips worked back and forth in my hand, and his eyes clamped shut. "Eva—"

I kissed him again, hooking my hand around the back of his neck to keep him on my mouth. It was forward of me—all of this was—but I didn't care. I was on the brink of madness. My core burned for Nolan, and I was beyond all sense of decorum or decency. Brazen or not, I had to have him.

But then he snatched my hand away at the wrist and stared into my eyes as we panted at each other. I had crossed some line or upset him somehow, but I was too far gone. An apology was the last thing on my mind because I couldn't regret touching him like that. I wanted him. Every inch of him.

Nolan smashed his lips over mine.

Overcome with lust, he backed me against the side of the pool with kisses that were more like bites. My lips, my chin, my throat, all were a feast for him. I purred for every nibble. When he cupped my breasts over my sarong top, I shuddered, and when his thumbs strummed my nipples, the pleasure bolted through me straight to my core.

Groaning, I could not stay still.

As his hands grazed down my waist and over my hips, he murmured in my ear, "You touched me. I want to do the same to you."

"God, yes, please," I whispered.

He stared into my eyes as his hand drifted down. I gasped when he pressed his finger to that sensitive spot I'd heard the maids talk about. Despite their descriptions, I'd never imagined it would feel so good.

When we'd kissed before, and his manhood had rubbed that spot through the sarong, I'd damn near lost my mind. But now, with his fingers touching me, it was even better.

"There?" he asked.

"Yes," I hissed.

Nolan kissed me roughly as he rubbed me just the way I needed it.

I saw stars.

Soon, I was the one biting and nibbling whatever I could find. His tongue, his lips. Something hot inside of me shifted. It was like the nights when I was too wound up to sleep and touched myself. The rapture built inside of me. Only this time, I didn't have to bite my pillow. When I bit his neck, he growled at me.

As his thumb took over, pressing on the center of my pleasure, his other finger edged inside of me, and I rolled my hips to take him in deeper.

He gasped with me. "So warm," he murmured against my lips.

I couldn't speak. I merely nodded and tried to ride his fingers. Heat flashed through me. Breathing became secondary. Weakly, I panted, "You're gonna make me—"

"Come for me," he demanded.

My body broke on his order. Euphoria took hold, and I gasped before I bit his shoulder to muffle my moans. Pleasure coursed through me, making me mindless. My whole body was limp from the impact. When I looked up at him, breathless and elated, his eyes were fierce.

Primal.

Nolan kissed me, stealing my air and any thought I might have tried to have. Slowly, his fingers left me, making me squirm. Blissful fog rolled into my brain.

He panted. "I need you."

"You have me."

"Are you sure about this?"

Nodding, I murmured, "Absolutely." I reached for him, but he shook his head.

"Not like this. Not this time. I want you on the bed."

I almost smiled. "Nolan, I'm not freaked out by your tail."

He kissed me. "I know. It's not that. I just...you said to pretend we're fated for each other. To pretend you're my mate. The way I always pictured the first time with my mate, was on my bed. Not in the water."

That made me smile. "Did you picture it with me?"

He nodded, and the look in his eyes captivated me. "The night I met you." Nolan leaned to my ear and whispered, "I couldn't stop. I had to touch myself when I thought of you. The way you made me feel that night...." Quietly, he chuckled. "I've not been able to think of anything but how it would feel to be inside of you. I've dreamt of you, your lips, you in my bed. I was obsessed with you. I still am."

His jumbled words were better than any poetry he could have recited for me, sending a delicious thrill through my body. I kissed him until my lips were raw.

36

NOLAN

"*T*hat was the nicest thing anyone has ever said to me." Eva leaned toward me and pressed her lips to mine.

I wrapped my arms around her and kissed her gently, pouring all my love into it.

I loved her and believed she loved me back, but we'd just met, and she thought it was a dream. Perhaps once we made love, she would realize that this was real.

I just hoped she wouldn't panic.

There was no future for us, and I was sealing my fate by going forward with this, but I'd reached the point of no return.

There had to be a way, though.

If she couldn't be with me down here, I would find a way to be with her up there. We could move to a desert country where it never rained, and I would keep a tub in our bedroom for when I needed to dip.

Yeah, that could work.

I would lose the crown, but hopefully, I wouldn't be banished and could still visit my family from time to time.

She pulled away and looked into my eyes. "What's wrong?"

"I'm not willing to let our differences stand in the way of our happiness. I will find a way for us to be together."

A smile bloomed on her beautiful face. "I know you will. You can do anything you set your mind to, and I will be right there with you. I'm not some helpless shrinking violet."

"I know." I cupped her cheek. "Unique in every way."

Her smile broadened. "That I am." She hoisted herself up and out of the pool. "Come to bed with me, Nolan."

Grabbing three towels, she tossed one to me and took the other two with her.

I sat on the edge of the pool, rubbing the towel over my tail to dry it faster while watching Eva.

She spread the towel on the bed, sat down, and started to untie her top, but I stopped her with a shake of my head.

She frowned. "What's the matter?"

"I want to be the one to undress you."

Her cheeks blushed pink. "Oh."

As my tail shimmered and split to become legs, she gasped, but I wasn't sure whether she was startled by the magical transformation or by my nudity.

I stood up and walked up to her slowly, giving her ample time to change her mind, but her eyes remained on me—wide like saucers and roving over my entire body before fixating on my manhood.

When I reached her, I started to lean down to untie her top, but I jerked up as she surprised me with a quick lick to the tip of my shaft.

I gasped. "What are you doing?"

"I don't know what came over me." She giggled. "I thought I'd try what the maid did with the guard in the closet."

"You have a mischievous streak a mile long, don't you?"

"I wouldn't be here if I didn't." She reached out for me with a surprisingly sure hand and stroked my length. "Is it okay if I taste you again?"

Was she kidding me?

"Yes, please do."

As she licked up my shaft a few times, making me shudder with pleasure, I fought the urge to push into her mouth. I didn't want to scare her or have her stop what she was doing.

It was the sweetest torture I'd ever endured.

As something dark passed through my mind, a distant echo of a memory of being tortured, I forcefully pushed it away.

Where had that come from?

It must have been a remnant of a bad dream that had gotten triggered by that word.

When Eva swirled her tongue around the tip, all thoughts left me, and I felt like I might pass out from pleasure, but then she took me in her mouth, and the new level of bliss nearly buckled my knees.

I hissed, "Eva, fuck, this is good." Mortified by my coarse language, I pulled out from her lips. "My apologies. I should not have said that word."

Holding on to my shaft, she looked up at me. "Don't censor yourself for me, Nolan. I want you to be yourself." She smiled with mischief in her eyes. "I like the way you say fuck, as if that encompasses everything you cannot put into words."

Hearing her say the word was sexy beyond reason.

As I bent at the waist and kissed her hard, she wrapped her arms around me and pulled me down with her, and as I lay on top of her, she lifted her long legs and wrapped them around my waist, pulling me even tighter.

Her sarong was still on, covering where I wanted to feel her the most, but maybe it was a good thing that there was still this small barrier between us.

I braced on my forearms and looked into her eyes. "Are you sure about this?"

"I've never been surer about anything, Nolan." She smiled.

"This is the best dream I ever had, and I intend to see it through to its marvelous conclusion."

She still thought this was a dream?

I couldn't do this as long as she believed that there would be no consequences for her actions. It was like taking advantage of a drunk woman.

Then a thought struck me. What if she was right?

No one had ever brought a human to Poseidon City before, and Eva had accepted everything about my world too readily.

Perhaps this was a dream?

37

NOLAN

*N*o, it wasn't a dream.

I couldn't hide behind the flimsy excuse. In my heart, I knew the truth.

I was with my mate, and I wouldn't start our relationship with a lie. I brushed her hair back and regretfully said, "Eva—"

She stole my hand and kissed my palm. "I want you."

"What if this is not a dream? Would you still want me if this was real?"

"Yes," she said with no hesitation. "You are the one for me, in the dream world and in the real one." She smiled. "As soon as I wake up, I'm going to seduce the real Nolan."

"What about consequences?"

"What about them? One way or another, the real Nolan and I are going to live happily ever after, right?"

"Yes. But just to be clear, I'm the real Nolan," I tried one last time.

"You are my Nolan, and that's all that matters."

Well, that settled it. Dream or reality, Eva wanted a life with me.

"And you are my Eva." I dipped my head to kiss her.

Her smile faltered. "My full name is Eveline. I just thought you should know that."

"My beautiful Eveline." I kissed her again. "My Eva," I added.

That was her name when I fell in love with her, and that was what I was going to call her.

Absorbed in her scent, I kissed her chin, her throat, and down to her collarbones. Untying her top, I pulled it off her to reveal her beautiful, soft breasts. As I licked her pink nubs, Eva moaned and arched up, and when I massaged the tender flesh around them, she purred like a kitten.

"I'm so hot inside," she breathed.

Kissing and nibbling downward, I untied the sarong at her waist. But before I peeled it from her body, I looked into her eyes, and only when she silently nodded, did I tug it off.

Every inch of her was perfection.

I kissed and lightly nibbled her inner thigh while my fingers feathered over her sleek lower lips.

She growled, "Nolan, please! I need more."

"Your wish is my command."

As I licked her center, my eyes rolled back in my head at the taste of her.

With a gasping whimper, she reached down and dug her fingers into my hair, holding me to her. When I found her most sensitive spot and lightly flicked my tongue over it, she rocked her body against my face.

My chest swelled with male satisfaction, and I kept at it, pleasing my mate until she tugged my hair upward.

Eva looked like a dream from that angle, and I wondered again if she wasn't onto something with her insistence that we were in a dream.

"Nolan, I want you."

Kissing her sweet lower lips one more time, I climbed over her body.

Chest to chest, skin to skin, she felt so good. Every thought melted away as I touched her cheek and positioned my shaft at her welcoming entrance.

Soft, wet, calling to me.

When Eva cocked her hips to take more of me inside of her, I thought I might spend myself right then, even though it was just a fraction of my length.

"Now, Nolan," she commanded.

I pushed a little further, careful not to hurt her. We were both virgins, but the first time was supposed to be more difficult for females.

I wouldn't let it happen. Eva would enjoy this as much as I did, even if it drove me insane to go slow.

Excruciatingly slow, as it was.

Watching her expression, I refused to advance even a fraction of an inch until she was ready for more. When I was finally fully seated, we both cried out.

I could understand now why some merfolk were willing to risk their mating bond for the pleasures of the flesh, why poets wrote epic verses dedicated to one mer above all others, and why wars had been fought over love.

With this final act of joining, Eva became everything to me. I would never let harm come to her, do anything to protect her, and everything to make her happy.

I was hers, and she was mine.

I kissed her sweetly as I gently retreated and thrust into her again, a little deeper this time. I curled my arms under her, clasping over the top of her shoulders to keep her pinned to me. But I went slowly, carefully watching her expressions as I moved inside of her, memorizing them so I'd have them forever.

Her body moved in sensual waves beneath me, and her legs tightened around my torso, her small feet digging into my buttocks.

Some primal memory guiding my hand, I reached between

us and rubbed my finger over that sensitive spot while thrusting into her body. In response, the small muscles inside her feminine core tightened and squeezed me.

It was intoxicating. The rush of ecstasy made me dizzy.

I kept rubbing, becoming distracted by her writhing, and paused my thrusts just to experience what my touch was doing to her.

Focusing on her pleasure helped stave off my climax so I could bring her over the edge with me, but she got impatient and arched up, forcing my length into her.

Her eyes became half-slits as she whimpered, "You feel so good inside me."

"You're my heaven," I managed.

I couldn't hold back any longer.

Lacing my fingers with hers, I held her down as I surged back and forth deep inside my mate.

Our bodies worked in perfect synchrony as we climbed toward the peak, and when she arched and threw her head back with a silent scream, I erupted inside of her with a roar.

Wave after wave of euphoria flowed through me until there was nothing left.

Grinning, ecstatic, and spent, we panted in each other's faces.

I had no words.

There was nothing else in the world besides Eva.

My mate.

38

EVELINE

I was in love.

There was no doubt in my mind that the feeling in my chest, that incredible swelling of emotion, was love for Nolan.

He kissed me slowly and sweetly, taking his time while his erection softened inside of me. I nearly told him I loved him when I'd come, but I couldn't speak more than his name at the moment. There wasn't enough air in my lungs to say more when I climaxed.

He had told me that I was his mate and that he was going to spend the rest of his life with me, but but we were only pretending, right? He hadn't told me he loved me.

Was he waiting for me to say it first?

As something leaked out of me, I frowned but then realized what it was and felt my cheeks heat up.

"What is it?" Nolan asked

"Your um, your—I need to go to the bathroom." I wiggled under him,

Chuckling, he pulled out, and there was even more leakage.

I slapped my palm over my center and scooted to the side of the enormous bed.

Rolling onto his back, he looked as if he was stifling laughter. "I can help you clean up if you'll let me."

"No, thank you." I dashed to the bathroom.

It was so easy to get clean using all those marvelous devices, and as I looked at myself in the mirror, I was struck by the thought that I'd never seen myself fully nude like this. When I'd lived in the palace, a maid always helped me dress and undress, and it would have been awkward to parade in the nude in front of her.

I had to admit that I liked what I saw. My breasts were plump, the nipples tight, and my waist was narrow and flared into hips that were generous but not overly so. I was quite pleasant to look at, especially now that I was still glowing from making love to Nolan.

Unabashed by my nudity, I sauntered back into the bedroom and was struck again by how handsome he was. The cover was pulled up over his hips, hiding his manhood, and as he lay there smiling at me, all I could think of was how I put that smile on his face.

As he lifted the cover for me, I scooted in next to him, and he kissed my nose. "You were gone too long. I missed you."

Had I spent so much time admiring myself in the mirror?

I chuckled. "There was a lot to clean, and your bathroom is too incredible to rush through it."

He nestled against my ear. "I've never come so hard in my life."

Since he'd been a virgin, I assumed that, like me, he had indulged in self-pleasuring.

"I've often imagined how my first time would be," I admitted. "I always thought it would be painful, or at least uncomfortable. Yet it was none of those things. It was incredible. You made it so."

"It was the two of us. It felt like we were one. You're incredible, Eva."

Pride warmed my cheeks. "So are you."

He kissed my bare shoulder. "What I'm about to say is meant as a compliment."

I tensed. "With a preamble like that, you've got me worried."

"It's just that you seemed more experienced than you should have been given your virginity. I was pleasantly surprised."

I nodded. "The same occurred to me about you. I guess our bodies just knew instinctively what to do."

He nuzzled into the crook of my shoulder. "My body tells me that it wants to pleasure yours again."

I giggled. "I thought men needed to recuperate between bouts of lovemaking."

"We do." He turned me onto my side and pressed himself against my back. "But my hands don't have to rest, and I need to see you come again." Reaching around my hip and between my legs, his fingertips stroked me to life as he kissed my neck.

I groaned wordlessly as he touched me.

Needing to pleasure him too, I rolled my hips, rubbing against him, and as his shaft hardened against me, I panted, "Nolan?"

"Eva?"

"I want you again."

"Aren't you sore?"

Why would I be sore? After all, this was a dream, and everything in it had been wonderful so far. Even losing my virginity had been pleasurable. But I didn't say any of that because Dream Nolan didn't like to be reminded that he wasn't real.

"I'm not sore." I turned around, pushed him onto his back, and climbed on top of him, straddling his lap.

I felt empowered by how shocked and aroused he was by my assertiveness. Seeing him on his back, his muscles all pumped, and his shaft primed, I felt myself get wet for him.

He rasped, "Gods, Eva, you feel incredible."

"So do you."

I rubbed my wetness up and down his shaft and then took him in my hand and lowered myself over him, just the tip at first, and then I was riding him, going up and down. He gripped my buttocks, helping me lift and pulling me down.

The angles were so different this time, but he still felt amazing inside me, brushing up against a sensitive spot I hadn't known I had.

When my leg muscles began to protest, which baffled me since they shouldn't have done that in a dream, I lay onto Nolan's chest. He kept thrusting up into me with an upward roll of his hips, and every time I moaned, I could hear his heartbeat skip.

Nolan's breath shimmered in the air as he gasped, "I am yours, Eva."

I purred, "I belong to you, Nolan."

He reached up and cupped the back of my neck, pulling me to his lips and kissing me deeply. His hands slipped down to my hips, and he held me there, controlling our pace.

Being on top was fun, but the truth was that everything felt better when he was in charge. I wanted to give him everything and do anything he wanted.

If it was mine to give, then it was his.

If this was a dream, I never wanted to wake up, and if it wasn't a dream, I never wanted to sleep again for fear of spending one moment without Nolan.

As I neared my climax, my body tightened on him,

He held me close and murmured, "I can feel it. You're close again."

"Yes," I purred against his chest.

I was shaking, unable to contain the pleasure in my body. The way he held me, the way he touched me, all the ways he made me feel like I was the only woman in the world for him.

The coil inside of me tightened until I could barely breathe, but the edge eluded me.

"Come for me again, sweetheart."

As his words shattered me into a thousand pieces, I let out a scream of ecstasy, unable to stifle it this time.

Nolan wrapped his arms around my back to keep me tethered to him, and as the tension left my body, I collapsed onto his chest, weak and helpless in his muscular arms.

Holding me to him, he stroked my hair as I recovered, but then it suddenly occurred to me that he hadn't climaxed. He was still hard inside of me.

Gasping, I sat up.

"Rest, my love." He pulled me back down over his chest.

Hearing him call me his love was such a delight that I felt rejuvenated.

"I want to try something." I sat back up on him fully to see how that felt and then rode him that way.

Every new angle brought its unique pleasure, and this was no exception.

Nolan's lips were slightly parted as he watched me on top of him, and when he reached out and cupped my bouncing breasts, his eyes rolled back in his head.

He thrust up from underneath. "Gods, Eva, you feel so good!"

Raking my nails down his chest, I rocked harder on him, and he growled like a beast, pumping up rougher. The more primal he became, the more unhinged I got, and soon, I was soaring to another screaming orgasm.

This time he joined me, letting out a howl of his own as he came.

Sitting up, Nolan wrapped his arms around me and kissed me passionately.

When we came up for air, he leaned away and looked into my eyes. "Are you alright?"

"I'm amazing."

"Yes, you are." He laid me down next to him and fetched towels for us both.

After we gathered our breath and cleaned ourselves, I felt sleepy, but I was afraid to close my eyes. What if I woke up and all of this was gone?

I would die from a broken heart.

I wasn't sure what scared me more, this being only a dream or the thought that it might not be. Each possibility held its own obstacles and joys, but the only thing I wanted was for my connection to Nolan to be real.

I didn't care about the consequences, and I understood why so many would risk so much for this. It was the only thing that truly mattered in the world—the deep connection to another person.

It wasn't even about the sex. It was the closeness. The oneness. The sense of endless love.

I was in love with Nolan.

I no longer knew whether this was a dream or reality, and frankly, it no longer mattered to me. As I laid my head on Nolan's muscular chest, all I knew was that I wanted to always be where I could feel the soothing rhythm of his heart.

39

NOLAN

*F*alling asleep with Eva in my arms, I had never known such contentment. As I drifted away, I knew there could never be another for me. As impossible as it was, we had bonded.

It was said the mating bond could only happen with another mer. No one thought it was possible with a human. It was considered such an absurdity that a common taunt revolved around the idea.

Mer children would curse at one another, "You son of a human!"

And yet, my bond with Eva was undeniable.

She and I would not fit so well together if we were not fated. Every cell in my body told me she was mine and I was hers, and neither of us was complete without the other.

During the haze of passion, I resolved to make it work somehow, but now that I was thinking rationally again, I wondered how in the six hells it could be done?

Eva's problems were easier to overcome than my own. She had been a barmaid on the run from her father. Simple enough.

But as a prince of Poseidon City, I had responsibilities. I loved my people, and they counted on me to lead them one day.

Still, every mer knew that one's mate was one's highest priority.

No one questioned that law of nature.

My father, however, wasn't just anyone.

He was the King. He could question and tear asunder anything in his path. With a word, he could banish Eva and prevent me from going after her.

I shuddered at the thought.

The throne did not matter to me. Theo could have it for all I cared. But I could not withstand being apart from her.

I remembered thinking that we could live in a desert and that I could make do with several discreet baths a day, but what if someone spilled water on me by accident?

The moment water touched my legs, they would transform.

That being said, Theo and I had risked it plenty of times by going to taverns along the beach. We had never tested whether spilled ale would trigger the transformation the same way water did, but since ale contained water, it made sense that it would.

We'd been careful not to spill anything on each other, but sometimes patrons had gotten rowdy, and we had been forced to leave before things grew too chaotic and sloppy.

All it would take was one splash of mud on my skin, and my tail would form.

Such a thing would expose the secret existence of the mer, and humans would hunt my people to extinction.

I could not let that happen. Shirking my duties and handing the crown to Theo was one thing, but betraying my entire kind was quite another.

I sighed, trying to come up with a solution, but there was no compromise to be made between the ocean and the land. Our bodies had different needs.

I could not reach out to my father for help either. He would not see things as I did, even if he believed me that Eva was my mate, but I needed the help of someone more powerful than me.

The only mer who was nearly as powerful as my father, had the gift of magic, and might be more sympathetic to my plight, was my Uncle Osiris.

With his magical powers and his penchant for nonconformity, he was the perfect mer to turn to.

Hell, with his powers, he could turn me into a human or Eva into a mermaid and solve all of our problems.

I smiled so hard that my face ached.

I kissed Eva's forehead. "I will be right back, my love," I whispered.

Theo had said his father had been traveling, but I suspected it was a lie to cover up the fact that he was back to his old habits, creating potions and monsters in his illegal laboratory.

Uncle Osiris was a mischievous mer, and he liked the privacy of the borderlands to conduct his risky experiments.

I knew that I would find him there.

Exiting my quarters through my private hatch, I crossed the city to where I knew I would find the borderlands hatch.

It was a forbidden area for residents of Poseidon City, but a tunnel connected the dome with the various borderland encampments for our guards to patrol the lawless communities, search for dissidents, and arrest thieves and smugglers.

The tunnel had three exits leading to various parts of the borderlands, and I took the one that led to the worst part—the caverns.

Each cavern had air trapped inside, so I could breathe there, but not for long. Fearsome creatures dwelled there, cursed by my ancestors to be forever trapped in the caverns.

Winged, luminous, sightless, and venomous, the jetsflom did more than bite mer. Their bodies were small and sticky, near impossible to remove, and once they attached to a mer's skin, trying to pull them off resulted in tearing off flesh. If given a chance, they would attach themselves to a mer's mouth and nose, asphyxiate their victim.

Thankfully, they didn't venture underwater.

When they heard me, they floated in the air like butterflies hunting for blood, and I quickly gobbled air down before diving beneath the surface once more.

Not much further now.

An explosion ahead told me I was right about my uncle's location.

It was the cavern at the very end that was alight with a green glow.

No jetsflom would dare bother Osiris. I suspected that he chose these caverns not only for the privacy they provided but also because of the protection of the nasty little creatures.

No ordinary mer could go this far into a borderland cavern without risking a miserable death by jetsflom. Only royals had the breath control required for such a feat. But even with my gift of powerful lungs, I had to risk the occasional breath to make it all the way to him.

I found Osiris in the deepest part of the cavern, looking so much like my father that it was difficult to believe how different they were.

They had the same long gray hair, the same broad back and shoulders. But where Father had grown softer around the middle, Osiris kept himself in top shape.

It had long been said that had ruling been a contest of skill, Osiris would have been King. He was fitter, more agile than Father, and better looking as well.

But Grandfather had a feeling about his sons and had chosen my father despite him being the younger son.

Father was kinder, less selfish, and he loved our people.

Osiris loved himself and the magic he wielded more than anything else.

After he had lost Theo's mother to a magical accident, he had grown even colder and more reclusive. In fact, as I traversed the water nearer to him, I could swear that it became cooler.

Wearing only a pair of black breeches and no shoes, he stood atop a platform, stirring ingredients into a black cauldron and murmuring incantations. Purple and green flames burned beneath the cauldron, illuminating the space.

He was with his back to me, and I didn't want to startle him, so I softly cleared my throat to alert him to my presence, but he only held up a finger to make me wait.

I sat on a piece of driftwood, waiting for him to be done with whatever he was cooking in that cauldron, and hoping there would be no more explosions.

"Tell me, Prince, what prompted you to come all this way to bother an old man?"

I laughed. "You're not old, Osiris."

He faced me, smirking, his lined face belying my words. "If I'm not old, then you're not the prince, this isn't a cavern, and you didn't risk a terrible death to come to see me."

I chuckled. "It's good to see you, Silly One."

He laughed. "You as well. To what do I owe the pleasure of your company?"

"I have committed a crime."

His eyes widened, and he pointed a finger at me. "You?"

"Aye. I need your help."

Slyly, he folded his arms over his muscular chest. "I can't wait to hear what mischief the son of my sanctimonious brother has committed."

"I need your vow that what I'm about to tell you will remain between us."

"Of course."

"Vow it to me."

He arched an eyebrow. "You're making me your accomplice, but my curiosity is greater than my fear of the law."

Osiris didn't fear the law. He'd proven that many times over.

"I vow that I will tell no one about what you are about to tell me, and I also vow to help you in complete secrecy." As he spoke, his voice came out in a purple shimmer. I'd seen no one else's voice do that. It was silver for everyone else. "How is that for a vow, my nephew? Better, no?"

"Yes. Thank you for making your vow so thorough."

"My pleasure. Now, how may I be of service to you?"

"I have brought a human to Poseidon City."

He snorted out a laugh. "Bullshit!"

I was glad that Theo hadn't told him. I trusted my cousin, but Osiris was his father, and the two were close.

"She is my mate."

His eyes widened, and he shook his head in disbelief. "That's quite a scandalous thing to do, but you didn't break the law because what you did is so absurd that no one ever bothered to explicitly prohibit it."

"I know there is no law, but I also know what my father's reaction will be, nonetheless." I raked my fingers through my hair. "That's not even the biggest issue, though. She's my mate, and I want to build a life with her, but unless you can turn me into a human or her into a mermaid, that's not possible."

His eyes started glowing with an emotion that seemed very much like glee to me. "I can do either, but there is a stiff price to pay."

"Name it."

"It's not my price, nephew. I would never charge you for my help. It's the price magic demands. Sorcery requires balance. If I turn you into a human, you can never return to the sea. And if I turn her into a mermaid, she can never return to the land."

"So...I could never see my family again, or vice versa?"

He nodded. "I wish I could give you a better option, but it is not up to me."

"If it were you, which would you choose?"

He smoothed his hand over his beard. "There isn't really a choice. Humans are often more attached to their families than the mer are to theirs. It would be cruel to separate your mate from her family. Also, since she's human, she doesn't share our beliefs about the importance of mates, and she might choose to leave you to be with her kind, even if she truly loves you. You, on the other hand, won't be able to live without her. You will have to be the one to make the sacrifice."

My heart was heavy from his words. I wasn't sure about his claim that humans valued their families more than the mer, but he was right about the other stuff. "I must consult with Eva first. We should make this choice together."

"As you wish, nephew. But remember what I said. Even if she chooses to sacrifice her family connection for you, she will resent you for the rest of her life for it. Resentment is powerful magic, and since she will become a mermaid and susceptible to everything the mer are, her resentment will wither your mating bond." He smiled sardonically. "There is a good reason why the mer are more devoted to their mates than any other species. The bond requires nurturing, and once it is withered, there is no repairing it."

I'd already decided that I would make the sacrifice for us to be together, but I couldn't take the choice from Eva. "Thank you for everything, uncle. I will return after consulting with my mate."

He nodded. "Good luck, nephew."

40

EVELINE

"*P*lease wake up, love," Nolan's deep voice penetrated through my dream.

Waking up with him close was the only way I ever wanted to wake up again. I smiled, satisfied, but also ready for more.

"Come here." I reached out for him before opening my eyes.

He took my hand and kissed my palm. "I know what you have in mind with that tone, but we have much to discuss. Please, wake up."

Only then did I open my eyes. He looked like a dream, his gorgeous face and powerful body framed in the soft light coming through the windows of the surreal room. But there were worry lines on his face.

I frowned. "What's wrong?"

"I have a lot of things that I need to tell you, and we have some hard choices to make."

Well, that certainly made me wide awake. As I sat up, I saw that he was still naked. "I can't think clearly with you like that. If you want to talk, you will have to cover up." I waved a hand over him.

Nolan laughed and kissed me. "It is a terrible burden." He pulled his side of the covers over his lap. "Better?"

"A little, but not by much. What's going on?"

"There are things I have not told you about myself. But I do not wish for you to feel misled. I had my reasons for withholding them."

A sentiment we shared. But I wasn't about to go first. "I think you know by now that you can tell me anything. You can trust me."

"Of course." He sighed. "I'll start with the easiest part. This is not just a random building. This is the royal palace."

"Oh. Huh. Well, that explains the extravagance. You mentioned that you're a lord."

"No. You asked if I was a lord, and I said that I didn't like to talk about it. And that's because I am not a lord."

"But we're in a palace."

"I'm a prince. The crown prince of Poseidon City."

A gasp slipped past my lips. "Oh."

"I do not like it when people treat me differently when they find out. That's why I didn't tell you when we met, and after that, well, it never seemed like the right time. But we are mates, and there should be no secrets or deception between us."

I swallowed. "But we are just pretending, right?" I said in a small voice.

He shook his head. "I'm not pretending, and I don't think you are pretending either, Eva. You are my mate. There will never be another for me."

I let out a breath. "I feel the same way, Nolan. I will never want anyone else."

"Thank you for admitting that." He lifted my hand and kissed the back of it. "There's more."

"More?"

"I think it is time you realized that as unbelievable as all this is, you are not dreaming. I am really a merman prince, and you are a human, and although we are mates, we cannot be together because of our differences. Where would we live? What would we do?"

Frankly, I had realized that this wasn't a dream some time ago, but hiding behind that excuse felt less scary than admitting to myself that I had fallen in love with a merman.

The logistics were impossible.

I didn't have a solution, and I didn't know what to say. "You're right. We are fucked."

"Don't say that word right now, please. I am too vulnerable to hear it."

It was a crass word, but he'd said it before, and he'd seemed pleased when I said it.

I pouted. "Make up your mind. If you don't want me to say words like that, let me know."

He huffed and readjusted the blanket over himself. "I love it when you say naughty words. But right now, I can't afford to get distracted, and that word evokes yearnings that are very distracting."

I enjoyed having such power over him, but everything else was a mess. "Okay then. I'll save it for a more appropriate time. So, what do mer do in cases like this?"

"To my knowledge, this has never happened before. Only mer are fated for one another. That being said, the oracle told me that my mate would be unique in every way, and there is no denying that you are unique."

Usually, that would have been a compliment, but not in this case.

"What can we do?"

"I spoke to my uncle, Theo's father, and he can help us, but it's going to cost us. He's a powerful sorcerer, and he can either change you into a mermaid or me into a human so we can live together either here or up there."

"That's great!"

"As I said, there is a price to pay. Whoever changes can never see their family again. I don't know why, but I assume it is because their body will be incapable of completely existing in the other realm. Osiris explained that magic requires balance, and everything has a price."

I didn't have to see my awful father again? Perfect. But then I thought of my mother and sister and sighed. "That's a lot to give up."

"I know. But I will give my family up for you, Eva."

I gasped. "You're the crown prince of your people, Nolan. I can't ask that of you."

"I love my people, but you are my mate, and you come first."

I wasn't sure what to say to that. I didn't want him to be the only one sacrificing for us to be together. It wasn't fair. "You have a responsibility to your people."

"I've already transgressed against the crown by bringing you here and making you mine. I might have lost the position already. And if I didn't yet, I would give it up for you in a heartbeat."

"Why? I'm just a tavern girl you met a few days ago."

He winced and gathered my hands in his. "You are my mate. Nothing else matters. I love you."

My heart pounded in my chest.

I had to speak the words that might change his mind about me and make him resent me. Then again, he hadn't told me about being the crown prince until a few moments ago. He would understand why I had kept my real identity a secret for so long.

"Nolan," I began, "I must confess something as well, and I hope you can forgive me."

"You can tell me anything."

I took him in my arms to feel his warmth one more time before he might choose to push me away. "I'm not a tavern girl. I'm a princess."

His blue eyes bulged. "What?"

"I'm not Eva Trovalia. I am Princess Eveline, daughter of King Prosper III and Queen Gwendolyn."

His frown turned into a broad grin. "A pleasure to meet you, Princess." Then he leaned down and kissed the tip of my nose.

I was stunned. "You're not angry?"

"Why would I be angry? Now it's clearer than ever why fate thought that we were a good match. We grew up in similar circumstances, and we understand each other." He leaned closer again and kissed my forehead. "You are my mate. There is nothing you can say or do that would undermine my devotion to you."

"I know the feeling." As relieving as sharing our truths had been, there was still a decision to be made. "I will become a mermaid. Nothing else matters to me because I love you, Nolan." I sighed and shrugged. "I will miss my family, well, my sister and mother, but—"

He shook his head, "Osiris says that you would resent me and, over time, that resentment would wither our mating bond. I cannot risk that."

Something started to smell fishy. "Your uncle, whose brother is he?"

"My father's."

"So, with you out of the way, he is theoretically in line for the crown?"

"Grandfather had to choose and chose my father, even though Osiris was the first-born. He deemed Osiris too selfish for the role."

That's what I thought. "So, if you relinquish your title, who gets the crown?"

"Theodore. Osiris disqualified himself by breaking the law."

"Which may be why your uncle told you that my resentment would wither our mating bond. If you become human, you will no longer qualify as the next king, and his son will get the throne."

He frowned deeply. "I do not think he would deceive me. Besides, Theo doesn't want the crown. He's an artist, and he loves what he does."

"I don't know how things work down here, Nolan, but where I come from, royalty is at each other's throats, regardless of blood bonds. They are vicious, and assassinations are common. My concern is that this would be an easy way to clear a path to the throne for Theodore. I don't mean to malign your uncle or make you doubt him, but if he has a reputation for lawlessness and selfishness, you must consider it a possibility."

"I suppose you're right." His lips pursed as he was considering my words.

"We should speak to your father before doing anything that cannot be undone."

"He will banish you and forbid me to follow after you. I cannot be apart from you, Eveline."

I smiled. "Hearing you say my real name is nice, but I prefer Eva."

"Why? Eveline is a beautiful name."

"Yeah, but I heard my father say it too many times with anger in his voice."

He grinned. "Then you need to hear it said with love, my Eveline."

I rolled my eyes. "Fine. Just don't say it too often."

"As you wish, love."

"I like that one. You can call me love whenever you want."

"I'll keep that in mind."

I sighed. "Even if your father banishes me, what's the worst that could come of it? I'm not a mermaid. So, if he does, you can go to your uncle and ask him to turn you into a human. But if your father doesn't banish me and has a different solution for us, then it's worth a try."

"I don't know...."

"Nolan, would your father ever make you marry someone you didn't love? Or even someone you hated?"

He frowned. "Absolutely not. Mer marry their mates, the person they are fated to love."

"Then he is miles better than my father, and it seems unlikely he would deny your request to keep me here."

"As the prince, I'm supposed to make sacrifices for my people, and my father will demand that of me. If he believes it is in the best interest of his people, he will sentence me to a life of misery without my mate. You are a link to the outside world, Eveline. If he does not banish you, then the people will question his loyalty. He cannot afford that kind of generosity."

I held his hands. "You may underestimate your father. In your place, I would put my trust in the hands of the one who loves me and wants the best for me and not the one who looks after the best interests of his own son and has a less than stellar reputation."

NOLAN

*a*s we dressed to visit my father, I regretted not having an outfit for Eveline befitting her station and her beauty. I wanted my father to see her as I did, a stunningly beautiful lady who was smart, regal and a presence to reckon with.

To me, she was as beautiful in the borrowed maid's outfit as she would be in the most alluring of gowns, and wearing a pair of sarongs, she shone like a star, but she would have felt more confident wearing something fancier.

"How do I look?" she asked nervously. "Back home, I would never wear something like this to court, and I don't know what's appropriate here." She looked down at her bare feet. "I can't believe that I'm going to an audience with the king barefoot."

"He's going to be barefoot as well." I kissed her and grinned. "You are beautiful no matter what you wear. And there is nothing official scheduled for today at court, so there will be less pomp and grandeur all around."

"That's good." She glanced at the mirror one more time. "Are you sure that I look good enough to meet your father?"

I took her hand in mine. "You look good enough to rule Poseidon City, Princess Eveline."

She rolled her eyes. "I think you're getting ahead of yourself."

"I usually do."

As we walked out of my quarters, Eveline regarded everything with greater care and more attention now that she knew where we were.

I wasn't sure what had captivated her more, the aquarium-style wall sections that flowed into aquarium-style flooring and back again, or the occasional mer servant who bowed to me on our way to the throne room.

When we walked past the enormous double doors, she let out a faint gasp. "Is that…"

"Mm, hmm." Next to the throne, my father reclined in his pool, gold tail splashing from side to side.

"Nolan, my boy," he boomed. "Come, sit with me."

"Hello, Father," I said as we strolled toward him past the murals on the walls and the oversized windows.

The floor was my favorite part of the throne room. The glass surface showcased the large jewels and pearls encased underneath that sparkled and gleamed in the natural light. And by the look in Eveline's eyes that impressed her the most as well.

But as we approached the pool my father was luxuriating in, though, she kept her eyes on him, curtsied, and smiled politely.

A servant held a towel out for Father's privacy as he flipped his tail out of the pool, and another servant toweled it dry until it shimmered, turning into a pair of legs.

He wrapped his sarong around him behind the towel, picked up his trident, and used it to walk up the stairs to the dais.

Sitting on his throne, he smiled at us. "I see you have brought a friend."

"Yes, Father, this is—"

"My name is Eveline," she said firmly, then curtsied again. "Daughter of King Prosper III and Queen Gwendolyn."

Dark blue eyes skewered me as Father rose to his feet. "You brought a human to our city? To my palace?"

"I had no choice, Father."

"No choice?" he boomed.

"Eveline is my mate."

Father frowned. "That's not possible."

"I feel the bond with her, and it's unmistakable. She is my other half, Father."

He scoffed. "You think you're the first mer to be attracted to a human?"

"This is not a simple attraction, Father. This is a powerful bond." I squeezed her hand. "We both feel it."

"It is not possible. The bond only occurs between mer."

"The bond occurs when the fates so choose." I smiled and looked into Eveline's eyes. "Despite the difficulties we face, I'm grateful to the fates for choosing you for me."

But Father barked a laugh. "And where will you live? Pray tell, my son."

"Uncle Osiris has agreed to help us. He can turn me into a human, or he can turn Eveline into a mermaid. But the price is that whoever makes the change will never get to see his or her family again."

My father's face turned red with anger. "Bring me my brother and my nephew. Now!" he barked at a guard.

"It is not Osiris's fault, Father. He didn't choose Eveline for me. Besides, even the Oracle thinks that Eveline is my mate."

He arched one white brow. "The crone told you that?"

"She said my mate will be unique in every way. Who could be more unique than a human princess?"

"Bring me the Oracle, as well," he commanded another guard.

My father turned back to us. "How did you two meet?"

"I was working as a barmaid in a tavern—"

"But you're a princess."

Eveline nodded. "Yes, I am. Or at least I was until I decided to run away. My father wanted me to marry a horrid man, and I just could not abide by that. I snuck out of the palace wearing a maid's outfit and walked all the way to a village just beyond the border of our kingdom, hoping to secure employment as a barmaid. That was the night I met Nolan. He gallantly rescued me from a band of bandits."

Father arched a dubious eyebrow at me. "Have you been flitting off to the surface?"

"Tell me you didn't do those things when you were my age."

He pursed his lips, annoyed. "Go on."

"Theo and I helped her fight off the bandits. Had they not outnumbered her six to one, I believe she could have handled one man on her own."

He laughed. "Is that so?"

"She knocked one of the attackers into a tree, Father."

"Impressive," he said, regarding her more intently and seeing her in a new light, "but running away because your father wishes to marry you to someone you don't like is hotheaded and foolhardy."

Eveline stood tall and proud, chin jutting out defiantly. "I may be a princess, but I am the queen of my destiny, and I will choose my path in life. No one will choose it for me."

"Is that so?" My father seemed amused, which was an improvement over anger.

"It is. And I do not accept Prince Osiris's bargain, either." She turned her gaze to me. "I am sorry, Nolan, but I must disagree with his plan. Something about it does not sit right with me. It is too self-serving. There must be a better way."

"What if there isn't?" Father asked. "Would you give up your land life for an eternity with a tail and fins?"

Eveline's smile had a hint of sadness to it that shattered my heart. "I love Nolan with everything that I am. So yes, I will. But I would like to say goodbye to my family first."

"And you, Nolan? Would you say goodbye forever to me? To your mother?"

I smiled at Eveline, wondering if my smile had the same sadness to it.

The thought of never seeing my parents again was like a crushing weight on my chest, but saying goodbye to my mate was a worse fate than death. "I love you, Father. And I love Mother with all my heart, and it will be the most difficult thing I will ever have to do, but a mer has to follow his mate, and without her, I would wither away and turn into sea foam. I've never believed in that myth, but now I know that it is an allegory for what happens to mer who refuse or are refused by their mates. They turn into nothing."

"Alright." My father thumped the floor with his trident. "It is evident that the two of you love each other. But this is an impossible situation."

"With magic, all things are possible," Uncle Osiris said as he strutted into the throne room with Theodore by his side. "Good day, brother." They both bowed.

"What is this that I hear about you conspiring to turn the Crown Prince into a human?"

It was a rare moment when Uncle Osiris was speechless. But only for a moment. A smirk flickered on his lips when he looked at me. "So, you made me vow not to reveal anything, but you told him everything anyway? Shame on you, Nolan."

He sniffed and scrunched his face for a beat. "Well, I was only trying to help the lad. True love and all that, you know, Oswald. You were young once and in love. We are but mere pawns in the hands of the fates."

Father stood once more. "You orchestrated this, didn't you, Osiris?"

"And how would I manage that? You know that I don't venture to the surface."

"I know nothing of the sort. You have done nothing but be a thorn in my side for years. It would not surprise me if you used your powers to make this happen. You have always wanted the throne for yourself, and now you've found a way to disqualify Nolan."

Uncle Osiris only chuckled. "I am flattered you think me powerful enough to stand in the way of fate, brother, but I assure you, I am not."

We all turned as the Oracle's cane knocked against the glass floor behind us.

Step by step, knock by knock, the old woman made her way across the throne room to us.

She attempted a curtsy, but it looked more like a bad bow. "My King. I understand there is some concern regarding a prophecy for your son."

He narrowed his gaze on her but said, "Everyone except the Oracle, leave now. Guards, close the chamber doors behind yourselves and make sure that not a word leaves the throne room. I am to have absolute privacy until I come to open the doors myself. Go. Now." He struck the floor with his trident with such vigor that I was surprised it didn't crack.

As we scurried out of the room, the guards closed up behind us, and everyone was silent until Theodore scoffed, "You'll be lucky to get out of this with only a banishment, Nolan. I've never seen your father so angry."

Neither had I.

42

EVELINE

I had been called a troublemaker by my father plenty of times, but it had never been more true than now.

Being the firstborn, I'd been doted on as a child, and I hadn't been deemed difficult until I hit my teens and started voicing my opinions.

To get booted out of a throne room moments after meeting the man I hoped would become my father-in-law was a new low for me.

It did not help that Theo and Osiris kept exchanging sly smirks when Nolan wasn't looking.

It was difficult to keep focused on the situation at hand while surrounded by so many marvels. Throughout the glass palace, a path for fish spiraled around the walls, ceilings, and floors as though I needed a reminder that we were underwater. It was fascinating to see them so close. Oddly, the nearest floor portion of the path was littered with starfish. One of my favorites.

"Sorry, my boy," Osiris said. "Your father is unfortunately not as enlightened as the rest of us. He does not understand how love can cross boundaries and flourish between people of disparate origins."

Theo nodded. "I hope Father did not get your hopes up on the matter, Nolan. I don't imagine your father will be open to having a human-turned-mermaid become our queen one day."

Nolan turned to me. "They are right, Eveline. That only reinforces my conviction that I should be the one to turn."

"Let's wait for your father's judgment on this." I tried to sound supportive when all I felt was suspicious.

Had Osiris orchestrated this?

Oswald wouldn't have said that without proper cause, would he?

But how?

There were too many moving parts for one person to arrange.

I would not have run away had it not been for my impending arranged marriage. The bandits would not have attacked me, and Nolan and Theo would not have been there to defend me. Too many coincidences were involved.

But at the heart of everything was my ill-fated betrothal to Eghurt, and the fact that his mother was a witch.

Osiris was a sorcerer, so maybe the two knew each other and had conspired together?

The Queen of Verdona would have gotten involved only if she had something to gain from it, though. My reputation for being a hothead was well known, so if she'd wanted me to run off, arranging a betrothal to her wretched son was a perfect way to do that.

But what would she stand to gain by that?

My mind considered and dismissed one possibility after the other as the men discussed how cruel it was of Oswald to deny us a life together.

I was listening with only half an ear, but it sounded to me as if they kept planting seeds in Nolan's mind to make him abdicate.

The King of Verdona had died not too long ago under mysterious circumstances. Could Osiris's sorcery have been involved?

If the Queen had done it, she would have been under suspicion, but she'd been away while the king had died, and she played the role of a grieving widow quite well.

Having Osiris do it for her was smart. Who would ever suspect the involvement of a merman sorcerer?

Perhaps arranging our meeting was payment for him killing her husband?

He had done a favor for her, getting rid of her king, and she'd repaid him by getting rid of Nolan.

Then an even more terrible thought popped into my head. What if Osiris used magic to make us fall in love with each other?

What if our bond wasn't real?

I had to know. "Nolan, you said you thralled me to make me fall asleep. How does that work?"

"We can put humans under a thrall that convinces them to do what we tell them. It's like compulsion, only they think that they are in charge."

"Can mer do that to each other?"

"No. It doesn't work like that. And it depends on the mer doing the thralling. Some can do it to only one person at a time. I can manage five, seven at the most, but it gets more difficult the more people I have to thrall."

I nodded and fell silent again.

It was good to know that his feelings for me weren't Osiris's thrall at work. But that didn't change the fact that Osiris could have thralled me or used some other kind of magic to make us fall in love. He could have disguised himself to enter the castle and thralled me to plant the idea to run to Seaside and become a barmaid at McCoy's.

I shook my head at myself.

My parents often said I had a vivid imagination, capable of seeing conspiracies where there were none.

Besides, I loved Nolan with all my heart. Our passion and adoration were too deep to be a spell. Osiris could have triggered it, but we were always fated to be together.

I knew that beyond a shadow of a doubt.

Nolan squeezed my hand. "In the short time I've known you, Eveline, I have never known you to be quiet this long unless you were asleep."

I smiled. "I suppose that's true."

"I like that you speak your mind. But when you go quiet, it makes me worry that there is something you wish to say but are thinking of the best way to say it, which means there is something wrong."

"You've gotten to know me quite well in the short time we've been together."

"What's on your mind?"

I could not keep my thoughts from him, but we had a potentially hostile audience.

"I am thinking of court intrigue and the politics of my family." It was not a lie, but not the whole truth, either—a technique my mother often deployed in order to survive my father's wrath.

"Are you worried that your family will not accept me when I am human?"

"Among other things." I played along with that thought in front of Osiris and Theo. I could not say what was truly on my mind just yet. "For instance, where will we tell my parents you came from?"

"That is a good question."

"Overseas?" Osiris suggested.

"Perhaps underseas is more apt," Theodore teased.

I rolled my eyes at them both. "I was thinking about Cotania. We have no allies there, and we've never hosted visitors from there. It is a strange land with an unusual government, where the royal family toil on their own land alongside the farmers. They share everything with their peasants to ensure all are cared for."

Osiris laughed heartily. "What is the point of being a royal farmer?"

"Can you picture Uncle Oswald working the mussel fields?" Theo laughed.

But Nolan smiled. "That sounds like an interesting place."

"I've always wanted to go there and see how that works," I said. "Cotania is prosperous but small. I'm not sure if their system could work on a larger scale, but I believe that there is always something to be learned from a successful enterprise."

He nodded, but Osiris clapped his shoulder. "Do you wish to see your queen working like a common milkmaid?"

"If that is what she wishes to do, then why not?"

Theodore looked me over. "I saw her work as a barmaid, Father. Farming isn't that different."

"I hope to improve the lives of whomever I can," I said. "If that means working with farmers, then I work with farmers. I am not afraid of hard work."

"No, clearly not," Theo said. "You were sweating with the rest of the wenches. But tell me, Princess, what will you do when your husband's hands are callused and rough from all that work?"

I squeezed Nolan's hand. "I will be proud to hold his roughened hand and kiss his calluses."

They both rolled their eyes at us.

"You do whatever makes you happy, Princess. Don't let anyone stand in your way." Osiris's words were kind, but his tone was condescending.

"I never do."

He continued, "I for one will be glad when this matter is settled. Though it is nice being back in the palace. I've missed my home."

"As a prince of the realm, is your home not luxurious?" I asked Osiris.

"I have several homes. Some are luxurious. Some are not."

"Then I would imagine the palace is a nice place to visit."

His brow furrowed slightly. "It is. I grew up here."

"A palace this size surely has room for a wayward sorcerer, doesn't it?"

"As nice as that would be, you saw how Oswald speaks to my father. It's not a pleasant home environment."

Theodore was an only child, so of course he would think that.

"Siblings can be tough." I smiled at Osiris. "My sister and I used to fight all the time when we were younger."

Osiris nodded. "Sometimes it is best to keep apart from siblings. I was glad when Theo and Nolan became such good friends on top of being cousins."

"My sister and I would do anything for each other."

"How nice for you," Theo said.

"I mean anything. If I asked her to bury a body or cut off her hand, she would do it for me. It's important to have people like that in your life, don't you think?"

His frown reappeared. "A bit of an extreme example there, but we could all use a person like that, I suppose."

"Anyone like that in your life, Osiris? Anyone you'd do anything for?"

"We are not all as lucky as you, Princess. My list of people like that is rather short. My son, of course, and perhaps one or two others."

"What about the Queen of Verdona? Is she on your list?"

Nolan was confused, but both Theodore and Osiris were stunned and tried to hide it.

Osiris quickly covered with, "Who?"

"What did you do for her, Osiris? Did you help to bury the body? Or do you know a spell that makes a body disappear?"

Instead of answering me, he turned to Nolan. "Your mate has a wild imagination. Best to tame it before speaking to Oswald again. Come, Theodore." He escorted his son to the opposite end of the hall.

I didn't have a confession. But Osiris was guilty. I just had to prove it.

43

NOLAN

"*W*hat was that all about, Eveline?" I asked quietly.

"I think Osiris arranged our meeting," she whispered. "Maybe more. I'm not sure."

The truth was, I had wondered the same thing. I hadn't wanted to admit it to myself, but she was right. Everything was lining up too well for Theodore attaining the throne.

If so, Theo had played his role well.

Pushing back about joining the fight to save her, giving us plenty of time alone together that first night, saying he was a bit in love with her for helping him with the other girl. Even his apparent hesitation about helping me with her afterward. All of it was the perfect ploy to make me believe he was just my supportive cousin and not a usurper.

I sighed and quietly admitted, "You may be right."

"Thank you for believing me."

"But how could he have known we would bond?"

"He is a sorcerer. Could he have created the bond? If he can turn a human into a mer, and a mer into a human, it is not a stretch to assume that he can create a mating bond. Or he could have put a spell on you or on me." She sighed. "I don't know how magic works."

I frowned in Uncle Osiris's direction but kept my voice hushed so he wouldn't hear me. "Even if he could do that, I had not seen him for a very long time before I met you. To perform a spell on me, he would have to be near me."

Eveline thought on the matter for a moment. "Is Theo a sorcerer, as well?"

I watched my cousin speak to his father. They both wore concern on their faces, but each time I turned to Eveline, their expressions changed. It was as if they were sharing a private joke. The more I noticed it, the more I became convinced they were up to no good.

Still, Theodore did not have his father's powers. "No. In fact, he often laments his lack of powers. He has always envied those with more abilities than he has. Even though he's a royal, his thrall is weak, and that is one of our most basic gifts."

"Hmm," she mumbled and tried not to stare in their direction. "Is there any kind of magic that's...I don't know, portable? Something that can be loaned out? Don't sorcerers and witches use potions in their magic?"

"They do, but—"

"Then could Theo have put a potion in your ale?"

Her words dug into my heart. She did not trust our bond, and her distrust hurt my feelings. "Why are you so convinced that our love is not real?"

She took my hands in hers, and her lips formed a sweet smile that made me smile back. "Nothing of the sort, Nolan. I am merely trying to discern the nature of their plot. I know our love is real. You and I are...." She sighed happily. "There is not a power, magical or otherwise, that can undermine it."

"That's good to hear. I feel the same way."

"Good. Then help me sort this out and protect your throne."

"As I said before, Eveline, I would happily give it up for you."

"And as I said before, there is no need for you to do that. Osiris wants Theo on the throne. But the question is why? What does he hope to gain by crowning his son?"

I frowned. "Why is it so important to you? So what if Theo becomes the next king of Poseidon City?"

"Because people who plot against their family are usually not the people you want to rule. Think of Poseidon City. Do they deserve a king who used magic against his own family, or do they deserve a ruler who is wise enough to see through their machinations?"

I smiled proudly. "They deserve a queen who understands the difference and is not easily fooled."

She kissed my cheek. "You're so sweet."

"I'm serious, Eveline. You are so clear-minded. I had not considered what would become of Poseidon City if Theo were to rule. In all fairness to him, he is smart and could be a good ruler."

"Your tone indicates that there's a but coming."

"Indeed," I said. "If he were to come up against adversity, as all kings do from time to time, I am not sure how well he would handle it. He might use his father's magic as a crutch. When Osiris disgraced himself, Theo took to his apartment and holed up there for quite some time. The only chance I had of getting him out was to take him to the surface for some adventure."

"So, when he's upset, he sulks?"

I nodded. "Sadly, yes. A king who sulks is not a fit ruler."

"My father is that way. Sulking, pouting, railing against the heavens when he doesn't get his way." She shook her head in disgust. "He is angry all the time. He doesn't understand when people don't just go along with whatever he says. My father thinks that being a king means he can do whatever he wants, and no one will question it."

"Then I imagine having you for a daughter has been trying

for him."

She chuckled. "You could say that."

"Back to the topic at hand, do you suspect that Theo used a love potion on either of us?"

She nodded. "He always volunteered to get the ale."

"Love potions are fragile. They must be administered within minutes of their creation, and we had been traveling for quite a while before coming to the beach. Then we helped you, and it was a while longer before I had my first ale of the night."

"Not a love potion, then."

"More importantly," I said, kissing the back of her hand, "I fell in love with you while we were walking to the tavern."

"That's not possible."

"Perhaps not, but that is what happened. You were so strong and brave, Eveline. I was instantly enamored. You kept your head high and your sense of humor about it all. I suspect you could have handled the bandits even if Theo and I hadn't shown up."

She shivered. "They meant to murder me, or worse, Nolan."

"Even if they had murdered you, I suspect your ghost would have haunted each of them for the rest of their days. You would have been their eternal nightmare."

She laughed. "That is one of the nicest things anyone has ever said to me."

"Then I am glad to have been the one to say it." I sighed, coming back to the point. "Regarding potions or other magical tools. Even a sorcerer cannot create something out of nothing. He can turn me into a human, but he still needs my body to make a human from it. He cannot make one from nothing. So, I think that means Osiris could not have made a mating bond out of nothing."

"Are you sure?"

I nodded. "People have tried in the past, back when arranged marriages were common for the royal mer. If they could have created a mating bond for those marriages, it would have solidified them. But arranged marriages were a failure. We soon realized that we were at the mercy of the fates."

"So, arranged marriages are not common anymore?"

"Not for centuries. Once we realized holding to what the fates decreed was the best way for us, we forged ahead with fated mating bonds as the precursor to marriage. Since then, the mer world has been mostly peaceful."

She sighed. "I wish humans had that kind of wisdom."

"What do you mean?"

"Girls are often forced to marry men they didn't choose."

"You mean like what your father wanted to do to you?"

She nodded. "He wanted me to marry a prince of Verdona. Eghurt. He is an awful man, Nolan. Handsome on the outside, rotten on the inside. He is a spoiled princeling who abuses anyone he can. He takes after his mother in that regard. I pray my sister does not have to take my place in the arrangement."

"Before either of us becomes a different creature, we should visit your family and ensure that she does not."

"Thank you for that. But I am not sure how we will make it so."

"We will think of something."

She smiled again, but it soon faded. "Does my lack of royal mer lineage complicate things for us?"

"My mother has only a fraction of royal mer blood in her. But my parents' mating bond is as strong as anyone else's. I do not believe it will be a problem. If I were not royalty on land, would that be a problem?"

Another nod. "Humans are quite snobby about that. Especially about the men in the marriage. A royal woman cannot marry a commoner, but sometimes exceptions are made for men."

"The human world is a mess."

"I couldn't agree more."

4 4

EVELINE

A loud banging sound came from the throne room just before the doors whooshed open.

No one had opened them by hand, and King Oswald stood in front of his throne, with sparks still flying from his golden trident.

His voice boomed down to the reception hall, "Enter!"

Nolan squeezed my hand supportively. "It will be okay. No matter what he says, you are mine, and I am yours."

"Now!" the king demanded.

"Best we hurry."

I nodded, and we followed the procession of guards and men into the throne room. On our approach, I couldn't help but notice the apologetic glance from the Oracle.

Not to Nolan or me, but to Osiris.

Was she in on this too?

How far did this conspiracy go?

Had she bewitched Oswald?

Was he going to disinherit Nolan?

I tried not to panic, but there was too much magic involved, too many things that I didn't understand about the mer world, and too many intrigues to properly keep track of. But in the middle of all that, Nolan's hand kept me steady. He would let no harm come to me.

I sighed and smiled at him to reassure him, too.

As King Oswald struck the floor with his trident, sending more sparks flying, everyone fell silent.

"Our dear Oracle," he said with heavy sarcasm, "has finally told me the truth, though it took some doing." His annoyance at that last detail was clear to anyone with eyes or ears. "Hundreds of years ago, there was a prince who fell in love with a human princess."

Nolan smiled at me before his father continued. The familiar elements of the story made it seem like our love was a part of history, and I smiled too.

"In order to be with his princess, he gave up the crown to his—"

"Cousin?" Theodore offered.

His boldness shocked me, given his question was so on the nose.

"His younger brother, Theodore," King Oswald said angrily. He stroked his long white beard before continuing, "The abdication caused a great stir in the depths, as his younger brother was not fit for leadership. This became a part of the reason the mer began arranging marriages for our kin. The thought was that if only his marriage had already been arranged, then he would not have gone to the surface and found love there. He would not have ruined his kingdom." He sighed. "If only things were that easy…."

"Alas, love is never easy," Osiris said with a heavy heart.

I did not understand what he meant by that, but the earnestness with which he said it touched me. Maybe there was more to the sorcerer than jealousy.

King Oswald gave him a nod, then said, "But fate is not so easily circumvented, and we have since learned to move with the tides of fate, not against them. But I digress. When the princess became pregnant out of wedlock, something humans have a real problem with, she was quickly married off, with her family hoping to dupe her new husband. The ploy worked. Her child was born a human girl, and her husband never knew."

"You speak of the love story of Prince Tristan and Princess Adalara?" Theodore asked.

He nodded once. "Yes."

"But that is a fairytale, merely something for poets to muse upon."

"It is not a fairytale, Prince Theodore," the Oracle declared. "It is history."

"And as fascinating as that is, brother," Osiris said, "What does that have to do with any of this?"

The King said, "Their daughter is Eveline's ancestor."

Everything in the room stilled, including my heart and my breath.

The only sound was my gasp. "I am part mer?"

"A small fraction of you is mer," Oswald said.

Nolan grinned at me. "Do you know what this means?"

I shook my head.

King Oswald smiled kindly at me for the first time. "Since you are of royal mer blood, you are a suitable match for my son. It also helps that you are royalty on your human side, as that will diminish objections about your humanity. Regardless, this means Nolan will not have to relinquish his crown in order to be with you."

I wanted to believe it. All of it. But I had a feeling he invented my lineage using a popular mer myth.

And I was not the only one.

"Oh, seahorse shit, Oswald!" Osiris bellowed. "You made this up to make sure Nolan kept his throne."

Another trident strike sent a shower of sparks flying at the objecting sorcerer. He winced from the sizzling burns but stood firm.

"The Oracle has spoken!" King Oswald said. "And her word is beyond contestation!"

Osiris glared at her, and purple sparks shimmered around his hands. "You play every side to your advantage, don't you, Oracle?"

But the crone didn't wither under his glare or at the threat of whatever magic was in his hands. She spat back, "At least your brother did me the courtesy of learning my name. You couldn't even be bothered."

"Not only did the Oracle tell me of Eveline's true royal mer heritage," the King said. "She also told me of your betrayal. You have conspired against me for the last time, Osiris. You know what my trident is capable of. Do not make me remind you."

As his grip on the trident strengthened, I worried that a magical battle between the brothers was coming. Fascinating, to be sure, but I imagined it would be deadly, and I did not want that for any of us.

Osiris stretched his hands, and with that the purple sparks vanished. He stood straighter. "No one wants that, brother. It was only a flash of anger. Nothing more. My apologies."

Oswald's shoulders relaxed, as did his grip on the trident. He sat on the throne and huffed. "I should banish you for your interference. You could have destroyed my kingdom had Eveline not insisted they come to speak to me before allowing you to turn Nolan into a human. If you were anyone else, I would have taken your head."

Osiris's jaw gritted. "Why have you not?"

"Because, through your maneuverings, my son found his truelove mate. I dare say he never would have found Eveline had you not interfered. As troublesome as it is to admit, the Crown owes you an uncomfortable debt, brother. Thus, you keep your head and your titles and estates." He turned to me.

"As they say where you come from, all is well that ends in well."

I smirked. "The phrase is, all's well that ends well, my King."

"Ah. I suppose that makes more sense. But, Osiris," he glowered at his brother, "mark my words if you ever interfere like this again—"

"I won't."

"If you do, I will take your head. I don't want to do it, brother. But I will. I cannot permit this sort of chaos in my kingdom ever again. I vow this to you." His breath shimmered gold in the air.

Osiris gulped audibly. "Understood."

The King turned to us. "Nolan and Eveline, your royal wedding will be in one week. The kingdom will cheer and dance for their crown prince, the wine will flow, and the music will play so loudly that the humans may hear us all the way on land. Congratulations."

I grinned at Nolan just before he kissed me. The tension in the room dissipated as he held me in his arms.

This was it. The life I truly deserved.

As our kiss ended, I rested my head on his strong shoulder. I was happy, and I knew everything would be alright.

But then I realized there was one not-so-insignificant detail yet to be managed. "Um, what about turning me into a mermaid?"

King Oswald looked at his brother. "You can handle this, I trust?"

"Aye, brother."

"But with no caveats. She will be free to visit her family, just as any mer can go on land."

"My liege, the magic requires a balance. If I give her the full capacity of any mer, then the sorcerer must make a sacrifice."

"What is that? A finger? A limb?"

Osiris huffed. "I would have to cut my hair."

"That is the cost of one of us being able to see our family upon our transformation?" Nolan scowled at his uncle. "A lock of your hair? And you were not willing to sacrifice it for me?"

"I like my hair."

I snorted a laugh, and King Oswald barked, "Cut your damned hair, Osiris. Give my son his mermaid bride."

The sorcerer huffed again. "The things I have to do for my family."

NICK

W̶hat the hell? Where am I?
What's that thing on my head?

I blinked at the fog in my brain and the bright lights that replaced the thing on my head as my eyes tried to focus.

I wasn't in the throne room anymore.

I was someplace else.

"What is going on? Where is Eveline?"

"Take a deep breath, Nick," a man in a white coat said soothingly.

Nick. I'm Nick.

That's Shane, the technician.

I'm in the studio...Perfect Match.

None of it was real. The fog finally lifted as I took several deep breaths. "That's like coming out of the deepest dream I've ever had."

He nodded. "Take a couple of minutes to get your bearings. How do you feel?"

"Groggy. My leg is sore—right. The scars." I chuckled at myself for forgetting them. "Wow. That was…"

"Immersive?"

"Utterly."

The sparse room and the bank of equipment at the far wall helped to ground me back in reality.

Unfulfilling, non-merman reality.

Not that I didn't like my life, but waking up to a normal world felt cruel somehow. To go from merman royalty to a scarred human ex-soldier in seconds was the strangest sort of mental whiplash.

"Did you enjoy yourself?"

I chuckled. "More than I thought possible. This kind of fun...how is it even legal?"

"How do you mean?"

"I cannot imagine something more addictive than this. I want to go right back in."

Shane laughed. "Everyone says that. Working here, we get to use the equipment a lot, and we have to be careful about that aspect."

I need to see Eveline.

Jessica.

Her name was Jessica.

It was definitely her in the simulation. Minor tweaks aside, there was no mistaking that cherry chocolate hair and the way her voice sounded.

The way she made me feel.

The simulation was only three hours long, and maybe it was all just a fantasy, but there was no mistaking love.

Actual love.

The passion I felt for Eveline was undeniable, and it was still coursing through me.

I had to see Jessica as soon as possible, and I had to tell her everything.

It was the only way.

But did she know it was me?

My avatar didn't look like me. How could she know?

Could she have guessed it?

Her fantasy world was dense and detailed, like no dream I'd ever experienced. Not even the experiments we'd been subjected to in Special Ops had been that engrossing. I couldn't imagine the work that must have gone into such a comprehensive illusion.

I nearly snorted a laugh at myself.

I was still thinking like Nolan, with all his fancy words. But was that so bad? That was who Jessica had fallen for.

I wasn't sure of anything anymore.

Had she wanted us to be virgins for her fantasy?

Strange. Although our first time was…I smiled, thinking about it. Far better than my real first time. Maybe she wanted a do-over on that.

"Nick?"

"Yeah?"

"Are you sure you're alright? I asked you a question, and you didn't respond."

I laughed at myself and sat up. "Yeah, sorry. What was the question?"

"I asked if you were feeling well enough to go home. If not, we can get you an Uber."

"No, need. I'll be fine. Still kinda hazy, that's all."

He smiled. "Understandable. The first time is always a doozy."

I chuckled. "You can say that again."

On the drive home, the entire world seemed less vibrant to me. Muted. Dull, even. Nothing could match the lively blue world Jessica had created for Nolan. Or rather, the Perfect Match developers had created for us.

Still, when I thought of Eveline or Jessica, colors popped, and I felt more alive. More like myself. It was the strangest sensation.

Okay, so when I woke up, I was still in love with Eveline.

273

But now?

I was more convinced than ever that I needed Jessica in my life. I laughed at my rule about not getting involved with people who worked in my building.

I would sell the damn building to be with her.

We were a perfect match. She was smart and funny and an absolute knockout. She was perfect for me.

But what the hell did I bring to the table?

My leg gnawed at me as I parked and went up the elevator to my apartment on the top floor. Maybe that was why I had bought the building. To give myself other things to fix because I couldn't fix myself, and there was more than my leg that needed fixing.

Some things had been broken inside of me, but somehow they didn't bother me now. It was as if the virtual experience had cured me.

I would never be perfect for Jessica, and she deserved perfection, but maybe she was willing to settle for a broken ex-soldier who would worship her like a queen.

Or rather, a princess.

I huffed at myself and got in the shower, still thinking about the whole thing.

It was one thing to be engaged under the sea in a fantasy. It was another to pursue things in the real world.

Could I fit into her world? What was her world? Would her friends like me? Would I like them? My head was a tornado of jumbled thoughts.

I chuckled at myself when I lay down. I was hungry, but I couldn't eat. Sighing, I watched as the hours ticked by. Replaying the experience in my mind, I couldn't fall asleep.

As my phone flashed, I had a good idea who was calling me in the middle of the night and picked it up without looking. "Hello?"

"Did you do it?"

I smirked. "Ed, still working on those phone manners, I see."

"Come on, tell me. Did you?"

"Yeah. I did."

"How was it? Tell me everything. Spare no details."

I chuckled. "Whatever your concept of immersion is, this is bigger."

"Shit, really?"

"When I came out of it, I was still convinced that I was my avatar, so yeah."

"That sounds dangerous."

I frowned. "Dangerous, how?"

"Think about it. If someone got, say, a world leader in that chair, and they forget themselves…."

He had a point. "But it was just temporary. Took me a minute to come back to reality."

"And that could give someone a minute with the nuclear codes."

I chuckled. "There goes that paranoia again."

"It's only paranoia if they are not after you and, Nick, I've had a black van parked in front of my place for three days now."

"Black van? Come on. They wouldn't be so cliché."

"They are nothing if not clichéd, Nick."

"What about the line?"

"Secured. Stop testing my patience. I'm already on edge."

"You still have your escape route, right?"

Ed had built a tunnel that led from his basement to the sewers, where he had hidden a supply stash and a car for when an emergency exit would be needed.

"Of course. And there's room for two if you need it."

"I don't, but thanks. What are you so worried about?"

"My friend, who forgot who he was for a minute. A solid minute, Nick. And crazies could take my country over with this kind of tech."

I smirked. "I'm fine. And our country is as fine as it will ever be. You have got to stop reading so many conspiracy websites."

"Black. Van," he enunciated.

"Is it marked plumbing? Because those are the real bad guys. You ever see what they charge?"

He chuckled. "Mock me, why don't you?"

"Thanks, I will," I teased.

"And it's marked TV Repair. As though anyone gets a TV repaired anymore. Amateurs."

"See? Amateurs. You've got nothing to worry about."

"So you say," he paused, "so it was that good?"

"My God, man. You need to do it."

He laughed. "No, thank you. I prefer to remain in complete control."

"You always did."

"Says the control freak."

I shrugged. "I don't know. Maybe I'm turning over a new leaf. I was completely out of control during the session, and I've never been happier."

"How so?"

"I won't get into what happened in there, but all I'm going to say is I am going to do everything in my power to make things happen with Jessica."

Dead silence on the other end.

"Ed?"

Still silent.

"Hey, man, you alright?"

"Since when are you this sprung on a girl?"

"You scared me."

"Shit, you scared me! Are you sure you're feeling like yourself now? Because you do not sound like you at all."

I chuckled, relieved that men in black ski masks hadn't come to take him away. "Yeah. I'm good. I'm fantastic, actually. This is it. The real thing. I feel it in my gut."

"Are you saying your hard-partying bachelor nights are over?"

"With any luck, yes. I had a good run, but once you know what it can really feel like, there's nothing else like that in the world. No more hookups, no more random women. I don't want to spend another night in a noisy club, buying overpriced drinks and pretending to make conversation just to get some woman to sleep with me. Jessica is all that I want."

"I don't think Nick came out of that simulation."

I chuckled. "Maybe not. But I'm good with that."

46

JESSICA

"So, how was it?" Sarah asked excitedly.

I'd waited to call her until I'd gotten home.

I could barely remember the drive back because all I could think of was the simulation and how much prettier everything was underwater. "I'm not sure."

"That is not a ringing endorsement."

I chuckled. "Well, here's the thing; when I woke up, I was still my avatar for a few seconds, which was kind of disorienting and freaky. When I found myself in the studio instead of the underwater palace, I wanted back in."

"Underwater palace?"

"It was part of the fantasy." I brushed past that. "Anyway, after I got my bearings, there were two things on my mind. One, I was madly in love with my Perfect Match. Two, he wasn't real."

"But isn't he based on a real guy? I mean, a real man partnered with you in the simulation, right?"

"Yeah, my so-called Perfect Match is out there somewhere. I asked the technician, Chloe, if I could meet him in a couple of days or a week. I'm not ready to meet him just yet. I don't think I can take it."

"How come?"

Valid question. "Because I'm in love with him. I mean, the real deal. Nothing fake about it. Even right now, when I think about him, I get butterflies, followed by a terrible sense of loss because I may never be with him because it wasn't real. It's crushing, Sarah."

"So, reach out to him, Jess. This isn't a deal breaker. Why aren't you on the phone with him instead of me?"

I sighed. "Because what if that's not who he really is? I mean, obviously, he's not a merman."

"A merman?"

"Fantasy, remember? But that's not the part of him I care about. It's who he was in there. His kindness and bravery, his gentleness when I needed that, and the passionate sex when I needed that."

Sarah squealed. "Uh, that sounds good."

"It was phenomenal. Earth-shaking. Take the best orgasms you ever had with a guy or with your BOB, and multiply that by your imagination."

She let out a gasp. "Wow."

"I'm still not over that part. And the worst of it is that after I woke up and came around, I wanted it to be Nick."

"The handyman?"

"Yeah," I sighed. "But it couldn't have been him. I mean, the personality was right, the chemistry was spot-on, and all that. But there's no way he could afford a trip to Perfect Match. So now I'm stuck in love with an impossible man who can never live up to what I created in the fantasy world. And I'm miserable, missing him."

"This sounds way more intense than what you were prepared for."

"Oh, yeah. Definitely. This isn't some kind of schoolgirl

crush thing, either. This is full-blown, what-I-should-have-felt-for-Charles, passionate, all-consuming love. The kind you don't get over in a hundred years."

"I have to do this."

I laughed. "This sounds like what you want? To be obsessed with a man you can never have?"

"You know me. Every guy I'm with is a total disaster. At least with Perfect Match screening them, I stand a better chance of getting it right."

"I suppose."

Part of me thought I should warn her that the whole thing felt like a trap or the best marketing around. It was like they dangled the perfect man in front of me and said, *'Yeah, but he's not real. Pine away forever.'*

"Tell me about this guy you've fallen for," Sarah said.

"Well, like I said, merman. A merman prince."

"Well, of course. Why not?"

I giggled. "Sun-kissed hair, luminous blue eyes. Great ass."

"Isn't that last part what you always said about Nick?"

"Yeah."

"Then maybe it is him."

I laughed. "Yeah, maybe. In my dreams."

"Wait, how did you see his ass if he's a merman?"

"They become human-like when they're out of the water. It's magic. Their tails turn into legs."

She giggled. "Oh, well, sure. Of course."

"More than anything else, Sarah, he was good. All the way through. There were no games. There was no guile. He was just a kind man. He and his cousin rescued me from bandits. That was how we met."

She giggled. "That's a hell of a meet-cute."

"Though to be fair, I clobbered one bandit into a tree right before he was about to attack Nolan."

"Nolan? Good name. And look at you, Little Miss Badass, clobbering bandits."

I chuckled. "Yes. And the sex...God, it was like nothing I'd ever experienced. Mind-melting, life-altering... There are no words, Sarah. None that can describe what it was like."

"Wow." She paused. "Wait, were you a mermaid princess?"

"A human princess."

She giggled. "That is quite the fantasy."

"I mean, if you're going to go, go all the way, right?"

"Of course."

"Anyway, now I have to decide. Do I meet the man I partnered with in my underwater adventure? Or do I let him stay a fantasy?"

"Why would you do that?"

I chuckled. "Who can live up to something like this? It's too much pressure. So if I don't ever contact him, he can't disappoint me in real life."

"And if you don't ever contact him, he can't make you happy in real life, either."

"Therein lies the rub."

"Honey," she said, "reach out to your fantasy man. He may not be a merman prince, but he could be a great guy. Or is it the merman-ness and prince-ness that does it for you? Not trying to kink-shame you, but you're in for a world of disappointment if—"

I laughed. "No. That's all just the fantasy element of it. It's him I want." My stomach twisted as I said the words. "But I am in love with a fantasy. No man can be that heroic and kind and funny and amazing. He doesn't exist." Just saying it out loud, I wanted to cry.

"Cheer up, Jess. He exists. Somewhere out there is the man of your dreams. All you have to do is reach out to him."

"What if he disappoints me?"

"Everyone will at some point. That doesn't mean they aren't

worth it. That just means they're human. And again, unless the merman-ness is your kink, then you know that."

I laughed again. "Thanks. I'm just not sure. I hear what you're saying, but it feels like such a risk, when I could let him remain a perfect fantasy. Something I can think about when I'm old and gray, this ideal, untarnished memory that can keep me warm at night."

"Well, that's the question, isn't it? Do you want a memory to keep you warm at night, or do you want a man to do that for you?"

"Since when did you get so smart?"

She laughed. "Since you started talking like a moon-eyed schoolgirl. Seriously, what did Perfect Match do to you?"

"Too much, and not enough."

"Oh, I am absolutely going to try this thing."

"Be careful. You might come out of it hung up on a dream."

"I always have been," she said with another laugh. "Do you need me to come over? You sound so lonely and sad that my heart goes out to you."

"Honestly, I have a presentation I need to work on that's due Monday." I huffed at myself, knowing it was just an excuse to stay alone tonight.

"Whatever you need. If you change your mind, I'm home, and I can bring our two favorite guys over."

I frowned. "Who?"

"Ben and Jerry."

I rolled my eyes. "Thanks. If I change my mind, I'll let you know."

We said our goodbyes, and I hung up, still moping. After deciding to treat myself to a long soak and a glass of wine, I lay in bed with my hand hovering over my phone as I debated calling Perfect Match and asking for an in-person meeting with my fantasy man. It was late, but I was sure I could leave a voicemail.

The question still lingered, though. Was it better to have a perfect memory or to risk a disappointment?

The bath hadn't unwound me like it usually did, and neither had the glass of wine.

Was this what purgatory felt like?

Hell could not be as bad as this. At least in Hell, you knew where you stood.

And I wanted nothing more than to go back to heaven.

47

NICK

*I*f anyone could have made this happen, it was Ed.

I could always count on him, no matter what he thought of my requests.

He knew all the right people for any kind of emergency, and even though he objected to my plan, he still made it happen for me.

Knotting my tie, I wondered why he agreed to it.

Maybe he was gunning for the Best Man nomination.

The suit was Ed's idea and he made that happen too. I needed to look sharp on short notice, and he knew a twenty-four-hour tailor who didn't ask questions. I'd half expected a John Wick-like experience with the guy, and was startled to get exactly that. I got a fantastic black suit and equally sharp shoes.

I had even worked on my hair and trimmed my stubble. My nails were short and clean, and my hands felt like skin again after copious amounts of scrubbing and lotion.

I couldn't present Jessica with my usual self if I was going to make this work. I needed to be clean, polished, someone worthy of her.

After all, I wasn't the merman prince of her fantasies.

The drive from the jeweler to my building left me a nervous wreck.

Between the traffic and the thought of what I was doing, I could hardly breathe. But it wasn't the thought of spending the rest of my life with Jessica that took my breath away. In fact, that thought made me happier than I'd ever been. The part that scared me about proposing was the thought that she might say no.

There was no plan B.

If she said she wanted to date first, okay, great. But I needed to know we were heading down the aisle sometime soon.

Having never proposed before, I did my due diligence and googled it.

What was expected, what was preferred? Public or private? Elaborate or simple? Flowers or no flowers? All the recommendations were meant to make her say yes.

I decided against nearly all of them.

Jessica was not an average woman, and more than that, I didn't want her to say yes just because I got her exactly the right flowers or some other frivolous reason. I wanted her to say yes because she wanted to marry me.

As much as I had wanted to wait until the end of the day for it, I couldn't.

Once I saw the ring, I knew I was doing the right thing, and I needed to get it on her finger. It was perfect. A mermaid and a merman on either side of a one-carat blue diamond solitaire the color of Nolan's eyes.

Now, all I needed was the woman to put it on.

I pressed the elevator button for her floor too many times. But I couldn't wait. I wanted my forever to start now.

When the doors opened, it was as if everything was in slow motion. People passing by, conversations in the air.

Jessica wasn't at her desk.

My eyes scanned the open floor plan room for her, and I couldn't breathe.

She wasn't there.

Shit.

But as I was about to turn around, she walked out of the conference room with a group of people trailing her, asking her questions.

Whatever it was, she seemed happy and gestured with her hands as she answered. But then Phelps called their attention to him and guided them to his office while Jessica walked over to her desk.

She glowed in her cream-colored pantsuit.

Whatever transpired in that meeting, it went well for her.

Was it a good omen?

Her desk mate clapped her shoulder in congratulations when she returned, and it clicked in my head. They must have picked her design for the governor's library.

I was so happy for her, and I knew that was the perfect moment to do this.

The stars were aligned, and fate guided my steps.

Taking a breath, I marched up to her desk.

She smiled when she saw me approaching. "Good morning, Nick. Are you going to a wedding?"

"I hope so." I pulled out the ring box and kneeled before her. "Jessica Dare, in all my life, I never thought I would meet a woman who made me want to give her the world. I thought love was a mistake or a gamble, a fairytale or a fantasy. But you are my fantasy. In fact, you are my perfect match." I opened the box, hoping the ring would tell her everything she needed to know. "Will you marry me?"

Jessica's eyes widened with understanding, and she gasped. "It was you! I knew it!" She dropped to her knees in front of me and wrapped her arms around me. "I knew it had to be you, Nick."

Behind us, I could hear Jessica's co-workers cheering and clapping, but I only saw and heard her.

"How did you know it was me?"

"I'm not sure. But I knew it in my heart."

I grinned and pulled back to put the ring on her finger. "Now, I know this is a bit fast—"

She laughed. "Fast?"

"I mean, technically, we haven't even kissed."

But she kissed me right then, and I could have died a happy man. "Now we have."

I held up the ring.

She held out her hand for me to put it on and stared at it for a long minute. "I love it. Oh my God, I love it so much."

"Really? It's not too much?"

"It's perfect. You're perfect."

I laughed. "Not really."

"You're perfect for me, Nick. That's all I care about."

My face hurt from grinning so hard.

Her desk mate said, "I didn't even know you two were dating."

Jessica smiled at him. "Neither did I." She turned to me. "You realize there's a lot we have to talk about."

"Definitely. But first, can we get off our knees? My leg is killing me."

"Oh, of course."

After we stood up and I put my arm around her shoulders, everything felt right.

Better than right.

It was perfect.

EPILOGUE: POSEIDON CITY

"You look perfect, Eveline," Theodore told me.

After the truth had come out about Osiris's meddling, Oswald had been true to his word and let him retain his titles and holdings. He'd even elevated him to the status of counselor, which was all Osiris ever really wanted. To feel important. He had accepted that his son would not be king and put his energies into ensuring his nephew had the biggest, most elaborate wedding the kingdom had ever seen.

With Theodore as my human-to-mermaid translator, I had a leg up on knowing the customs of their people.

My people, now.

I got an apartment in the palace for before the wedding, and it was almost identical to Nolan's. I had my own pool and everything, but I was still confused about making it work. "How do I move around in this thing?"

He laughed. "Don't think about it too hard. How do you move with legs?"

"I just do."

"Exactly."

I huffed. It was strange to adjust to the skimpy clothes—

sarongs left nothing to the imagination. But the tail was something else. I closed my eyes and tried to relax, which left me vulnerable to sinking. Unfortunately, I had not grown up underwater, so my lung capacity rivaled a shrimp's. I jetted up, sputtering and wiping the wet hair from my face. "Not the best advice, Theo."

He grinned. "Oh, really?"

"Yeah, why?"

"Look at you." He motioned downward.

Then I realized I was swimming. "Holy crap! Look at that!"

He laughed hard. "You're a natural. You just needed someone to annoy you enough to make you swim."

"With you around, I'll become a professional swimmer in no time."

"I'm happy I can be of service, my lady." He offered me a mock bow.

I rolled my eyes. "You will not start bowing to me when you see me, right? Not even when I'm queen?"

"Why wouldn't I when you're a queen?"

I sighed. "I know things got started on the wrong foot—flipper? Fin?"

"The wrong foot," he smirked. "Go on."

"But I also know that you're a good man who got caught up in his father's plot. And if Oswald can forgive Osiris, we can forgive you for your part. I want you to be a part of our family, Theo. Here at the palace. I don't want you to feel like your dad did and go off to hide in a cave. I want you around."

"Okay, but I'll have to bow to you when we do public functions. If I don't, the people will think there is something between us."

I laughed hard. "Oh gods, can you imagine?"

"It's not that funny."

But I couldn't stop laughing for a good minute. "Sure, sure. Bow in public. No one needs tongues wagging nonsense."

"Just remember, when you make friends down here—"

I parroted the words he had drilled into me: "Talk about you as our roguish artist cousin, so you sound dangerous and emotionally available."

"Leave that second part off, but yes."

"I've already played wing woman for you at the tavern, and now you want me to do it here? Don't I have enough political intrigue to manage?"

He chuckled. "The way I see it, if I hadn't played a part in you meeting Nolan, then this wedding would not be happening, so you owe me. And speaking of which, it's time to get your wedding sarongs on. You've got a prince to marry."

Theo exited the room to give me privacy and left me in the capable hands of my mermaid-in-waiting.

I grinned and got out of the pool. Feeling my legs come back was an enormous adjustment. It didn't hurt at all, but it was strange and felt like a miracle every time it happened. In no time my hair was done, and my wedding sarong came on.

It was white, simple, clean, and clingy.

"Okay, I'm ready."

Walking back into the room, Theo let out a gasp. "You're the prettiest bride I've ever seen."

"Aw, I bet you say that to all the brides."

"Of course. But with you, I mean it."

I bounced on the balls of my feet. "Come on, let's go get me married!"

He laughed, and we headed to the throne room.

"I am so happy my cousin found you. You are as crazy about him as he is about you."

"Mates are like that, I guess."

"Not all of them, actually. But the fates like the two of you. I can tell."

"How so?"

He softly chuckled. "Because you're both like dolphins who

291

found another dolphin who likes to play the same games. Just plain giddy about each other."

"I hope to learn more about dolphins. And sharks. Whales, even."

"Here's a fun fact for you on whales. All killer whales are named Kevin."

I laughed. "Huh?"

"We're not sure why, but every single one is called Kevin."

"You're messing with me."

"Could be. But I'm not. And here we are."

The throne room doors stood tall, with guards at both sides, ready to open on my signal.

I grinned at Theodore. "Thank you. For everything. You weirdo."

He laughed. "I am happy to help. My future queen."

I nodded to the guards, and they opened the doors. Inside, all the mer royals stood at attention to watch me walk down the aisle. At the end of the aisle stood the man of my dreams. Crown Prince Nolan. Someone played the *Wedding March* on a conch for us—we'd had to get the music for it during a trip to the surface, as it was not a common song in Poseidon City.

The mer people had accepted me as Nolan's mate. None seemed to mind that I'd been born as a human. I'd worried I would face discrimination, but as things stood, everyone was happy to meet me. All they cared about was Nolan's happiness.

On my way to him, my mother and sister stood in the front row. I stopped there to hug them. It had taken some doing for them to understand and believe me when I'd explained it all to them. I was grateful that my father did not come to the wedding. Away on some diplomatic mission, almost as if by magic.

I had to remember to thank Osiris for that small favor later.

When Bernice met Theodore, I was sure she understood the allure of a merman. He helped us get them to Poseidon City for the ceremony, and she hadn't needed to be thralled to sleep in his arms. She was quite content to be there and not scared at all about traveling underwater.

My little sister was braver than most, and I held high hopes for my home kingdom when she became queen.

After our hugs, I turned to the man who would become my king. Butterflies fluttered in my belly as I held his hand. Throughout the ceremony, as Oswald gave his wedding speech, Nolan's thumb rubbed the back of my hand, and every stroke of his stoked a fire inside of me. Not just lust but the fire of deep and abiding love the likes of which few had ever known. He was a part of me, and I was a part of him.

We kissed at the end of the ceremony, and as we did, the royals cheered, and the sea life danced by the windows.

I had my merman, and he had me, and we were going to live happily ever after.

EPILOGUE: ONE YEAR LATER

"You made me leave my house," Ed grumbled. "And put on a tie. I hate you."

I laughed. "Thanks for being my best man."

"You owe me."

"Yes, but not for that. You made my engagement happen. Thank you." I straightened my tie in the mirror.

"Why aren't we in our dress uniforms?"

"I'd like to leave that part of life behind me. No more bombs, no more men in black vans, no more talk of the things we saw back then. Just moving forward."

He nodded, understanding. "It's not easy, you know."

I sighed at him. "I know. But I'm trying to get past all of that."

"Not that stuff. Marriage."

"How would you know? I've never even heard of you going on a date."

"I was married before I joined the service."

I stared at him before I blurted, "Oh, bullshit!"

He laughed. "Her name was Heather."

"Why...what happened?"

"You think any good can come from a marriage to a woman named Heather?"

I laughed and rolled my eyes. "Well, what happened with her?"

"Let's just say I joined the service for a reason. The point is marriage isn't easy. But do you want some advice?"

"I'm all ears."

"One, don't marry a woman named Heather."

Laughing, I said, "Got that covered."

"Two, if she makes you happy at all, she's done her job. It's your job to make sure she's as happy as she can be. Whatever it takes."

"I'll remember that."

"Three, if she can't cook, learn it yourself."

"We both like to cook."

He thought for a moment. "Then I think that you got it covered."

"So, happiness and food? That's your advice?"

"Pretty much all you need for a good marriage. That, and the Heather thing."

I clapped my friend's back. "Thanks, Ed."

"Why did you ask me to be your best man?"

"Without you, I couldn't have gotten engaged so quickly. And without you, I probably wouldn't have gone to Perfect Match in the first place. On top of that, without you, I'd probably be dead by now. I think that's enough reason for you to be my best man."

He chuckled. "Well then, I'm honored. Ready?"

"Yes! As much as I've been looking forward to this, I want to be married already. The wedding is just a formality."

Shaking his head, he advised, "Nope. Don't you treat it like that. There's a chance she's been dreaming about this day since she was a little girl, so if you act like this is all a big pain in the ass, she's gonna be mad."

"She's already been married once. That's why we're doing something nontraditional for our wedding."

"Still. You don't want to upset her. Not ever, but especially not today."

I took a breath. "You're right. Okay. It's a big deal, not a big pain in the ass. Got it."

"And come on. You're excited about today. You've been looking forward to this your whole life, too, you big faker."

I laughed. "You're talking out of your ass."

"I've seen years of your search history."

I paused and frowned at him. "That's still creepy, man."

He laughed. "People lie. Search histories don't."

"Let's go."

We walked out to the entryway at the top of the Governor's Library steps. As a part of the deal for being the architect of the library, Jessica had made arrangements for our wedding to be the first event held there upon completion of the building. Ornate pink and purple flower bushes flanked the front steps, and the building itself was a modern wonder.

Every time I'd driven past it, I was so proud of my mate. Fiancée. Whichever. After going back to Perfect Match so many times in the past year, we called each other mate as often as any other pet name.

At the top of the steps, the retired governor of our state stood ready to officiate our wedding. Laid out along the center of the steps was a blue carpet for an aisle. A crowd of one hundred of our closest friends and family sat along the sides of the steps by the flowers. There were even the photographers who followed the governor, standing just beyond the guests.

I had expected nothing as high profile as this for my wedding, but I was happy to have it. Jessica pulled every string she could to have the perfect day. Standing there and waiting for things to begin, Ed quietly scoffed in my ear, "I can't believe you're getting married by a damned liberal."

I laughed, and the music began. The *Wedding March* played on a conch shell. How she found someone to do that, I would never know. But I had a sneaking suspicion that Jessica had collaborated with Ed on the matter.

She arrived in a limousine, and when her best friend Sarah helped her out of the car, my breath caught in my chest, and, for some strange reason, my vision clouded as my eyes misted with unshed tears. I had seen no one as radiant as the woman I was about to marry.

Jessica was beautiful to me in any outfit and even more so in none at all, but in her simple white mermaid wedding gown, she rocked my world.

When she reached me, I took her hand and rubbed my thumb over the back of her hand, just as I had done at our first wedding in Poseidon City.

My mate smiled up at me, and I lost track of what the governor was saying. In fact, I lost track of anything but her smile. A few minutes later, Ed nudged me. I frowned at him, but he gestured with his chin to the governor, who smirked and said, "Let me try again. Do you take Jessica Dare—"

"I do."

He laughed, and the crowd joined him. Jessica giggled and said, "I do."

He smiled at us both and, per our request, ended the ceremony with, "I now pronounce you truelove mates."

Ready for the next Perfect Match?

The Dragon King

To save his beloved kingdom from a devastating war, the Crown Prince of Trieste makes a deal with a witch that costs him half of his humanity and dooms him to an eternity of loneliness.

Now, king, he's a fearsome cobalt-winged dragon by day and a short-tempered monarch by night. Not many are brave enough to serve in the palace of the brooding and volatile ruler, but Charlotte ignores the rumors and accepts a scribe position in court.

As the young scribe reawakens Bruce's frozen heart, all that stands in the way of their happiness is the witch's bargain. Outsmarting the evil hag will take cunning and courage, and Charlotte is just the right woman for the job.

Dear reader,

Thank you for reading *Perfect Match: The Merman Prince*. As an independent author, I rely on your support to spread the word. If you enjoyed the story, I would be grateful if you could post a brief review on Amazon.

Kind words will be greatly appreciated and get good Karma sent your way -:)

Love & happy reading,

Isabell

Also by I. T. Lucas

PERFECT MATCH
VAMPIRE'S CONSORT
KING'S CHOSEN
CAPTAIN'S CONQUEST
THE THIEF WHO LOVED ME
MY MERMAN PRINCE
The Dragon King

THE CHILDREN OF THE GODS ORIGINS
1: GODDESS'S CHOICE
2: GODDESS'S HOPE
THE CHILDREN OF THE GODS
DARK STRANGER
1: DARK STRANGER THE DREAM
2: DARK STRANGER REVEALED
3: DARK STRANGER IMMORTAL
DARK ENEMY
4: DARK ENEMY TAKEN
5: DARK ENEMY CAPTIVE
6: DARK ENEMY REDEEMED
KRI & MICHAEL'S STORY
6.5: MY DARK AMAZON
DARK WARRIOR
7: DARK WARRIOR MINE
8: DARK WARRIOR'S PROMISE
9: DARK WARRIOR'S DESTINY
10: DARK WARRIOR'S LEGACY
DARK GUARDIAN
11: DARK GUARDIAN FOUND

63: Dark Whispers From Afar
64: Dark Whispers From Beyond

Dark Gambit

65: Dark Gambit The Pawn
66: Dark Gambit The Play
67: Dark Gambit Reliance

Dark Alliance

68: Dark Alliance Kindred Souls
69: Dark Alliance Turbulent Waters
70: Dark Alliance Perfect Storm

Dark Healing

71: Dark Healing Blind Justice
72: Dark Healing Blind Trust

The Children of the Gods Series Sets

Books 1-3: Dark Stranger trilogy—Includes a bonus short story: **The Fates take a Vacation**

Books 4-6: Dark Enemy Trilogy —Includes a bonus short story—**The Fates' Post-Wedding Celebration**

Books 7-10: Dark Warrior Tetralogy
Books 11-13: Dark Guardian Trilogy
Books 14-16: Dark Angel Trilogy
Books 17-19: Dark Operative Trilogy
Books 20-22: Dark Survivor Trilogy
Books 23-25: Dark Widow Trilogy
Books 26-28: Dark Dream Trilogy
Books 29-31: Dark Prince Trilogy
Books 32-34: Dark Queen Trilogy
Books 35-37: Dark Spy Trilogy
Books 38-40: Dark Overlord Trilogy
Books 41-43: Dark Choices Trilogy

BOOKS 44-46: DARK SECRETS TRILOGY
BOOKS 47-49: DARK HAVEN TRILOGY
BOOKS 50-52: DARK POWER TRILOGY
BOOKS 53-55: DARK MEMORIES TRILOGY
BOOKS 56-58: DARK HUNTER TRILOGY
BOOKS 59-61: DARK GOD TRILOGY
BOOKS 62-64: DARK WHISPERS TRILOGY
BOOKS 65-67: DARK GAMBIT TRILOGY

MEGA SETS
INCLUDE CHARACTER LISTS

THE CHILDREN OF THE GODS: BOOKS 1-6
THE CHILDREN OF THE GODS: BOOKS 6.5-10

TRY THE CHILDREN OF THE GODS SERIES ON AUDIBLE
2 FREE audiobooks with your new Audible subscription!

THE PERFECT MATCH SERIES

PERFECT MATCH: VAMPIRE'S CONSORT

When Gabriel's company is ready to start beta testing, he invites his old crush to inspect its medical safety protocol.

Curious about the revolutionary technology of the *Perfect Match Virtual Fantasy-Fulfillment studios*, Brenna agrees.

Neither expects to end up partnering for its first fully immersive test run.

PERFECT MATCH: KING'S CHOSEN

When Lisa's nutty friends get her a gift certificate to *Perfect Match Virtual Fantasy Studios*, she has no intentions of using it. But since the only way to get a refund is if no partner can be found for her, she makes sure to request a fantasy so girly and over the top that no sane guy will pick it up.

Except, someone does.

Warning: This fantasy contains a hot, domineering crown prince, sweet insta-love, steamy love scenes painted with light shades of gray, a wedding, and a HEA in both the virtual and real worlds.

Intended for mature audience.

Perfect Match: Captain's Conquest

Working as a Starbucks barista, Alicia fends off flirting all day long, but none of the guys are as charming and sexy as Gregg. His frequent visits are the highlight of her day, but since he's never asked her out, she assumes he's taken. Besides, between a day job and a budding music career, she has no time to start a new relationship.

That is until Gregg makes her an offer she can't refuse—a gift certificate to the virtual fantasy fulfillment service everyone is talking about. As a huge Star Trek fan, Alicia has a perfect match in mind—the captain of the Starship Enterprise.

The Thief Who Loved Me

When Marian splurges on a Perfect Match Virtual adventure as a world infamous jewel thief, she expects high-wire fun with a hot partner who she will never have to see again in real life.

A virtual encounter seems like the perfect answer to Marcus's string of dating disasters. No strings attached, no drama, and definitely no love. As a die-hard James Bond fan, he chooses as his avatar a dashing MI6 operative, and to complement his adventure, a dangerously seductive partner.

Neither expects to find their forever Perfect Match.

My Merman Prince

The beautiful architect working late on the twelfth floor of my building thinks that I'm just the maintenance guy. She's also under the impression that I'm not interested.

Nothing could be further from the truth.

I want her like I've never wanted a woman before, but I don't play where I work.

I don't need the complications.

When she tells me about living out her mermaid fantasy with a stranger in a Perfect Match virtual adventure, I decide to do everything possible to ensure that the stranger is me.

The Dragon King

To save his beloved kingdom from a devastating war, the Crown Prince of Trieste makes a deal with a witch that costs him half of his humanity and dooms him to an eternity of loneliness.

Now, king, he's a fearsome cobalt-winged dragon by day and a short-tempered monarch by night. Not many are brave enough to serve in the palace of the brooding and volatile ruler, but Charlotte ignores the rumors and accepts a scribe position in court.

As the young scribe reawakens Bruce's frozen heart, all that stands in the way of their happiness is the witch's bargain. Outsmarting the evil hag will take cunning and courage, and Charlotte is just the right woman for the job.

FOR EXCLUSIVE PEEKS

FOR EXCLUSIVE PEEKS AT UPCOMING RELEASES & A FREE COMPANION BOOK

JOIN MY *VIP CLUB* AND GAIN ACCESS TO THE VIP PORTAL AT
ITLUCAS.COM
CLICK HERE TO JOIN

INCLUDED IN YOUR FREE MEMBERSHIP:

YOUR VIP PORTAL

- READ PREVIEW CHAPTERS OF UPCOMING RELEASES.
- LISTEN TO GODDESS'S CHOICE NARRATION BY C. LAWRENCE
- EXCLUSIVE CONTENT OFFERED ONLY TO MY VIPS.

FREE I.T. LUCAS COMPANION INCLUDES:

- GODDESS'S CHOICE PART 1
- PERFECT MATCH: VAMPIRE'S CONSORT

- Interview Q & A
- Character Charts

If you're already a subscriber, you'll receive a download link for my next book's preview chapters in the new release announcement email. If you are not getting my emails, your provider is sending them to your junk folder, and you are missing out on **important updates, side characters' portraits, additional content, and other goodies.** To fix that, add isabell@itlucas.com to your email contacts or your email VIP list.

Copyright © 2023 by I. T. Lucas

Published by Evening Star Press

EveningStarPress.com

ISBN 978-1-957139-68-5

www.ingramcontent.com/pod-product-compliance
Lightning Source LLC
Chambersburg PA
CBHW060524180626
46817CB00002B/479